MONOMOY MYSTERY

A Cape Cod Mystery/Thriller

By: F. Edward Jersey

ALSO BY
F. EDWARD JERSEY

(non-fiction)

Softwhere

(fiction)

Paines Creek Mystery

ObitUCrime

Cougar Attack

Unfinished Business

MONOMOY MYSTERY

A Cape Cod Mystery/Thriller

By: F. Edward Jersey

This book is a work of fiction. Names, characters, places, and incidents either are products of the author's imagination or are used fictitiously. Any resemblance to actual events or locales or persons, living or dead, is entirely coincidental.

ISBN: 1460925955
EAN-13: 978-1460925959

This book is dedicated to my readers who wanted closure to some of the stories in the first four mystery/thrillers.

MONOMOY MYSTERY

Chapter 1

A few months had gone by since Katherine Sterns had lost her fiancé. Detective Frank Jenkins, on his way to meet Katherine, was tragically killed in an automobile accident. Katherine went into seclusion after the funeral and burial, keeping to herself in her West Dennis home, only going out for basic provisions.

One afternoon, Katherine was shopping at the Stop and Shop supermarket in Patriot Square. She looked over the fruits and vegetables selecting those items on her list. As Katherine placed a head of lettuce into her shopping cart, she heard her name called out.

"Katherine, how are you doing?" Katherine turned to see Dee Crowe standing a few feet away from her doing her own shopping. Dee came around the end of the counter between the two and approached Katherine.

"I'm fine Dee, how are you?"

"Harry shut Sundancers down for the usual winter break so I have quite a bit of free time on my hands."

"Are you working anyplace else?"

"No, I schedule all of my projects for the few months Sundancers is closed. Plus, I try to get my vacation time in during the break. How about you Katherine? What have you been up to?"

"Not much since Frank died."

"Yeah, that was really too bad."

"I thought I had finally gotten my life together. Frank had asked me to move to Connecticut with him. We were going to get married."

"After all you've been through, it's too bad it didn't work out for you."

"Thanks for your kind words Dee. I really appreciate it."

"Where are you going after leaving here Kat?"

"I have to take my groceries home and then I was planning to take a walk at the West Dennis beach."

"I've got to put my stuff away as well. When I'm done, can I join you?"

"Sure, why not? I haven't had any company for a few months now."

"We didn't see you again after the funeral and Harry thought you might have moved."

"I didn't. I just couldn't find it in me to get involved in anything."

"I understand. I can meet you down at the beach in about an hour. Would that work for you?"

"Sure. I'll see you then."

Dee took her grocery cart and went in the opposite direction finishing up her shopping. Katherine continued her shopping as well and in fifteen minutes, she was paying at the register. When she finished, she saw Dee a few registers away and Dee said, "See you in an hour."

Katherine responded, "In an hour."

Both ladies went to their respective vehicles storing their groceries and heading home. It took Katherine about ten minutes to put her groceries away, then she went into her bedroom and put on a pair of walking sneakers and a warm sweat suit. She grabbed a pair of mittens and a wool hat. She locked the door to her house behind her, got into her car and drove to the West Dennis Beach.

As Katherine pulled into the parking lot, she parked next to Dee's red Ford SUV. Dee, having arrived a few minutes earlier, was stretching on the beach. She had gone home, put her groceries away, put on her jogging suit, gloves and hat and driven to the beach. As Katherine got out, Dee said, "Look at you. All pink."

"I picked this outfit up at the mall last fall during Breast Cancer awareness month. I only wear it when exercising. But I have to admit. I'm a closet pink lover."
"Did you bring gloves and a hat?" Dee asked.
"Yup."
Katherine opened the trunk of her Camry and reached in. She pulled out a gray ski cap and a pair of black mittens.
"Not pink?" Dee laughed.
"No, I didn't have a pink hat or gloves, but I'll put them on my Christmas list."
"Well, put on what you have. It's cold out here."

The two started to walk west along the parking lot. The West Dennis beach parking lot gets a lot of people walking, running and biking. The parking lot is over a mile, and long and flat. About the only time of year when there isn't much activity is when it's raining or extremely cold. The current afternoon had been sunny and around forty degrees making conditions tolerable for outside exercise.

As the two walked, Dee said, "So, Katherine, what're your plans now that Frank's gone?"

"I don't know. Maybe I'll travel a little. I have enough money from when Sam died. I just don't have any ambition."

"I can imagine after all you've been through," said Dee as they continued to walk.

An elderly couple passed the two going in the opposite direction. The man said good afternoon. Dee said Hi but Katherine didn't say anything. She was deep in thought. As the two approached the first restroom station at the end of the first straightaway, Katherine said, "Maybe I should get a job."

"I thought you didn't need any money?"

"I don't. But a job would take my mind off the bad things that have happened and I might meet some new people."

"What kind of work would you be interested in?"

"Maybe I should try being a bartender, like you."

"You'd have to put up with a lot of crap."

"I can imagine."

"Oh, it's probably quite a bit more than you think. But you do get to meet some interesting people."

"Maybe I'll come in sometime and talk with Harry."

"I'm sure that would make his day" Dee said sarcastically.

"Don't you think Harry likes me?"

"He has opinions stemming from the attacks on some of the patrons."

"Did he think it was me?"

"Let's just say he was happy when you were going to marry Frank and move to Connecticut."

"Well then maybe I should try someplace else."

"I have some contacts at some of the other bars in town if you want them."

"Oh, thank you Dee. I'd appreciate your help."

"Why don't you come over to my house after we finish walking and I'll give you some business cards. I'm sure you'll find something with one of my contacts. And use me as a reference for sure."

"Sounds great."

The two kept walking and talking about different, lighter, topics. When they reached the end of the parking lot, Dee stopped and looked across the river to the Yarmouth side.

"I'd love to own a house right on the river."

"I thought your house was on the river?"

"Well, I can see it from my back deck. Mostly, my house sits back well off the water. You'll see when you come over later."

Dee stood and started to walk back to their cars. As the two continued walking, Dee said, "I thought I saw something in the paper about Tom Bowman's appeal."

"What did it say?"

"Something about irregularities with the proceedings and a retrial may be granted."

"You're kidding, right?"

"No. It seems the judge who heard the case has been reprimanded for his handling of the trial and a new judge is considering a retrial."

"I hadn't heard. But then again, I haven't been reading the papers every day and I don't watch the news on TV."

"You might want to look into it."

"I will, thanks. I think."

They arrived at the cars after the forty-minute walk.

"Thanks for walking with me Dee. It's been a while since I got out and talked with another person."

"Glad to help. Don't forget to follow me home and I'll give you those business cards."

"I'll be right behind you."

Dee got into her SUV, started it and backed out. Katherine followed in her vehicle. They went down Lighthouse Road and made a left on to Lower County Road. When they got to the end of the street, Dee turned right on Route 28. Katherine followed. Dee made a left on Main Street and turned into the third driveway on the left. Katherine pulled in right behind her.

As Katherine walked behind Dee, Dee took out her keys and opened the door. Dee said, "Take a look out on the back deck and you'll see what I meant by being able to see the river but not living right on it."
"Ok."

Katherine opened the sliders and walked out on the back deck. She could see past the end of the back yard through a few trees that the Bass River was partially visible. As she turned to go back inside, she saw some clothing Dee had hanging on the outside clothesline. At the end of the clothesline, there hung a pair of black silk Playboy pajamas. Katherine walked over and looked at them closely.

"These are my pajamas," she said out loud, bewildered.

Just then, Dee had come out on to the back deck. She saw Katherine looking at the pajamas.
"Do you like them?" Dee asked as she approached Katherine.
"I had pajamas just like these the night I was attacked at my house."
"Really?"
"Yes. Where did you get these?"

6

"That's a story in itself," Dee said running her hand over the pajama bottoms.

"The night I was attacked in my home, I had them on, but I couldn't find them afterwards. I reported them missing to the police. They probably figured I was crazy."

"I got this pair from Sundancers. One night after closing, I was putting money in the office safe when I found them. When I went back into the bar I showed them to Harry. He had made us a nightcap and while we were talking, he told me I could have them."

"So Harry had them?"

"He said he didn't know how they ended up at the bar or who had left them there. I tried them on and he said I looked good in them and to keep them."

"Harry had them."

"Like I said, I found them in the office. I don't know how they got there."

"Dee, do you think Harry could have been the one who attacked me at my house?"

"Why would he have attacked you?"

"I don't know. But these could have been my pajamas."

"I'll have to ask him when I see him."

"When did you say Sundancers was going to open for the New Year?"

"He usually opens up by the end of February so I'm sure I'll be seeing him soon."

"Dee, do you have Harry's phone number? I'd like to talk to him about the pajamas."

"Sure. I'll write it down and add it to the stack of business cards I put on the table by the door for you."

"Thanks Dee. I really appreciate your help."

"Anytime."

The two walked back into the house. Dee went to the table by the door. She took out a pad and wrote a number on it.

"Here's Harry's number."

Then she picked up a stack of business cards and handed them to Katherine.

"You should be able to find something in these."

"Thanks again Dee."

"Don't mention it."

Katherine took the cards and left.

Chapter 2

Katherine left Dee's house and went home. Walking into her house, she put the business cards Dee gave her on her desk in the study. She kept the piece of paper with Harry's phone number on it in her hand and walked to the kitchen. She picked up the phone and entered the number.

"Hello. This is Harry. I'm not available to take your call right now. After the tone, leave your name, number and a short message. I'll get back to you as soon as I can."

Katherine left her name, number and told Harry she had something she wanted to talk to him about. Then she hung up. When she did, she noticed a blinking light on the portable phone base unit indicating messages waiting. She called in.

"Katherine, its Charles Chamberlin. I'd like to take you to dinner if your schedule allows. Please call me." Katherine looked the recent phone calls up on her caller ID. She wrote down the number corresponding with the time the message had been left. She wondered what Charles wanted. He never just wanted dinner.

A second message waiting was from her attorney, Steven Kennedy. She pressed the button and listened.

"Katherine, its Steven. I was notified from the Barnstable Court today that Tom Bowman is going to be granted a new trial. His attorney had appealed the case and a new trial has been scheduled to start in about three months. Call me."

Katherine had lost her husband to an incident where he had been ice fishing with Tom Bowman out on Cape Cod Bay. Her husband, Sam, and Bowman had ventured out one Saturday for a day of ice fishing and had become stranded on an ice floe when it broke away from land. Over the next few days, the two drifted on the ice out into the Atlantic Ocean until the ice finally broke up. At the last minute, Bowman was rescued alive while her husband Sam was brought back dead a result of hypothermia from falling through the ice into the frigid waters days earlier. Katherine had thought there was more to the story than was told. Bowman had a thing for her and she thought he had played a greater role in Sam's death. She felt so strongly about it, she had conceived a plan to attack women in the area leaving clues implicating Bowman. Additionally, she intimated to Bowman certain acts involving the victims and had told him she would look favorably on him if the acts were carried out by him, too. With sufficient evidence, Bowman had been charged with attacking some of the middle-aged women on Cape Cod. There were issues with his trial that were being reviewed upon appeal and it looked like those issues were coming to a head.

Katherine thought about it for a minute and realized she had a few things to do. She had to talk to Judge Benson and she had to see if Tom Bowman was going to be released while awaiting retrial. Since Frank Jenkins had died, she didn't think she had any real contacts at the Dennis Police Department she could rely on. Maybe she would try Captain Tomlinson or Detective Grimes.

First, she tried Captain Tomlinson. When the dispatcher answered at the Police Department, she asked for Captain Tomlinson. The officer on duty informed her that Captain Tomlinson had retired at the end of the last year. He then asked if she wanted to speak with the current chief, Captain Pam Trudy. Katherine declined.

Then Katherine asked if she could speak with Detective Grimes. The duty officer said Grimes had transferred to a department off Cape and he could get her a number if she could wait a few minutes. Again, Katherine declined. She thanked the officer for trying to help her and hung up.

Katherine thought about her relationship with Pam Trudy. She knew Frank had worked with Pam on a few occasions sometimes more closely than Kat would've liked. She had a hunch Frank had slept with Pam Trudy at least one time and she thought Pam Trudy held Katherine partially responsible for Frank's misfortunes. Katherine decided not to contact her.

Katherine then made a call to the Corrections Department in Barnstable. She asked how she could find out the status of an inmate. She was told to utilize the Internet and to go to the Barnstable Corrections Department site, barnstablecorrectionsdept.gov. There she could use an inmate search to view the current status of anyone serving a sentence at the institution. Katherine wrote everything down and hung up. She went to her computer, entered the web address and eventually entered "Tom Bowman" into the inmate search area. The response she got back startled her.

"No Match for Name Entered."

"How can that be?"

She tried again, this time entering "Thomas Bowman" into the search fields. Again, she received the same response. She looked further down the screen on the left side and found a Contact Us button. She selected it. A phone number was provided as one of the options. She called it.

"Barnstable Corrections Department."

"Hello, my name is Katherine Sterns. I was trying to find out the status of an inmate, Tom Bowman. When I put his name into the online search at your site, it returned with a No Match message."

"That means the person isn't here," was the response from the man at the other end of the phone.

"But I know he's in jail. He was convicted last year and is serving a sentence of over twenty years."

"Maybe he got transferred to another facility or maybe his sentence was commuted or maybe his attorney filed an appeal and he's going to be retried."

"How would I find out?"

"What's the name again?"

"Tom Bowman, or Thomas Bowman."

She could hear the man hitting some keys in the background. "Here it is. He's been released pending retrial."

"Oh no."

"Ms. Sterns, if you were involved with this person, your attorney should have been notified of a retrial, and he or she should have notified you."

"He was, and he did, but he didn't say Tom had been released."

"Well, he has. He posted bail yesterday and was released. Is there anything else I can help you with?"

"No. I guess not."

She hung up and called her attorney, Steven Kennedy.

"Steven, has Tom Bowman been released from prison?"

"He could if he can get someone to post his bail."

"So you knew he was getting out?"

"No. I just knew he had been granted a retrial. The Judge who granted the retrial had ordered bail and set it at $100,000."

"Who would put up $100,000 for him?"

"Well, the bail was $100,000. He probably only had to put up ten percent, or $10,000."

"Still, who would do that?"

"Maybe a friend or family. I can find out if you want."

"Please do."

"I'll call you when I know something."

"Thanks Steven. Goodbye."

"Bye."

Hanging up, Katherine thought about what she had learned. Her pajamas or an exact copy at Dee's house, a gift from Harry, Charles Chamberlin's phone message, Captain Tomlinson retiring and now Tom Bowman getting released from jail, what else could go wrong?

All of these things happening at the same time made her think about the horrible times she had experienced at the end of the last year. She lost her best friend, Dottie Masters, to cancer shortly after her fiancé, Frank Jenkins, had been killed in an automobile accident. All of her expectations had been upbeat, as Frank had been offered a job as a Police Chief in a Connecticut town. He had asked Katherine to marry him and to move to Connecticut with him. She had thought she would finally put all of the bad things that had happened in her life behind her. Now all of a sudden the bad things were coming back.

As she looked out her back window, her phone startled her from her thoughts.

"Hello."

"Katherine, its Harry. You called."

"Yes. Harry, I ran into Dee at the grocery store recently. She had me stop over to her house for something and while I was there I found pajamas that looked exactly like the ones I'd been wearing the night I was attacked in my house hanging on her clothesline. When I asked her where she got them, she said from you. Can you tell me how you came to have them?"

"Let me see. Were they black, silky material?"

"Yes. They had a playboy logo on them."

"Oh, yeah. I remember them. They were in the bar one night when we were closing up, probably after the Halloween party or something. I put them in my office in case someone stopped in to claim them. Then, Dee found them and asked if she could have them. I didn't know where they came from or who owned them, and they had been there awhile, so I told her she could."

"You sure you don't know where they came from?"

"Nope. People are leaving things here all the time. We have quite a few things in lost and found."

"But pajamas?"

"Katherine, you'd be surprised at the things people leave here. I found a bikini once and I'll bet there's four or five pair of women's underwear in the lost and found box. We must have a dozen sweat shirts and two-dozen baseball caps in there, too. Plus, people are always leaving their glasses somewhere in the bar.

"Harry, if those pajamas Dee got from the bar were the same ones I had on the night I was attacked, then the person who attacked me was at your bar that night."

"That was such a long time ago Katherine, I have no way of knowing who might have left them there. Plus, the day I found them may not have been the same day they were left."

"Well, think about it if you would and if you remember anything, let me know."

"Ok. I will. Anything else?"

"Well, there is one thing. Dee suggested I do something to get back into the swing of things."

"We didn't see you much around the bar after that Detective died. I wondered what you were up to."

"I haven't been going out much. I think I've been too depressed."

"What did you have in mind?"

"Dee thought I might look for a job and I thought about Sundancers."

"We're just getting ready to open up after the winter closing. Why don't you come in and let's talk about what you might be interested in doing."

"Ok. When should I come by?"

"How about Friday around 2 pm?"

"I'll be there."

"See you then."

Katherine's attitude improved suddenly. She had a bounce in her step as she went around her house straightening things up. On Friday, she would get out to Sundancers and talk with Harry about a job.

Harry, on the other hand, hung up the phone and shook his head. He had thought he was done with her and now he had invited her to come talk to him. What the hell was the matter with him?

Chapter 3

Katherine felt good for the first time in quite a while. After straightening things up at home, she took out a bottle of white wine and poured herself a glass.

"Maybe things are changing direction," she thought to herself.

She picked up her portable phone, looked up the caller-ID for Charles Chamberlin and pressed talk. As the number she called started to ring, Charles Chamberlin answered.

"Charles Chamberlin."

"Charles, its Katherine. You called?"

"Katherine, I'm glad you called back. I'd like to get together with you. I have some good news for you."

"What kind of news?"

"I'm back in the states."

"Where are you?"

"On Cape Cod."

"And you want to get together?"

"Yes. I flew in a few days ago and I've been busy getting things straightened out."

"Charles, when I saw you in Rio, I thought you were all set down there."

"I did have a good thing going, but Brazil isn't the same as the states. I decided to move back."

"How are you going to avoid the authorities?"

"That's what I wanted to talk to you about. Things aren't what they appear Katherine. You and the other women I've been accused of robbing have it all wrong. I'd like to explain everything to you."

"I don't know Charles. I think the police are looking for you."

"I have a plan. That's what I want to talk with you about. Can we have dinner? Please?"

"I don't know Charles; I haven't been out much since Frank died."

"I heard. I'm sorry for your loss."

"Thanks Charles, you're always the gentleman."

"I was on Cape Cod when it happened but I didn't want to contact you. The timing wasn't right."

"What were you doing here?"

"Trying to get my plans set."

"For what?"

"I wanted to come back but I had some things to take care of first. Now everything's in place."

"Sounds mysterious."

"There's no real mystery. I just had to get a few things taken care of before I came back." He changed the subject. "So I guess you were serious about that detective I saw you with in Rio."

"Yeah. We were engaged. He was coming over to my house when he was killed in an automobile accident."

"Again, I'm so sorry."

"Thank you for your kind words, but I'm not sure I'm ready to move on just yet."

"Katherine, getting out will be good for you. Plus, I think you'll be excited when you hear what I have to tell you."

"What could you want to tell me that would be better than your giving me back the two million you already returned to me?"

"Come to dinner and you'll find out."

"Alright. When would you like to have dinner?"

"How about tomorrow night?"

"Tomorrow, no, I can't make it tomorrow night."

"What night would be good?"

"How about Saturday night?"

"Saturday's fine for me. I'll pick you up at seven."

"I'll be ready, Charles."

"Looking forward to it Katherine."

"Bye."

Katherine hung up. She straightened things up at her home and then went to her bedroom closet. She took a few dresses out, holding each one up in front of the mirror, trying to decide which one to wear for her dinner date. After looking at a half dozen or so, she decided on a red dress that accentuated all of the right things. She took out a pair of black shiny heels to match the dress and her Louis Vuitton pocketbook. As she looked into the mirror, she commented to herself that it was time to get active again. She put Saturday night out of her mind for now, but this outfit might see another date, besides Saturday.

On Friday morning, Katherine got ready for her meeting with Harry. She dressed in a pair of winter white jeans with a nice pale pink cashmere sweater. She pulled her hair back into a ponytail giving her a kind of schoolgirl look. At 11:30, she left her house for Sundancers.

Pulling into the Sundancers parking lot, there were only two other cars there. She recognized one as Harry's Jeep

Grand Cherokee and the other as Dee's Ford Explorer. Kat went to the main door. Dee was working behind the bar getting things organized as Kat approached.

"Dee, is Harry around?"

"Hey Katherine. He's in the office. Go back out the door and across the parking lot. The last door on the left is Harry's office. I'm sure he's inside."

"Thanks Dee."

Dee knocked on the left-most door and could see through the blinds that the lights were on and someone was seated behind a desk.

"Come in."

Kat opened the door and went in.

"Dee said I would find you here," Kat said as she stood in front of Harry's desk.

"Have a seat Katherine."

She took off her coat, hung it on the coat rack in the corner and sat down.

"When do you plan on opening back up Harry?"

"It will take us a week or two to get everything organized and ready. I'm planning on being open the first of March."

"Do you think you'll have a need for me by then?"

Harry, not sure how to respond, was put on the spot. He already knew this was not what he wanted to have happening. Katherine? At the bar? And then he heard himself. "Sure. Our business usually picks up pretty quickly once we open back up. There are a group of regulars who will start coming in once the doors open. I'll need waitress staff, a hostess or two and maybe some kitchen help."

"I don't know about the kitchen. I don't think I'd be any good in there."

"I wasn't thinking of you working in the kitchen Katherine. With your looks, you should be a hostess or a waitress."

"Thank you Harry."

She smiled and held her head back looking confident.

"No really, looks count. I'll bet the better looking waitresses who can actually do the job make quite a bit more money than those who don't have the looks or can't do the job."

"And what about the hostess?" she asked.

"The right hostess can help alleviate stressful situations when we're packed. Men, especially, will be more tolerable and willing to wait, if the hostess is good looking and pleasant. Certainly steering them to the bar to wait is a good thing for everybody."

"Really? Harry, you've got this all figured out."

"I don't know about that but I know what's worked in the past and what hasn't. Are you interested in being a hostess?"

"I'd like to give it a try."

"Then why don't you plan on being here on March 1st at 3:00 pm. Dress nice and bring your smile. You know what kind of place we are. Don't underdress, don't overdress."

"I will. And thanks Harry for being so considerate."

"Kat, with your looks, I'm sure you'll fit right in."

"I'll be ready."

"Before you leave, you didn't even ask about the pay."

"I don't really need the money Harry. I'm more interested in keeping busy."

"Well, in any case, the pay's $12.00 per hour to start out."

"That'll be fine."

"Ok, then we'll see you on the first."

"See you then."

Katherine got up, put on her coat and left. On the way out, she stopped back in the bar. Dee was still working behind the bar restocking. Katherine walked up.

"Dee, it looks like I'll be working here as a hostess."

"Great."

"I'm starting when Harry opens March first."

"That should be interesting."

"I'll bet it will. I can't wait to see the look on everyone's face when they see me working here."

"Me either."

"Well, I'll let you get back to work. See you on the first."

"See you then."

After Katherine left, Dee went into Harry's office.

"Harry, what're you thinking? Offering her a job?"

"I think she could be a big asset if we can keep her under control."

"What do you mean *we*?"

"You'll have to keep an eye on her when she's working just to make sure her focus is on Sundancers' business and not her own."

"Oh, you're putting me in an awkward position. I get too busy to be a spy, too."

"Dee, you can handle it."

"We'll see."

Dee turned and went back to the bar to continue her work.

Chapter 4

Katherine had a storied history with a number of the patrons at Sundancers. She had dated or slept with many of the men and at one time had been close friends with a few of the middle-aged women who frequented the establishment. She would have to figure out how to interact with those she knew from her past in a manner favorable to Sundancers' interests, but for now, first things first. She focused on her upcoming date with Charles.

She went to the beauty parlor, had a pedicure and a manicure. Then she had her hair highlighted slightly strawberry blond. She wanted to look her best getting out.

On Saturday afternoon, she put on the deep teal jewel-toned dress she had selected adding a unique turquoise and silver necklace and earrings. She applied a new perfume she had recently purchased and declared herself ready. She looked stunning. A few minutes before seven, her doorbell rang. She opened the door asking Charles to come in.

Charles had dressed in dark slacks with a pair of black loafers. He dressed in a light blue dress shirt accompanied by a dark blue sweater vest. Over the vest, he had on a dark gray twill sport jacket.

He couldn't take his eyes off of her.

"Stop staring Charles."
"You look great Katherine."
"Like you haven't seen me before?"
"I guess it's been a long time."
"Not that long Charles. Remember Rio?"
"You're right. You looked great down there as well. What have you done with your hair?"
"I had it highlighted. And if I remember correctly Charles, I didn't have anything on the last time I saw you."
"Like I said, you looked great then and even better now. I'd like to see you in that light again if I could."
"Charles, I haven't been with a man since Frank died. You'll have to be patient with me. It's been a difficult time."
"I understand Katherine. I was just remembering."
"Well, I try not to remember too much. The memories are pretty painful."

Charles knew she was referring to the times Katherine had with Frank. In Rio, he had watched the two through their hotel room window from his apartment in the building next door, so he knew how involved Katherine had been with Frank. He changed the subject.

"I've made a reservation at Alberto's for 8:00 pm. We should be going."
"Let me get my coat."

Katherine retrieved her coat from the closet by the front door. Charles helped her put it on. He caught a whiff of her perfume. The two went out the door with Katherine locking it behind them. They got into Charles' car heading towards Hyannis. On the way there, Katherine talked a little about her seclusion after Frank died.

"I really shut down when he died."

"I'm sure it must have been difficult. It was quite unexpected." He tried to be sensitive to her plight.

"It was, and tragic. I haven't been out other than to get groceries."

Charles tried to lighten the topic a little. "About the time Frank died, I had gone out with your friend, Ann Benard. She told me about most of the things that had happened to you. I thought it wise not to call on you at the time."

"Oh Charles, you could've called me."

"It didn't feel right."

"So you were with Ann?"

"I thought she might not remember me from before. At first she went along with the Wes DonLevy thing but eventually, she told me she knew who I was."

When Charles had left the country after what had appeared to be a theft of large sums of money from a number of wealthy widows on Cape Cod, he moved to Rio and had changed his name to Wes DonLevy. He had changed his name in order to give him time to set up a new business operation and identity.

"Charles, she was probably just stringing you along. When I came back from Rio, I had told her about our encounter down there."

"Even our rendezvous at the cabana on the beach?"

"Yes. We tell each other everything."

"Did you tell her about my name change?"

"Yes. So you see, she knew Wes DonLevy and Charles Chamberlin is the same person."

"She never let on."

"That's so like Ann. Are you still seeing her?"

"From time to time."

"I'll have to call her. Does she know you're back again?"

"I haven't called her yet."

"I'll tell her when I talk to her if you haven't called her by then."

"Do you think she'll have a problem with my taking you out?" He looked at her with his eyebrow raised.

"Ann? No, we never have an issue over a man."

"Never?"

He had a puzzled look on his face.

"Never," she said.

"That's good to know."

"So what's all the mystery about your return?"

"I'll tell you over dinner, after our first drink."

They pulled into the back lot behind Alberto's. The valet opened Katherine's door and then the driver's door. Charles handed the key to the Valet and then the two went inside. Charles gave his name to the hostess. She seated the two at a table near the window looking out onto Main Street. A waiter approached.

"May I get you something from the bar?"

"I'll have a dirty martini, with onions, no olives" said Katherine.

"Make it two."

The waiter left, returning a few minutes later with two martinis. Charles raised his glass to her and said, "To a beautiful woman, whom I hope to make very happy."

"Charles, what are you saying?" said Katherine as she touched her glass to his.

"It's like this Katherine. When I left the states after securing funds from a group of widows, I went to South America and invested the money. In a fairly short period of time, I was able to achieve significant returns. Now I've come back to return the fruits of those investments to my clients."

"Clients? Charles, I don't know if I'd call the women you took money from clients."

"Katherine, if you remember when I first met you, I gave you documents I said I'd been working on with your first husband."

"Yes, I remember."

"Well, if you remember, I had you sign a document outlining what I had given to you."

"Well, yes."

"One of the things in that document was a paragraph identifying me as a financial consultant."

"I remember something like that."

"It also contained language indicating that I would make every attempt to fulfill the intentions of your deceased husband's business with me."

"But I thought you were just turning the files over to me leaving any decision about proceeding to me."

"That isn't the way it was presented. The temptation was there to just take the funds and disappear but I couldn't let that happen."

"I don't understand. The authorities said you somehow took funds out of my account and the other widows' accounts and left the country."

"I realize it appears that way. I did install software on your computer to keep track of what you were doing but that was only to help you manage things."

"Why didn't you tell me?"

"And how would you have reacted."

"I guess I wouldn't have liked it."

"So I didn't. Anyhow, I invested your money and the other widows' money. The investments panned out. Now I'm back to return the investments along with a very nice return."

"But you already gave me my money back."

"I only gave you back the principle."

"And now?"

"And now I'm going to give you your returns."

"What kind of a return are you talking about?"

"Fifty percent."

"Exactly how much are we talking about?"

"That's a million dollars."

"No kidding?"

"No kidding."

"When do you plan on doing this?"

"Shortly."

"I guess things are looking better."

She picked up her martini, slid an onion off the toothpick, and took another sip. Charles did the same. The two had a wonderful dinner. Katherine was all smiles for the rest of the night. Alberto's had a piano player in the lounge they could hear from the dining room.

After dinner, the two went into the lounge and ordered after dinner drinks, Chambord for Katherine, J&B for Charles. About 11 pm, the piano player finished for the night. Charles paid the tab and the two left after having a nice evening out.

When they got back to her house, Charles walked her to the door. Katherine opened the door. Charles leaned into her to give her a kiss. As he did, she said, "So when do you plan on giving me the interest?"

"I can do some of it right now if you let me use your computer."

"Come on in. The computer is in the study. It's already turned on. I'll pour some red wine."

Charles went into the study. He logged into his account from her computer and issued a fund transfer transaction to her checking account. When she came into the room with the drinks, she handed one to him.

Katherine looked at the computer screen and saw that it said "Transfer Completed."

"That's done. Half of the interest has been sent to your account."

"What about the other half?"

"I'm waiting on a few fund transfers from settling on the investments I made in Brazil. I'll get you the rest of the money as soon as those funds come in. It should be all set in a few weeks. Plus, I just need to double check a few things first."

"What do you need to check?"

"Until the investments get liquidated, I won't have the actual gains amounts finalized. I want to get it all right."

"Great. I'll check my account in the morning and await your second transfer."

She raised her glass. He did the same.

"Thank you Charles. You've made my day."

"You're welcome."

The two finished their drinks. Charles stood and put his arms around her. He gently kissed her. As he did, he reached around her back and started to unzip her dress.

"Not tonight Charles. I'm not ready just yet. Give me some time."

"I understand."

"I'm kind of tired. It's been that kind of day. If you don't mind, I'd like to go to bed. Why don't you call me sometime and we can get together again."

"Sure. I have to go out of the country for a few weeks to finish up some business. I should be back in April or in the beginning of May at the latest."

"Why don't you call me then, when you get back?"

"I will."

With that, Katherine walked Charles to the door. As she locked the door behind him, she leaned against the door and smiled. She went right to her computer. She clicked a few keys and let out a whoop of delight."

The software she had purchased at Staples did its job. She had captured the URL, account number and password Charles had entered to transfer the funds to her account. It was payback time.

Chapter 5

Katherine spent Sunday doing her grocery shopping for the week and checking out her clothing for what she would plan on wearing as a hostess at Sundancers. On Monday morning, she opened the file cabinet in her study and took out a file she had saved. Frank had given her after the widow incident. She opened the file and began to read. The file contained fact sheets on each of the victims. She recognized the names since she and Frank had talked about them numerous times in the past.

As she read, she came across her fact sheet. It contained contact information including her name, address, phone number, e-mail address and bank account information. The fact sheet had additional pages attached to it, each dated with specific meetings held between Katherine and various members of the Dennis Police Department. She looked at the other victim fact sheets which all contained similar information. She decided to contact the other women.

One by one, Katherine went through the fact sheets and called the women at the phone numbers found on the sheets. The other women all knew about each other from conversations they had with the police department. When Katherine told them she had information for them and thought she knew of a way in which they all could get their money back plus a nice return, they were all interested. Katherine suggested they get together at her house a few days later for lunch.

Having successfully talked with all of the women, Katherine made a list of the names along with the amount of funds Charles Chamberlin had stolen from each one. She looked over the list when done. Then she tallied the list on her calculator and wrote it on the bottom of the list.

Sharon Kelly	$1,500,000
Carol Tindle	$2,000,000
Katherine Sterns	$2,000,000
Theresa Lee	$6,000,000
Ann Pierce	$2,500,000
Sarah Jacobs	$245,000
Total	$14,245,000

On Thursday, she picked up a lunch platter of cold cuts and fresh rolls, and an angel food cake with chocolate sauce for dessert. She set up a simple buffet in her kitchen along with a few bottles of wine.

At 11:45, her doorbell rang. Katherine opened the door to find Ann Pierce and Theresa Lee there. She greeted them and asked them to come in. Before she could close the door, Sharon Kelly and Sarah Jacobs walked up and she greeted them. They all went inside. Formal introductions were done. Katherine opened a bottle of white and a bottle of red wine. She asked that they make themselves at home and to get a plate and drink in her kitchen.

About that time, the doorbell rang again. When Katherine opened the door, Carol Tindle greeted her. The group was now complete. Katherine escorted Carol to the kitchen and introduced her to the other women. After everyone had fixed a plate and poured a drink, Katherine asked them to join her at her dining room table. They each took up a seat with Katherine at the head of the table.

Katherine stood up and said, "I've asked each of you to come here today to see if you're interested in getting your money back that had been lost when your husband passed away."

Carol Tindle said, "I'd love to get back what was taken from me. I can't believe I fell for that guy's story."

"We all fell for it," was a response from Ann Pierce.

"Except for me," said Sharon Kelly. "I didn't meet Mr. Connors or should I say, Charles Chamberlin, as a result of someone dying. I met him as the result of an automobile accident."

Katherine continued, "Well, as it turns out, our Mr. Chamberlin actually did something with the funds he got from us."

"How could you know that?" asked Sharon Kelly.

"I talked with Mr. Chamberlin recently. He gave me back my funds. Plus, he said he's going to give me a 50% return on my investment. Yesterday he gave me half of the interest and said I'll get the rest in a few weeks. He says."

"Investment? Is that what he called it?" asked Sarah Jacobs testily.

Katherine spoke up. "Did each of you sign a paper when Mr. Chamberlin turned over the so-called information he had gathered for your husband when he met with you?"

Each woman, except Sharon Kelly, nodded in agreement.

She continued, "Well, you probably didn't carefully read the lengthy document Chamberlin had you sign, and buried a few pages down in the document was an authorization to continue as a Financial Consultant with authorized access to your accounts."

"You're kidding?" said Theresa Lee.

"No, I'm not kidding. Chamberlin has documents on each of us authorizing him to continue as a Financial Advisor," Katherine continued as she looked around the table at each of the women.

"So what he did was legal?" asked Carol Tindle.

"Well, legal might be too strong a term. I think what he did was unethical, we were all vulnerable," commented Katherine.

"So why are you telling us all of this and where does this leave me?" asked Sharon Kelly.

"Because it's time we each got our money back including interest and then some," added Katherine. "Charles recently told me that he intends on paying us all back plus interest. I think I have a way of getting everything he has in his account including what he took from you Sharon."

"And just how are we going to do that?" asked Ann Pierce.

"Let's just say I have a way of getting your funds back. If each of you can write down an account number including the numbers in front of your account which designate the financial institution you want your funds sent to, I'll see to it your funds plus at least fifty percent interest are deposited in your account in a few weeks."

"How are you going to do that?" asked Carol Tindle.

"Let's just say our Mr. Chamberlin let his guard down once too often. As soon as the timing's right, I'll get all our money back. Charles has gone out of the country for a few weeks and before he returns, I'll get everyone's money back."

The women all cheered. Katherine retrieved the wine bottles from the kitchen and passed them around. Everyone refilled their glass and Theresa Lee made a toast.
"To Katherine. I hope you're right."
"Oh, I'm right. It's payback time."
They all laughed.

For the next hour, they talked about their time with Charles Chamberlin. With each story, they would all laugh. At the end of the luncheon, the women all thanked Katherine for having them over and for letting them in on the plan. Katherine passed a blank page of paper around the table for the transfer information from each of the women. Katherine said she would keep them all informed via e-mail over the next few weeks.

After the women had left, Katherine spent an hour on her computer entering the e-mail addresses of each woman into her address book. She created a group list with each woman's address in it and labeled the group "Chamberlin Victims."

When done, she took out sticky note with Charles' account URL information from her top desk drawer. When prompted for the User ID and Password, she referenced the sticky note again. The screen refreshed with detailed information about the account. It had a balance of $27,410,922.01.

"It looks like the investment liquidation has shown up, Charles. Now, how much are we each getting back?"

She entered the number into her calculator and then subtracted out the amount Chamberlin had taken from the women. That left a balance of just under $13,000,000. Charles had been right. He had made quite a bit. In fact, he had nearly doubled the amount he had taken.

She thought about it for a few minutes and then realized Chamberlin was going to pay the women back with interest, and still keep $6.5 to $7 million for himself. She would take care of that.

Katherine opened an Excel spreadsheet. She entered the names of the women along with the amount of money each had lost. Then she created a formula allocating the total from Chamberlin's account to each woman based on each woman's fund amount divided by the total of all the funds taken. She adjusted the formula under her name for the funds already paid back. Katherine allocated the entire balance of Chamberlin's account proportionately to the women based on how much he had originally taken from them.

"I don't believe in an eye for an eye; I believe in two eyes for an eye" Katherine commented to herself.

When she was done, she smiled.
"I'm sure everyone will be very happy with the job you did for each of us Mr. Chamberlin." She picked up her wine glass and had another drink.

Chapter 6

On March first, Katherine started her hostess job at Sundancers. She dressed smartly in a pair of black skinny jeans below a forest green short sleeved cashmere sweater. Knowing she would be on her feet for a few hours, she put on a pair of comfortable black flats. She had pulled her hair back into a ponytail. A pair of medium gold hoop earrings and a delicate gold necklace with a letter "K" completed the look. She knocked on Harry's office door promptly at 3 pm.

"Come in," Harry barked from behind his desk.
"I'm ready to start."
"Great. Go inside and see Dee at the Bar. She'll get you started."
"Thanks Harry. I really appreciate it."
"No problem."
Harry watched her as she walked out of his office. He thought with her looks, things might work out.
Katherine left Harry's office and went into the bar. She stood at the opening to the bar and waited until Dee was finished doing what she had been doing.

"Dee, Harry said I should see you to get started."

Dee came out from behind the bar. She walked Katherine over to the hostess station.

"The job's pretty straight forward. Here's the stack of menus, and the Today's Specials papers. There's a phone under the podium. When it rings, answer it."

"What do I say?"

"Sundancers, how may I help you?"

"If it's for information or a reservation, then you handle it. If it's for Harry, press hold, then 1, and the call will be transferred to Harry. If it's for the kitchen, press hold, then 2, and it will ring in the kitchen. You'll need to know who's in there each time you work, so you only transfer it if that person is working. If it's for one of the bartenders, press hold, then 3, and it will ring at the bar. If someone wants to make a reservation, enter it in the reservations book on the podium. When you first come on duty, look at the reservation book to know if you have to put a reservation card on a table. If you do, put it on a table with the appropriate place settings for the reservation. Other than that, seat whoever comes in. Smile and be as polite as you can, even to the grumpy ones."

"Do we get many grumpy people?"

"Not many. Just the old ones actually. They think you should always just have a table available for them, cuz its them. But some of the same grumpy people come in here time and time again. So I don't think its Sundancers. I think they're just always grumpy."

"Ok, I think I've got it."

Dee went back behind the bar and continued preparing for the night, chopping lemons and limes, and dumping ice. Katherine went to the hostess station to familiarize herself with everything. About twenty minutes later, an elderly couple came in.

"Here for dinner?"

"Can we have a table for two by the windows?"

"Inside or out?"

"Inside please."

"Sure. Follow me please."

Katherine picked up two menus, a specials sheet and seated the couple in the back corner of the dining room. She told them their waitress would be right with them. She went to the waitress station and informed the waitress for that table of the presence of the customers. Then she returned to the hostess station. Dee, having observed Katherine, came over to the hostess station.

"Kat, when you seat customers, make note of it on the seating chart right here on the top of the podium. Also, make note of the waitress assigned to the table. Then, as more customers come in, you'll get used to spreading the business around to all of the waitress staff. It's the hostess's duty to ensure the workload, and tips, get spread pretty evenly to the waitress staff."

"Thanks Dee. I'll make sure everyone gets a fair share of the workload."

"You catch on pretty quick Kat."

"Oh, she catches on quick," said Kenny Brown.

Kenny had just come into the bar. He stood at the podium as if he were waiting for a table.

"Kenny, is there something I can do for you?" Katherine asked.

"Kat, there are always things you can do for me. Where should I begin?"

"Kenny, I'm working."

"Yeah, Kenny. Give her a break," said Dee from behind the bar.

"Ok, Ok. I just don't see you as this kind of working woman," Kenny said to Katherine.

"I needed something to do with my time, that's all."

"You should have called me. I could have helped you out there," Kenny said smiling at her.

"I'll bet."

Kenny walked past Kat and then looked back at her. He took up a stool at the corner of the bar ensuring he had a good view of the hostess station.

"What will it be Kenny honey?" Dee said in a wise-guy way.

"Give me a bud and a shot of Jack."

Dee got his drinks and put them in front of him.

"Look Kenny, Kat has been through a lot lately. Go easy on her."

"I will. But doesn't she look great?"

"You guys are all alike. Always thinking about sex."

"Is that such a bad thing?"

"Could be."

The door to the bar opened and in walked Tina Fletcher, Sue Kent and Linda Sage. The three were friends of Katherine's.

"Hi girls," said Katherine.

"Kat, are you working for Harry now?" asked Sue.

"Yeah, I needed something to help me get going again and this seemed like a good start."

"Well, if we can help, let us know," added Linda.

The three took up a high table near the DJ station and ordered drinks from Dee. It had been a while since any of the three had seen Kat let alone talk with her.

Tina said, "Kat looks terrific, doesn't she?"

"She sure does," responded Linda.

"I'd like to ask her how she worked her way into looking that good. The last time we saw her when her fiancé died, she looked like hell," said Sue.

"She must be working out," said Tina.

"Yeah, but with who?" asked Sue.

They sipped their drinks and changed the subject.

The night went on without a hitch. Katherine did a good job seating the customers as they came in. She was pleasant to everyone and greeted every customer who came in the door promptly with a smile. All the waitresses had customers, and tips, and didn't complain. For a change. Harry sat at the corner of the bar for a while observing.

At one point he said to Dee, "Looks like it's all working out fine with Kat."

"Yeah, she has a way with people, especially the men."

"Hey, that can't be a bad thing."

"I guess."

"Any problems with any of her past boy toys?"

"Not that I've seen."

"Well, let me know if there are any."

"I will."

Harry left the bar and returned to his office. Walking past Katherine, he said, "Keep up the good work Katherine."

She smiled at him.

At 9 o'clock, Harry came into the bar area and told Katherine the kitchen would be closing in fifteen minutes and not to seat anyone else for dinner. Her shift would be done at 9:30 and he asked her to join him for a drink at the bar. At 9:30, she straightened things up at the hostess station and joined Harry.

"So what did you think of your first day?"

"I enjoyed it."

"Did anyone give you a hard time?"

"Not really although I thought Kenny was going to be difficult."

"He can be an ass sometimes."

"Sometimes," added Dee.

"I do have a history with Kenny, so I think I can handle him."

"That's just what he wants you to do Kat, handle him," said Dee.

"Ha, Ha," said Kat.

"Well, if anyone gets out of line, let me know," Harry added.

"What can I get you Kat?" asked Dee.

"I'll have a dirty martini."

"And you Harry?"

"I'll have a bud."

Dee got the drinks and handed them to Kat and Harry.

"To a job well done," toasted Harry, touching Kat's glass.

"Thank you Harry," Kat said.

"You did fine," added Dee.

Tommy Anderson, Bobby Jones and Ed Phillips all came into the bar around 10 pm. Bobby took up the stool next to Kat. Tommy and Ed sat next to Bobby.

"Kat, we haven't seen you in here for a while," commented Bobby.

"I know. I've been in seclusion."

Ed turned to Tommy and said, "I wonder who she was secluded with?"

"I heard that Ed. You could at least have some respect for the deceased," said Kat angrily.

"Yeah, that was uncalled for Ed," came a strong response from Harry.

"I'm sorry Kat. That was insensitive of me."

"Thanks Ed. I know you really didn't mean anything by it."

"So what brings you out tonight Kat," asked Tommy gently.

"Today was my first day working here at Sundancers Tommy."

"Really?" said Tommy in a surprised voice.

"Yeah, she did a great job," added Harry.

Katherine finished her drink. She looked at Harry and said, "I'm going to get going. I'm beat."

"You'll get used to it after a week or two," said Harry.

"Probably."

"See you tomorrow, 3 pm."

"See you then."

Katherine got up and retrieved her purse from the hostess station. She got her coat from the kitchen and left. As she walked to the door, Dee said, "See you tomorrow Kat."

"See you tomorrow."

Katherine left and went home.

Tommy took up the stool Kat had been seated at and said to Harry, "So, you hired Kat."

"Yeah, she wanted to be kept busy and I needed the help."

"And she sure looks good. That should be good for business, right Harry?" Tommy commented.

"Plus, she actually does a good job," said Harry.

"So you going to keep her on?" asked Tommy.

"For now."

Harry got up and walked to the kitchen. After he left, Tommy said to Dee, "Did I say something wrong to Harry? He seemed annoyed."

"He's alright. He just wants things to work out the best for Sundancers."

"Don't you think Kat will be good for Sundancers?"

"We'll see."

Chapter 7

On Saturday morning, Katherine got up and took a hot shower. She felt refreshed although her legs told her she had been standing for quite a long time the day before. She took some aspirin to help her feel better. She went to her closet looking for the right clothes for her workday. She picked out a black pencil skirt and a white button-down blouse. She went with the black flats again, mostly because just the thought of heels made her legs hurt more. When she finished dressing, she put on makeup and jewelry, and brushed her hair. She left it long resting on her shoulders. She was ready for day two.

At 2:30, she got into her car and drove to Sundancers. She parked at the far end of the lot and went in. She stored her purse under the podium and took out the reservation book to see if any reservations had been entered for her shift. There were two reservations, one for 6:30 and one for 7. The 6:30 was for a group of six people and the 7 for a couple. She went into the dining room and pulled two tables together on the right side of the dining room. Then she made sure the setting was for six. She put a reserved card on the table. Even though it was early, she could always pull it if a group of six came in between now and 6:00 pm. She decided not to put a reserved sign on any other table as all the other tables were already set up for four people and the chance of all of them being filled at 7:00 was slim. She would just take one of those tables when the 7 o'clock couple came in, but she would have to keep an eye on them just in case.

Having taken care of the reservations, she organized the hostess station, putting the specials menu inside each regular menu. She reviewed the specials menu ensuring she had an idea of what was being offered for the night. She checked the waitress station to make certain ample special menus were there for the waitress staff. Then, she went around to each empty table in the restaurant making sure they were all properly setup with condiments and drink menus. Everything was in order.

The phone rang and she walked back to the hostess station.

"Sundancers, how may I help you?" she said.

It was a customer inquiring about coming in for dinner. The caller wanted to know the hours of operation for the night and if a reservation would be necessary. Katherine told the caller the hours of operation and that reservations probably would not be necessary. After hanging up, Dee stopped over at the hostess station.

"Ready for your second night?"

"I think so. I've checked the reservations log and put a reserved on a table for a group of six. There's another couple coming in at 7, but I didn't think a reserved table would be necessary."

"As long as you are keeping track of the seating on the chart there, you should be able to ensure a table's ready when they come in."

"I'm all set there. Say Dee, how do you think I'm doing?"

"Things seemed to go fine last night."

"Good. I want Harry to be pleased with my work."

"He was very positive when I spoke to him last night."

"When was that?"

"Right after you left. He was talking with Tommy and I heard him say some good things."

"Oh, Tommy. He tried to come on to me while I was working last night."

"What did he do?"

"Just little things. Every time I walked past him, he would make a comment. Or he would have his elbow out where I had to make contact."

"I think he was just teasing you."

"I hope so. I don't want anyone from my past to present a problem for me or Harry, especially with regards to my work."

"Harry can handle them."

Just then, the door opened and in walked Tom Bowman. He stopped in front of the waitress station and just stared at Katherine.

"Will it be a table or seat at the bar Tom?" asked Katherine.

"What? Are you working here now?"

"I'm the hostess."

"You're kidding? Didn't you inherit enough money when Sam died?"

"That's none of your business Tom."

"I'll sit at the bar."

He walked past her and took up a seat on the far side of the bar where he could see the whole place. He ordered a beer and sat there by himself watching Kat. After serving him the beer, Dee said, "Harry doesn't want any trouble."

"Don't worry. I'm not going to create a scene. But sometime soon, she's going to have to answer for everything she's done."

The front door opened and Kenny Brown walked in.

"Hey Katherine," he continued walking. He took up a stool near the hostess station.

"Dee, can I have a Bud?"

"Sure Kenny."

Dee took a cold mug out of the freezer and poured a cold one. She put it in front of Kenny. He took a drink and set it on the bar.

"Kat, everyone says you did a good job last night," Kenny said turning around to speak to her.

"Everyone did, did they?"

"Yeah. You're a natural. Harry should be real happy."

"I'm just trying to do a good job Kenny, that's all."

"I'm just saying, you are."

"Thank you."

"Say Kat, why don't we get together after your shift's over?"

"That's alright Kenny. I'll be tired when my shift's over. I'll just want to go home and rest."

"I could help you."

"I'll bet."

"You know what I mean."

"Yeah, that's the problem."

"What problem?"

"Let it go Kenny," said Dee as she came around to the waitress station.

"Ok, Ok."

Kenny turned around and went back to drinking his beer. Dee talked to Kat for a few minutes. Then she went back to bartending.

"I'll have another one," said Kenny.

When Dee put the beer in front of him, he said, "What's he doing in here?" He pointed at Tom Bowman.

"Who knows," said Dee.

"I thought he was in jail."

"Something about his appeal was granted and he's getting a new trial. But I'm not a lawyer, so who knows."

"The girls aren't going to be happy to see him around," said Kenny before taking a drink from his beer.

"You're right. They were in here last night and I heard them talking about it. They're still ticked at him for what he did to them."

"And didn't he keep saying Kat had a lot to do with those attacks on them?"

"Supposedly that's his story. It should be interesting to see how his retrial ends up."

"This is strange. Kat working here as a hostess and here this guy is at the same place."

"For now, he's not creating a problem."

"Maybe not, but if Harry knows he's here, he'll blow a gasket."

"I think we're going to find out," said Dee as she was looking into the kitchen door just as Harry was coming through it.

"Kenny," said Harry.

"How are things Harry?"

Harry looked around and said, "I thought good but I see a problem." He was staring at Tom Bowman. Harry walked to where Tom was seated.

"You're not welcome in here Mr. Bowman."

"Isn't this a public place?"

"It's a bar and restaurant. My bar and restaurant. And I say you're not welcome here."

"You can't kick me out."

"You don't think so?"

"No I don't."

"Look Bowman. There are other places you can go near by and not bother my staff or me. Why don't you just leave?"

"Harry, is he giving you trouble?" asked Kenny.

"No. Mr. Bowman is just leaving."

"I'll finish my beer. Then I'll go."

"There's no charge for the beer Bowman. Just leave."

Harry motioned to Dee to take the glass. Dee did. Tom Bowman stood up and walked out. On his way, he momentarily stopped at the hostess station.

"This isn't over Kat."

Tom walked to the door. Harry followed close behind him. As he opened the door, he looked back at Harry and said, "I won't be any problem for you Harry. I'm going to Virginia for a few weeks to see my kids."

"Well, I don't think you should come around here when you come back to Cape Cod."

"You'll see things differently after my retrial Harry. She isn't good to have around."

"Just keep going Bowman."

Tom Bowman got into his car and left.

"I'm sorry about that," Katherine said to Harry after Tom had departed.

"You didn't do anything wrong Katherine. Don't worry about it."

"I just don't want to create any problems for you Harry. You have been good to me."

"Like I said, you're not creating any problems for me plus Bowman said he's going out of state for a few weeks."

"He is? Did he say where he was going?"

49

"Something about seeing his kids."

"He must be going to Virginia. That's where his ex lives now."

"You shouldn't have to worry about him for a while."

"Yeah. You're probably right."

"Like I said, it's not a problem."

Harry turned back to Dee at the bar and she said in a low voice, "Yet."

Harry just looked at her, turned and walked back into the kitchen. It sounded like Dee had some premonition, and that worried him.

The rest of Kat's shift went without incident. A few people came in whom Katherine knew and she made small talk with them. She was able to give the couple that came in for the 7 o'clock reservation a good table by the windows. She wrapped up her shift around 9:30 and then asked Dee to make her a drink as she took up a stool at the bar. Kenny was still there. He moved to the stool next to Katherine.

"So how did your shift go?" he asked her.

"Just fine."

"Did Bowman give you a hard time?"

"Not really. Harry took care of it."

"Want me to take you home?"

"No. I can take care of myself."

"I'm not trying to be difficult Kat. I just want to help."

"Kenny, you just want to get laid."

"Well, I wouldn't pass it up if the opportunity presented itself."

"I'm sure you wouldn't." She picked up her glass and took a sip.

"So what are your plans for the rest of the night?" Kenny asked as he set his beer down.

"I have a date."

"Anyone I know?"

Just then, Kenny looked over her shoulder and saw Harry coming towards them. When Harry stopped right behind Katherine, Kenny said, "She has a date."

"I know," was Harry's response. "You ready to go?" Harry said to Katherine.

"Yep."

Katherine stood and left with Harry. When they had left, Kenny said to Dee, "Harry and Kat on a date?"

"What's wrong with that?"

"Oh, nothing. Nothing at all."

Chapter 8

Harry and Katherine were out on their first date. Katherine drove her car to her house and parked it in the driveway. She got out and got into Harry's car. Harry took her to a place he knows in Harwich, the Hot Stove Saloon, that had a singer that night. They got a table for two in the lounge area and ordered drinks. When the drinks came, Harry made a toast.

"You're doing a great job Katherine. I really appreciate it."

"You saying that as a boss or a friend Harry?"

"Both."

"You take all of your female employees out on dates?"

"Nope. Only the interesting ones."

"I interest you?"

"Yes."

"How so?"

"You're a mysterious person Katherine. I think I had the wrong impression of you in the past. You're really a hard working, conscientious person."

"You really don't know me Harry."

"But I know people. You get to see things in people's actions that tell you a lot about the person. I've watched you working."

"And from watching me, you think you can tell things about me?"

"Yes. For instance, you're concerned about neatness and attention to detail. You take the time to make sure the tables in the dining room are all arranged properly and orderly."

"I guess I do. That must be the Virgo in me."

"Plus, you're pleasant to everyone who calls or comes in. Even to people who have been rude."

"That's just my nature."

"See what I mean. I picked that all up just by watching you."

"And what about me as a woman Harry? Does that interest you?"

Harry was quiet for a minute. Then he looked her in the eyes, "Katherine, you're a very beautiful woman. Any man would be happy to be with you. You look terrific and you take care of yourself."

"Why thank you Harry."

"You have a charm that's alluring."

"Really?"

"Yes, really."

"You sure it isn't just your male hormones?"

"It's probably some of that too. But I like you."

"If you keep up those kind words Harry, you'll break down my resistance."

"Katherine, are you resisting me?"

"Not just you, Harry. Since Frank died, I have resisted all men."

"In time, maybe you'll see things differently."

"We'll see."

They sat and listened to the singer for the next few hours. They laughed about some of Harry's stories, even the ones including Katherine. At the end of the night, Harry drove Katherine home. When they got to her house, he walked her to the door. She allowed him to kiss her and then she went into the house, alone. Harry got into his car and drove away.

With the door closing behind her, she leaned against it and said, "What a gentleman."

Katherine put her coat away and walked into her kitchen. She saw the light on her phone blinking indicating a message waiting. She called in for messages.

The first message was from Charles Chamberlin.
"Kat, its Charles. I'm still in Rio. I'm finishing up down here and I expect to be back on Cape Cod in about two weeks. Call me when you get my message."

She remembered Charles had told her she had to enter the country code before a phone number when calling internationally. She used her computer to look up the code for Brazil and entered it, along with the rest of Charles's number, and pressed call. At first, she thought he wasn't in as the phone rang four times. Then he answered.

"Charles, its Katherine. I got your message to call. What's up?"
"I should be able to wrap things up down here soon and then I'll be coming back."
"Have you returned any of the funds from your other clients yet?" she asked already knowing the answer.
"No. I want to do it in person. That's one of the things I plan on doing when I get back."
"How about the other half of the interest you said you would be giving me?"

"I'll take care of it as soon as I get back, too."

"Can't you do it from there?"

"Not really. I'd prefer to handle all that business when I'm back on Cape Cod. Please be patient. I promise I'll make everything right for you and my other clients."

"Is there anything else you wanted to tell me Charles?"

"Just that I'm coming back in a few weeks and I hope we can pick up where we left off."

"I don't know Charles."

"Katherine, I know you're still hurting from your loss. But I think I can fill that void for you."

"We can talk when you get back Charles."

"Yes, we can. I'll see you in a few weeks."

"Alright. See you when you get back. Safe trip."

"Bye."

She hung up the phone. There was another message waiting. It was from Sharon Kelly.

"Katherine, have you heard from Chamberlin? Give me a call."

There were no more messages. She selected the caller-ID for Sharon Kelly and pressed call. The phone rang at the other end.

"Sharon, its Katherine Sterns."

"Hi Katherine."

"I got your message. I talked with Charles recently and he's coming back into the country in a few weeks. He says he's going to make everything right for his clients when he gets back."

"So we're still *clients*?"

"Yeah, that's how he refers to us."

"What do you think?"

"I think everything will work out when he returns."

"It's different for you Katherine. He already gave you your money back."

"Yes, but I still have a lot more coming."

"And you feel OK he'll make good on his promise?"

"Let's say I'm confident we will all get what's ours."

"You're so sure of yourself Katherine."

"I am.   Be patient Sharon and you won't be disappointed."

"Ok. I'll wait a few more weeks."

"Look, I'll send an e-mail to you and the other women after we hang up. Hang in there. The money's on the way."

"Keep me informed if you will Katherine."

"I will."

They hung up. Katherine went to her computer and opened her e-mail account. She selected a new message and entered the group name Chamberlin-Victims into the "To" field. Then she entered a message to the group.

She thought about issuing transfers right then and there based on the funds in Charles's account but she was unsure if there would be any more funds to be transferred into his account. If he saw it was gone, their chance to get more could be gone too. She decided to wait until he said he had all the funds.

She typed,   "Talked to Charles recently.   He's returning to the states in a few weeks and intends to return all funds plus interest to his clients upon return. I have every reason to believe we will all get what's ours when he returns. Be patient for another few weeks. Katherine."

She pressed send.   The e-mail was sent to the recipients identified in the list.

Before logging off, Katherine noticed she had something in her in-box. She clicked the "Inbox" tab. There was an e-mail from her attorney, Steven Kennedy.

"Katherine, we should talk about Tom Bowman. He has been released from prison. I don't know yet who posted bond. You should be on-guard as you may run into him in town. Call me. Steven."

She deleted the e-mail and picked up the phone. After three rings, the phone was answered.

"Steven Kennedy."

"Steven, its Katherine."

"Oh, Katherine. You got my e-mail."

"Yes. That's why I'm calling."

"As I said, Tom Bowman's been released."

"I know. I tried to look him up on the Internet. I couldn't find him there. Then I remembered Frank had told me any detention center could find anyone within the system using their computers. So I tried the Barnstable Corrections Department."

"And what did they say?"

"They told me Tom had been released on bond."

"I figured he'd be out soon."

"Do you know who posted his bail?"

"Not yet. I'm still trying to find out. I should know more in a day or two."

"Well, let me know. I'd like to know if someone I know is secretly helping Tom out. If it's a friend, it won't be for long."

"Ok. You need to be careful as well. Bowman may not take too kind to you if he runs into you."

"I already saw him at Sundancers."

"Really? Did he do anything?"

"No. But he's itching to do something."

"Why do you say that?"

"He made it pretty clear he isn't happy with me."

"Well, be careful."

"I will.   Steven, Tom told Harry, my boss at Sundancers he's going out of state for a few weeks to see his kids. Can he do that?"

"I'm sure the court's keeping close tabs on his whereabouts but yes, they probably would let him see his children."

"Then I shouldn't have anything to worry about from him for a while."

"Don't worry about Bowman for now and I'll let you know if I find out anything more."

"Thanks Steven."

"You're welcome.   I'll call you when I have something."

"Bye."

Chapter 9

For the next few weeks, Katherine continued to work at Sundancers without incident. The place had opened up for the season and everything was running fine. She didn't hear from Tom Bowman, Steven Kennedy or Charles Chamberlin at all during the period. As a result, her life settled into a peaceful routine.

Towards the end of the second week, Harry decided to ask Katherine out for another date. She had off the upcoming Saturday.

"Katherine, do you have any plans for Saturday?"
"Not yet. Why?"
"Are you interested in doing something with me?"
"Like what?"
"Oh, I don't know. How about we make a day trip up to Boston."
"I'd like that. It's been a while since I was up there."
"The Red Sox have a game Saturday afternoon, and then have a nice dinner somewhere."

"I like the sound of that."

"I know a good club we can visit if we're still up to it after dinner. They have a band playing I want to hear. If they're good, I'd like to try to get them to come to Cape Cod over the summer to play."

"What time does the band go on?"

"I think 10 pm."

"That would be pretty late to drive back to Cape Cod, wouldn't it?"

"Maybe."

"Why don't we stay the night and come back Sunday morning? I have no pets Harry" she suggested.

"You sure you wouldn't mind?"

"I think I'm ready."

"Then I'll take care of getting tickets, making a dinner reservation, and making a reservation at the Copley Marriott."

"Ok. Then it's a date. You can give me the specifics tomorrow."

"Have a good night Katherine."

"Night Harry."

"Bye."

Katherine left Sundancers and went home. She had a special bounce in her step and smiled at everyone she passed. Harry continued to sit at the bar. He asked Dee to get him a beer. When she did, she stood in front of him with her arms crossed and lips pouting.

Harry said, "What?"

"So you're going to Boston with Kat Saturday and staying overnight with her?"

"Is there a problem?"

"No, no problem at all. Just be careful."

"Of what?"

"Harry, bad things seem to happen to the men in her life. Think Sam, think Tom, think Frank."

"So, now I'm a man in her life?"

"Hey, you made the move, not me."

"Just because I asked her out?"

"Yeah, just because." Dee shook her head and went back to bartending the other patrons.

Friday night turned out quiet at Sundancers. A rainy, cold spring night. As Katherine was cleaning up, Harry walked up to the Hostess station.

"I'll pick you up tomorrow at 11:00. It's a 2:05 game and that should give us time to grab a bite on Yawkey Way. Does that work for you?"

"Sure does. I'm excited. Haven't been to a game, or Boston, in a while. Thanks Harry."

"Not a problem. Thanks for going with me. See you in the am."

"Night Harry," Katherine whispered into Harry's ear, as she scooped up her purse, umbrella, and jacket and headed out the door.

On Saturday morning, Harry picked Katherine up at her house. She had an overnight bag packed. Harry put it in the back of his BMW.

"Where's the Jeep?" she asked.

"That's my work car," said Harry. "I keep this one for non-work stuff. Would you park this in the 'dancers lot?"

"Nope. Good choice, and nice car," was all she said.

They got in and headed out for Boston.

"Did you have any trouble getting tickets?"

"No. It's early in the season and I used the same guy I always use for tickets. Since I buy so many, I get a good deal from him."

"Where do we get to sit at Fenway?"

"Right on the first base line past the dugout."

"Pretty good seats."

"Like I said, my guy takes care of me."

"I'm looking forward to it."

"Just make sure you keep watch. Last time I was in those seats, a player landed on the guy seated next to me trying to catch a foul ball."

"That must have hurt."

"He was ok. But it could have been bad."

"I'll watch out. Were you able to get a room at the Marriott?"

"They were pretty full so I had to take the penthouse."

"No kidding?"

"No kidding. Course they probably just said that to rent it out. I'm kinda cynical."

"I don't think I've ever been in a penthouse suite."

"You'll like it. You'll fit right in."

"Sounds like you've been there before."

"Once."

"Harry, now you're the mysterious one."

"No mystery here."

"I'll bet you'll have the place stocked with drinks and snacks."

"I think the penthouse comes with all that stuff."

"Harry, are you trying to impress me?"

"Really Kat, it was the only room they said they had open."

"Ok. But don't get your hopes up too much."

"I promise to be a perfect gentleman."

"I wouldn't have thought otherwise."

As they continued to drive, they passed a group of people kayaking.

"Look at those people Harry. Kayaking in the cold weather."

"It doesn't have to be warm to kayak. Remember, you're using your body to paddle the kayak. It heats you up. As long as you don't fall into the water, it's not bad."

"Have you ever tried it?"

"Sure. You know Clint Somers, don't you?"

"Yeah."

"He owns the tour boat parked outside the bar in the summer time. He also owns the kayak and canoe rental business over by the Bass River Bridge. I've taken one of his kayaks out on a few occasions."

"Harry, you actually know how to kayak?"

"Hey, if you want to give it a try sometime, let me know. I'm sure I can arrange it. How about we try it when we get back on Sunday?"

"Ok, let's see what Sunday's weather brings. Are you sure it's not too cold to try something like kayaking in springtime?"

"I'm sure."

"I guess I have to try new things to get back into the swing of things."

"I guess."

"If it's a nice day tomorrow, take me kayaking."

"Like I said, we'll see."

They continued to drive. Off in the distance, they could see the Boston skyline come into view. The radio was tuned into an old rock station out of Springfield, 102.1. Both sang along to every song they knew.

"Here we are."

Harry had exited the highway and pulled into the Marriott lot. He parked near the front door.

"Let's get our room first and then go to the ball park. We can drop our stuff off and not worry about it later. Plus, we'll want to change for dinner."

"Ok. You do think of everything, don't you Harry?"

They went to the front desk and checked in. Just as Harry said, he had gotten the penthouse suite. They got in the elevator, and Harry turned to Katherine.

"Here, you use the key to get us to our floor." Harry handed her the key card. Katherine swiped it, and a bell indicated it was approved. They were whisked to the floor for penthouse suite tenants only. As the elevator doors slid open, Katherine gasped.

"This is breathtaking," said Katherine as she looked out the massive windows surrounding the room on three sides. I can see the Atlantic, all of Boston and way down by Cape Cod."

"It's impressive."

"Now I know you're trying to impress me Harry."

"Really Kat, this is all they had left."

"Sure."

"Let's put these things away and then go see the game."

They both unpacked their belongings. Kat took the bureau in front of a very large mirror. Harry put his things in a dresser by the closet. She went into the bathroom for a minute. Harry could hear her talking to herself.

"Look at this place."

He went in to the bathroom to see what she was talking about. On the left was a walk-in shower for two surrounded by glass from floor to ceiling. Next to it was an oversized tub and jacuzzi. A vanity along the far wall had two sinks and a mirror that must have been fifteen feet long.

"I could get used to this," said Harry.

"Maybe later we can try these things out," said Katherine as she ran her hand along the top of the tub.

"I'm looking forward to it."

The two exited the hotel room. They got a cab from the bellman in the lobby and went to Fenway. The place was mobbed. They walked down Yawkey Way with the other early season fans. Another good game was anticipated between the Red Sox and Twins. They picked up a bag of peanuts, two beers, and headed to their seats.

"We're so close to the field. I can't believe how big this place actually is," exclaimed Katherine.

"Remember what I told you Kat, be attentive during the game. I wouldn't want you to get hurt by a foul or one of those guys coming into the stands."

"I'll pay attention Harry."

They watched the game. Only once did a ball come into the stand near Harry and Katherine during the game. The man behind Harry deflected it just before it could hit his companion. Both Harry and Kat cheered the Red Sox during the game. They had a good time. The Sox won 5 to 3. After the game, they went back to the hotel.

As they opened the door to the penthouse suite again, Kat said, "I'm a little tired Harry, do we have time to rest before dinner?"

"Sure. I'm gonna see what's on the TV."

"I have a better idea Harry. Come with me."

She led him by the hand into the bedroom. She walked over to the windows and closed all the drapes. Then she came back to Harry who was seated at the end of the bed. She started to unbutton his shirt.

"Do you really want to do this?"

"I think I'm ready Harry. It's time."

She took her top off. Then she reached around and undid her bra allowing it to fall to the floor. She unzipped her jeans and slid them down after kicking her shoes off. As Harry rose, she undid his belt and slid his pants down. The two embraced and kissed. Then they fell back into the bed in each others arms.

After an hour of love making, Kat had curled up into Harry's arms and had fallen asleep. Harry carefully moved his arm from around Kat and got up. He went into the bathroom and took a shower. Just as he was about finished, Kat joined him.

"I woke and heard the shower running. Thought I'd join you."
"Please do."

They lathered each other's body, laughing, poking and teasing each other. Harry started to get aroused again. Kat reached down and said, "I'll see you later."
She got out of the shower, dried herself off and began to get ready for dinner. An hour later, the two were on their way out of the hotel for a night out.

As promised, Harry took her to a nice restaurant and then out to the club. Harry had wanted to see a new act to evaluate them for a possible engagement at Sundancers over the upcoming summer. The band went by the name "Ultimate Sound." The band did not disappoint. Harry and Kat were impressed by the band's ability and by the approval the band had on the crowd. At one point during the night, Harry went and talked to the bandleader during a break. When he came back, Harry was all smiles.

"Looks like we can get them to come to Sundancers this summer."

"Great. I think they'll be a big hit on Cape Cod."

"So do I. This really worked out well."

"You talking about the game, the dinner, the band or the weekend?"

"All of it."

"Then why don't we go back to the hotel?"

"I'm ready when you are."

"We'll see about that," said Kat as she took Harry's hand while exiting the club.

The two took a cab back to the hotel. When they got back into the room, Kat led Harry to the bedroom where they picked up from earlier that afternoon.

Katherine took off her clothes and stood in front of the mirror naked, brushing her hair back. As she looked into the mirror seeing Harry getting undressed in the background, she said, "Do you like this?"

He looked up at her and said, "What's not to like?"

He was staring at her breasts.

"Not those silly, I mean my hair?"

Harry looked up at her head and said, "Sure. You look great."

She could see he was ready as he stood there naked.

"You guys are all alike," she said pulling the covers back on the bed and getting in.

He joined her.

Finally at one in the morning, Harry was exhausted. The two of them lay in bed naked next to each other just talking. It felt right.

Chapter 10

They got back to Cape Cod around noon the following day. Being Sunday, there wasn't much traffic on the Cape. It was a sunny day, little wind with temperatures in the upper 50's. As they crossed the Bass River Bridge, Katherine looked over towards the Sundancers' side of the Bass River and said, "Are those Clint's kayaks?"

"Yeah. That's his spot right there at the end of the docks. Looks like he's open for business, too."

"It's such a nice day Harry, why don't we go out for a while?"

"Let's see if Clint's in."

Harry pulled into the Bass River parking lot and parked by the small shed Clint had set up by his kayaks. He got out of the car and walked over to the shed. The door was open so he called in, "Clint, you in there?"

"Yep. I'll be right out."

A minute later, Clint came out and greeted Harry with a hearty handshake.

"Hey Harry, what're you doing over here?"

"I'm just coming back from Boston. I thought if you're renting kayaks today, we'd like to take two out for a little while."

"Harry, you can use them whenever you want."

"Thanks Clint. We're going to Sundancers for a quick lunch, and then we'll be back. Can I bring you anything?"

"No thanks. I'm going over as soon as my help arrives."

"Then we'll see you at the bar."

Harry walked back to the car and got in.

"We're all set. After we grab a quick lunch, we can take two of Clint's kayaks out for a few hours."

"Great. I can't wait."

They left the Bass River Park and drove the few hundred feet into Sundancers' parking lot to get a quick lunch.

"How was Boston?" asked Dee.

"We had a very nice time," responded Katherine.

"And the Red Sox won," added Harry.

Katherine excused herself to use the restroom. When she had left, Dee said, "So Harry, how was your weekend with Kat?"

"Couldn't have been better."

"Does that mean you got lucky?"

"Dee, come on."

"Well?"

Just then, Katherine came out of the restroom and joined Harry at the bar.

"What will it be Kat?" asked Dee.

"I'll have a draft, the same as Harry's having."

"No martini?" asked Dee.

"No. We're going kayaking so I'm taking it easy."

"Kayaking," Dee shot Harry a quizzical look.

"Yeah," responded Harry. "We're taking a couple of Clint's kayaks out for a little while."

Clint opened the door to the bar and walked in. He took up the stool on the other side of Harry.

"My help finally arrived," said Clint.

"What are you having, Clint," asked Dee.

"Shock Top," was his response.

Dee poured the draft and set it in front of him.

"Dee, can I get a burger and fries, with cheddar instead of American?"

"Sure Clint."

"I've got to get back to finish cleaning up the shed after lunch. I hate opening. No matter how clean I think everything is when I close up, it seems someone messes it up over the winter."

"Why don't you have your help do it?" said Harry.

"Last year I let the help get things set up and we couldn't find the oars for the canoes. The kid had put them all in one of the kayaks. Boy did I look stupid to the customers who wanted to rent a canoe. No oars."

"So you do it all yourself?" asked Harry.

"Less stressful that way," replied Clint.

Dee went into the kitchen and came out with Clint's burger and fries. She put them in front of Clint. He added ketchup and then ate his lunch. Kat and Harry got their lunch around the same time. Harry had a burger also and Kat had a Caesar salad. All three finished around the same time.

"You two still want to go kayaking?" asked Clint.

"We're coming over in a few minutes," said Harry.

"I'll have two kayaks waiting," said Clint. "Dee, can I have my check?"

"Put it on my tab Dee," said Harry.

"Thanks Harry," replied Clint. Then he got up and left. He walked back to the Bass River Park.

When Harry and Katherine had finished their drinks, they got up and walked outside, too.

"Why don't we walk to Clint's rentals from here?" asked Kat.

"Sure," said Harry.

The two walked past the Marine Corps memorial to the Bass River Park. When they got to Clint's shed, he had two kayaks already in the water at the dock. His helper got them life vests, gave them the basics on using a kayak and helped Katherine into one of the kayaks.

"Let's head across the river to the golf course," said Harry.

"I'm following you."

Harry led the way paddling across the river towards the Bass River Golf Course. When they arrived along the shoreline, Harry waited for Katherine to catch up.

"How you doing?" he asked her.

"This is fun. I can't believe I'm not cold."

"The sun's pretty warm this time of year, and the paddling helps."

"Let's continue up river a little further."

"Around the bend, stay to the right and we can paddle past Cove Road."

"Everything looks so different from this perspective."

The two paddled side by side through the narrow part of the river. As it opened up, they paddled to the right. As they got between what looked like a road missing a bridge, Kat said, "What happened to the bridge?"

"I don't know," said Harry. "That's Cove Road on the left right there where it goes into the water and that's Cove Road on the right by the embankment. Maybe there was a bridge here at one time. I hear the guys talking about clamming here during the winter months and they always talk about Cove Road north side or south side. I'll have to ask someone to see if the two ever connected."

They paddled around the cove looking at the homes and enjoying the day. The water was calm with virtually no wind. They were on the water for about two hours finally returning to Clint's rental place at the Bass River Park.

"Was it fun?" asked Clint as he offered a hand to Katherine to get out of the kayak.

"Sure was. What a nice afternoon," Kat added.

"We're going back to Sundancers Clint. Care to join us?"

"I wish I could, but I'm going to get things put away and call it a day."

"What do I owe you?" asked Harry.

"It's on me Harry. Come again anytime."

"Thank you Clint."

Katherine walked over to Clint and kissed him on the cheek. "Yes, thank you Clint."

The two walked back to Sundancers and went inside. They took up two stools at the bar.

"Dee, now I'll have that martini."

"Beer for you Harry?"

"Sure."

Dee got them their drinks. The two sat for an hour or two talking about their weekend. As the sun went down, Katherine said, "Harry, can you take me home. It's been a nice weekend and I have to get some things ready for the week. I have to work, and my boss is a slave driver you know."

"Just give me a minute and we can go" he chuckled.

Harry went into the kitchen to talk with Antonio about something and then he returned.

"I'll be back later Dee. If business gets too slow, go ahead and close up around 10."

"Ok Harry. See you later."

The two left in Harry's car.

As they drove to her house she said, "Harry, thank you for such a nice weekend."

"You're welcome."

"I'd like to go kayaking again sometime. That was fun."

"It's even better when the weather's warmer."

"Next time, can we try going down river?"

"Sure. Better yet, I know a place where you can see seals and sometimes other wild life."

"From a kayak?"

"Yep."

"I'd like to try that sometime."

"Clint said we can use his kayaks anytime."

"Maybe we should buy our own from him?"

"Why? When we can just use his?"

"Doesn't he get real busy in the summertime?"

"I guess."

"Well, if we had our own, we could go whenever we wanted and not have to see if he has any available."

"You have a point."

"Well, I have a birthday coming up in a few weeks. You could buy me a kayak as a present."

"A birthday huh."

"Yes. I'm going to be 29. Again."

Harry laughed.

"What's so funny?"

"You."

"Why? Because I like to think I'm 29?"

"No. You actually look like you're in your 30's"

"Oh, so I'm not 29?"

"Trust me Katherine, 30's is just fine."

When they arrived at Katherine's, Harry got her bag from the trunk and walked up to the porch. Katherine opened her door.

"Coming in?" she asked him.

"No. I've got to get back to Sundancers and close out the weekend."

"I thought you told Dee to close around 10."

"If business was slow. But I still need to get back and see how the weekend went. And there's paperwork, orders, payroll…"

"Ok Harry. If you must."

She put her arms around him and gave him a big kiss.

"I had a wonderful time and I'd like to thank you properly."

"We did have a nice time. And I think you thanked me advance."

"Then I'll owe you one," she said as she kissed him again. He closed the door behind him then walked to his car. Harry had a big smile on his face as he started his car and put it into gear.

Chapter 11

Two weeks later, Katherine had just finished up her shift and was seated at the bar having a drink. Harry came out of the kitchen with a small wrapped box and card. He put it on the bar in front of her.

"Happy Birthday."
"Why thank you Harry. I thought you forgot."
"I didn't forget. Open it."

Katherine opened the package and on the inside, she found a picture of a new pink kayak.
"A pink kayak?"
"You said you wanted one for your birthday. Come with me."

Harry walked her out through the kitchen to the corner of the building. There behind the building was a brand new pink kayak. Along side it was another new bright green kayak.
"The paddles and life vests are in my office."

Katherine turned to Harry and put her arms around him. She planted a big kiss.

"I can't wait."

"Next day off when the weather's nice, we can give them a try."

"I have off on Thursday. Want to go then?"

"I'll have to check my schedule and let you know," said Harry as he turned to walk back inside.

The two went back to the bar. Antonio came out of the kitchen and stood next to Harry.

"What gives with the pink kayak behind the building Harry?"

"It's a birthday present for Katherine," said Harry.

"Oh, I didn't know it was your birthday Katherine," said Antonio looking in her direction. "How old are you anyway?"

"Let's just say I'm in my late thirties," said Katherine picking up her drink.

She walked to the back of the restaurant looking out on the Bass River. Harry walked back with her. After they had walked away, Antonio said to Dee, "Late thirties my foot."

"A woman never tells," responded Dee.

"If that one gets her claws into Harry, who knows what will happen," said Antonio.

"You don't know the half of it Antonio."

"And I don't want to know. I'm going back to the kitchen and mind my own business."

"Probably wise," said Dee as she looked at Harry and Katherine walking back from Harry's office. Dee overheard Katherine talking with Harry about kayaking.

"So you'll pick me up Thursday around noon and we'll kayak the lower Bass River?"

"Sure. Then we can come back here for lunch."

"I'll be ready."

Katherine picked up her pocketbook and left Sundancers. She was done for the night. After she left, Harry sat at the bar for a few minutes. Dee came over to talk.

"So Harry, you bought two kayaks."

"I can use the exercise."

"Are we talking about kayaking or some other kind of exercise?"

"I don't know what you mean."

"Oh sure you do Harry."

"Look Dee, Katherine wanted to try kayaking. We used Clint's stuff the first time and we liked it. So I worked it out with Clint to purchase those two kayaks. We can store them behind the bar and use them right here on the Bass River whenever we want."

"Harry, you don't need to explain anything to me. Are you feeling guilty about something?"

"No, no. I just don't want anyone to read more into the situation."

"I think everyone knows the situation for what it is."

"Be nice Dee."

"I am."

Harry went back to his office. He took a magic marker out of his desk. He wrote "Adams" on one of the life jackets and "Sterns" on the other life jacket, both in big letters. Then he went out of the office to where he had stored the kayaks and wrote the names on the outside of the two kayaks near the back of each one, again in large letters. As he was finishing, Antonio came out of the kitchen and said, "What'e you doing Harry?"

"I'm putting our names on the kayaks."

"I can see that, but why?"

"One time when I was kayaking down the Swan River, I had stopped by the mouth of the river and got out of my kayak. I had pulled it up onto the sand. Then I took a walk along the beach. When I came back, some guy was getting into my kayak. He had mistaken it for the one he had rented. He had just started to paddle away and I was able to stop him. My wallet and keys were in that kayak and I would hate to think what would have happened if he had tipped over."

"So putting your names on the kayaks will save your wallet and keys?"

"It might just deter someone from taking our kayaks."

"Say Harry, how many pink kayaks have you seen around?"

"I see your point Antonio, but it doesn't hurt to take extra precautions."

"Precautions, you're kayaking with Katherine. There's where you should be taking precautions."

"Antonio, why don't you like her?"

"Oh, I like her. Just not the same way you do."

"Are you saying you wouldn't go out with her if you had the chance?"

"Just the opposite. If I could, I'd do whatever it takes to go out with her just one night. I hear she's the best."

"Where do you get this stuff Antonio?"

"Around. I pick up things here and there. Don't you hear things Harry?"

"I try not to judge."

"Maybe you should," said Antonio as he turned and walked back into the kitchen.

On Thursday, Harry picked Katherine up at her place a little after eleven thirty. They went to Sundancers to pick up the equipment. Harry went into his office and got the life jackets and paddles. Then he put the carrier rack on the roof of his Jeep. The two got the kayaks out from behind the bar and put them on the vehicle.

As they were doing that, Antonio had looked out the back door seeing Harry and Katherine strapping the kayaks in place on the Jeep. He turned and went back to work. A few minutes later, he was taking a plate to the bar for one of the patron's order. As he handed it to Dee, she said, "Have you seen Harry?"

"Yeah. He's out back loading those kayaks with Katherine onto his Jeep."

"Is he still there?"

"I don't know. They were when I last saw them."

Dee went into the kitchen and looked out the back door. No one was there. She went back into the bar.

"Did you see him?" asked Antonio.

"No. They must have left. Antonio, do you know when he'll be back?"

"I'll guess they'll be back in an hour or two. He told me they would be back for lunch in a little while."

"Did he say where they were going?"

"Yeah. They were launching their kayaks down by Uncle Freeman's landing. You need something Dee?"

"It can wait."

Harry and Katherine drove the short distance down to Captain Freeman's landing. The dropped off their kayaks by the ramp and parked the Jeep. After putting on their life vests and getting their paddles out of the vehicle, they were ready.

"Let's paddle all the way to Nantucket Sound."

"Sure. It's only a mile or so down river."

They got into their kayaks and started to paddle.

"What's that place with all the boats over there?"

"That's Ship Shops," said Harry pointing to the gray buildings in the back. "That's the Bass River Yacht Club to the left."

They paddled down river weaving in and out of the boats already on their moorings. At each home along the river, Katherine would stop paddling and look at each property.

"What are you thinking about Kat?" asked Harry.

"I was wondering what it would be like to live on a river like this."

"Do you like the homes?"

"What's not to like? Some of these places are gorgeous. Any celebrities live along here?"

"If you want to know those things, take one of Clint's tours on his boat the Starfish. He knows everyone along the river."

"I just might do that."

They
paddled further.

"Look, a windmill," she said pointing to a building on the west side of the river that looked like a windmill.

"I don't think it's real," said Harry.

To their left was another waterway. Just south of it was an island consisting of grass and sod but no trees or shrubs.

"What's over that way?" asked Katherine pointing to the east.

"That's the Weir Creek extension. It goes to Kelly's Pond. The West Dennis Yacht Club is over there. That development to the left is a place called Wrinkle Point."

"Why do they call it Wrinkle Point?"

"I'm not sure, but I'll bet Clint knows."

"I'm going to have to take his tour."

They continued to paddle south. In another fifteen minutes, they could see the mouth of the Bass River. To the right was another boat launch adjacent to a big parking lot. To the right of the lot were large expensive homes. Some of the homes had big boats parked at private docks on the river. Next to the last house there was a large platform high in the air with a big bird perched on it.

"What's that big bird up there," asked Katherine pointing up at the platform?

"That's an Osprey. The town put up a few of those platforms at different places so the birds can nest."

"Looks like it worked."

"Yeah, we see them flying up river by the bar from time to time looking for food."

"You'll have to point them out to me the next time you see one."

"Sure."

"Harry, can we go past the mouth of the river into Nantucket Sound?"

"There's nothing keeping us from doing that legally, but to be honest, I wouldn't without checking out the water conditions on the Sound first. Wouldn't want to tip over in this cold water if its rought."

"Maybe next time then."

"Let's head back up river and go get lunch," said Harry turning his kayak around.

"I'm right behind you," said Katherine.

They paddled back the way they had come. It was a little more difficult going back up river as the tide was going out and the Bass River has a pretty good tidal flow. As they landed at Captain Freeman's Landing, Katherine said, "My arms are really tired."

"It's what happens when you go against the tide," commented Harry.

"I need a drink," was her response.

They loaded the kayaks on Harry's vehicle, stowed the life jackets and paddles and then headed back to Sundancers. After putting the kayaks back behind the bar, Harry said, "I'll be right in after I put these things away. Have Dee get us a drink."

"I'll have them waiting," said Katherine as she turned and walked to the front entrance.

They took up stools by the windows. Dee brought them both beers. Katherine picked hers up and drank half of it down. Harry took a sip of his. Then he said to her, "I guess you were thirsty?"

"I'm beat," was her reply.

"Kayaking got the best of you?" asked Dee.

"Paddling against the tide," added Harry.

"But the view was great and I got to know more about the river than I never knew before," said Katherine.

"One of these times you should take her to Stage Harbor, Harry. You can see the seals."

"You can paddle right up to seals?"

"Sure can," said Dee turning to wait on another patron.

"Harry, let's try Stage Harbor on one of our trips."

"I don't see why not."

"When do you want to go again?"

"Let's go next week."

"I can't wait," she said.

Dee came back over and added, "There's a cut at the south end of the harbor that gets you out to the Atlantic Ocean. We used to be able to go through there with our boat but the sand has filled the cut in somewhat and now the waterway's only a foot deep at low tide. I think you can make it through in a kayak."

"You said the Atlantic's on the other side?" asked Katherine.

"Yeah, it's a short distance. If you do make it through, there are usually a lot of seals on the other side."

"Can we see seals in Stage Harbor?"

"Sure. Just more on the Atlantic side."

"Sounds like an interesting trip," exclaimed Katherine. "I'll have another beer Dee."

"Me too," added Harry.

"I'm not off again until a week from Saturday, Harry. Can we go then?"

"Like I said, let's see what next week brings."

"I can't wait."

Chapter 12

A few days later Katherine noticed her phone blinking when she came home after getting off work. She picked it up and called in for messages. There were two waiting. The first was from Charles Chamberlin.

"Katherine, I've finished up my business in Rio and expect to be back on Cape Cod next week. Can we get together for dinner?"

She deleted the message.

The second message was from her attorney, Steven Kennedy.

"Katherine, I heard from Tom Bowman's attorney. They're asking for a meeting with us next week regarding his re-trial. Call me."

She deleted the message. She would have to call Steven in the morning.

After changing into pajamas and making herself a drink, she sat in her living room relaxing. As she sat there, it dawned on her that Tom Bowman must be back on Cape Cod if his attorney was requesting a meeting. As she thought about it, the hairs on her arms raised a little sending a chill up her body. Now she would have to be on-guard.

The next morning, she woke, made herself coffee and got dressed. She put on a jogging suit and sneakers intending to take a walk at the West Dennis Beach. She made a mental note that she would call her attorney when she got back. She got into her car and drove to the beach parking lot near the concession building. Then she started her walk to the west along the mile long parking lot. As she walked, a chill ran up her body again. She wasn't sure what caused the chill. It could have been the damp morning air as there was no sun out or possibly the thought of Tom Bowman coming back to Cape Cod.

As she looked out towards Nantucket Sound, the water blended in with the sky a few hundred yards off shore. She didn't know it at the time but a fog bank was rapidly moving north across the Sound heading right in her direction. She continued to walk at a brisk pace. After fifteen minutes, the paved lot made a slight turn to the right. She continued with her walk. At one point when passing the still 'Closed for the Season' rest rooms, she looked back and could no longer see her vehicle due to the slight turn in the lot. She continued walking anyway. After the next quarter mile, the lot makes a slight turn again but this time to the left. From this vantage point, she could see the end of the parking lot near the mouth of the Bass River. As she walked to the end of the lot, the fog moved onshore and quickly diminished the line of sight. In fact, she could only see a few hundred feet in front, the fog was so thick.

The hairs on her arms went up again. Then she heard footsteps coming from behind her through the fog. She knew she was only a short distance from the end of the parking lot and also knew there was no place to go from there. At the end of the lot was the Bass River. To the north, marshland followed by the Weir Creek extension and Nantucket Sound to the south. She quickly thought about her options, go along the beach or just turn around and walk back in the parking lot. She decided to turn back but to jog instead of walk.

Katherine started to jog. The fog was very thick. It seemed like only seconds had gone by and her ability to see ahead was decreasing faster and faster. She quickened her pace. Within a few minutes, she was about a quarter of a mile from where she had turned around and was out of breath. She stopped for a minute to rest. Then she thought she heard footsteps behind her running.

She thought to herself, "How could that be. I didn't pass anyone. Could someone be following me?"

She immediately started to walk at a brisk pace again. In a few minutes, she walked past the closed restrooms she passed on the way out. Now she knew she would be in the main part of the parking lot with her car at the end. She kept pushing forward all the time looking back into the fog to see if she was being followed, and feeling the beads of sweat on her neck and down her back.

At one point, about halfway back down the main stretch of parking lot, she turned back and thought she saw someone behind her through the fog. If someone was there, they quickly vanished. She kept up the rapid pace for another ten minutes and then her car materialized in the fog in front of her. She took her keys out of her pocket and opened the door.

She got into her car and left quickly. Afraid.

When she got home, she locked doors and locked windows. Katherine kept looking out the home's windows.

The fog kept advancing north across Cape Cod and took over everything including her house. She could barely see the street in front of her home. Whenever a vehicle would go by, she would look out the windows. She swore the same vehicle kept driving by. At one point upon hearing a vehicle on the street out front of her home, she opened her door and ran out to see who it might be. She recognized the vehicle going by as one belonging to one of her neighbors a few houses down the street. She went back inside feeling better but still on guard.

The fog stayed around most of the day. Then around three in the afternoon, it lifted. She felt better and began to get ready to go to work. Her shift started at four.

When she got to Sundancers, she told Dee about her experience at the beach.

"Dee, I was taking a walk at West Dennis Beach today when the fog rolled in. It kind of gave me the willies. I thought someone was following me. Even after I got home I thought someone was driving past my house watching me."

"That's creepy Kat. I thought everything was going ok for you."

"It is. That's part of what's bothering me."

"Well, here comes something else that'll bother you," said Dee, pointing to the door. Tom Bowman was walking in.

"Oh my God. Maybe it was him," said Katherine in a surprised and shaking voice.

"Don't worry about him Kat. Harry will take care of it."

Dee picked up the phone and pressed Harry's number in his office.

"What is it Dee?" asked Harry.

"Harry, can you come in right away. We might have some trouble brewing."

"Be right there."

"Harry's coming," said Dee to Kat.

Tom Bowman walked up to where the two were talking and pulled out a stool.

"Can I get a beer?"

Dee went to get him a beer. When she did, Tom turned to Katherine and said, "Did you have a nice walk on the beach?"

The hairs went up on Katherine's arms. She was about to say something when Harry walked up to them.

"I thought I told you not to come back Bowman," said Harry in a harsh voice.

"I thought this was a public place."

"I told you before. It's my restaurant and I can exclude anyone I want if I think they might create trouble."

"I'm not going to create any trouble," said Tom as he picked up his glass and took a long drink.

Harry reached in and took the glass from him.

"Not here you won't," said Harry handing the glass back to Dee.

"Don't serve him anything," Harry said to Dee.

Kenny Brown had been sitting across the bar listening to the whole exchange. He came around and said to Harry, "You want me to take care of this Harry?"

"No Kenny. Bowman was just leaving."

Tom Bowman got up and left. He got into his car and pulled out of the parking lot. When he did, he turned right and then right again into the next driveway belonging to the public boat launch. He parked his car and turned it off. He sat there for hours just watching Sundancers.

Katherine worked her shift, eventually shedding the fears she had earlier in the day. Work tends to have that kind of effect. At the end of the shift, she neatened things up at the hostess station, picked up her purse and left. She got into her car to head home. As she turned out of Sundancers parking lot, another car came out of the adjacent boat ramp launch lot following her. Harry, walking back to his office from the kitchen saw Katherine leave and saw the other car come out of the next door lot following her. He recognized the second driver, Tom Bowman.

Harry quickly ran into his office to get his keys. He came out and got into his car. He peeled out turning left out of the lot trying to catch up to the other vehicles but they were not in sight. Harry pushed the speed limit and quickly got to Katherine's street. He raced around the corner past a vehicle parked on the street. When he looked in his rear view mirror, he recognized the car he had just passed as the same one Tom Bowman had been in.

He pulled into Katherine's driveway and got out. He stood there for a minute when he heard a car down the street start up, turn around and leave. When he walked to the end of her driveway and looked down the street, the car Bowman had been driving was gone.

Harry walked back to the house. Katherine was standing on her porch.
"Harry, what are you doing?"
"Someone followed you when you left work."
"Do you know who it was?"
"I have a pretty good idea. I think it was Bowman."
"Should I call the police?"
"No. Let me look into it first. If you're all right, I'm going back to Sundancers. I was in the middle of doing something."
"Can you come over later?"

"Not tonight. I made other plans. Go inside and lock your doors. I'll call you later."

"Ok. Thanks for coming over."

Harry left, checking a variety of side streets and parked vehicles as he did. He went back to Sundancers and walked into the bar. When he did, he walked right over to Kenny Brown.

"Kenny, I want you to do something for me."

"Sure Harry, anything."

"Have a talk with Tom Bowman. Let him know if anything happens to Katherine involving him, there will be no safe place for him to hide."

"You want me to put a hurt on him just as a reminder?"

"Nah. Just make sure he gets the message."

"I'll take care if it."

"Let me know how it turns out."

"Will do."

Harry went back to his office to finish the tasks he had been working on. About two hours later, near mid-night, Kenny knocked on Harry's office door.

"I saw Bowman over at the Bridge Bar. We had a nice chat. He got the message."

"Was there any trouble?"

"Nope. He went down like a ton of bricks."

"Kenny, I didn't want you to get into a fight with him."

"Harry, it's been a long time coming. Actually, I enjoyed it."

"Thanks Kenny."

"Don't mention it."

"Let's go into the bar so I can buy you a drink."

The two walked to the bar and took up stools by the door.

"Dee, two beers," said Harry.

"And a shot of Jack," added Kenny.

"What's got you all riled up Kenny?" asked Dee.

"Oh, nothing."

"He handled something for me tonight. That's all," responded Harry.

"Let me know if you want more pressure put on that jerk, Harry."

"Thanks Kenny, but I think what you did tonight should get my message across."

"Oh, I'm sure he got a message."

"Kenny, do you always have to settle things with a fight?" asked Dee.

"Sometimes it's the best way," commented Kenny.

"Who was it anyway?" asked Dee.

"Bowman," was all Kenny said.

"I saw him following her home when she left work. So I went right over to Kat's house. He was parked on her street as I drove over there. I know it was him."

"So Harry, you asked Kenny to have a little talk with him?"

"Yes, but just a talk. I didn't ask Kenny to beat the guy."

"Harry's right. The beating was my idea."

"You're a lost cause Kenny," said Dee.

"Well, anyway, thanks Kenny," said Harry.

During the wee hours of the morning, Katherine was woken by a noise of someone trying to break into her house. She got up and went to her front door. When she got there, she could see the door handle turning. Thankfully, she had secured the deadbolt preventing the intruder from getting in. She turned on her porch light and heard footsteps leaving quickly. She peered out her front window just in time to see a figure of what looked like a man going down her driveway and turning down the street. She opened her door and heard a car start up, and then peel out.

She went back inside and called Harry's cell phone. To her surprise, Harry answered right away and sounded wide-awake.

"Harry, someone just tried to break into my house."
"Did you get to see who it was?"
"No. When I turned on my porch light, the person ran down the driveway. I looked to me like it was a man but I can't be sure."
"Did you call the police?"
"No. I called you first."
"Do you want me to call them for you?"
"No. Whoever it was is gone now. I think I'm ok for the rest of the night. Can you come over?"
"It isn't a good time right now. I'm in the middle of something."
Katherine thought for a minute and then realized Harry must be with someone.
"I think I understand. I'll see you tomorrow," she said trying to let Harry off the hook.
"If you think you're in danger Kat, call the police."
"Thanks Harry. If anyone else comes here tonight, I'll call the police."
"I'll see you tomorrow."
"See you tomorrow."

Chapter 13

The next day, Katherine showed up for work promptly at 4 pm. She organized things at the hostess station, and then put a few reservation cards on tables for the reservations already called in for the night. When everything was in place, she sat at the corner of the bar talking with Dee.

"Someone tried to break into my house last night."

"Harry told me. Did you see who it was?"

"No. Harry said he saw Tom Bowman follow me home from work yesterday. Maybe it was Tom."

"Didn't Harry have Kenny talk with Tom?"

"Kenny did have words with Tom."

"And Kenny can be pretty convincing."

"From what I heard, Kenny punched Tom."

"That's so Kenny."

"You think Tom was so mad he came back to my house to get at me?"

"Who knows Kat? I'd be careful if I were you."

"You're right. I can't wait for all this stuff to be over."

"You mean his re-trial?"

"Yes."

"If he thinks he will be vindicated at retrial, why would he be coming after you now?"

"I don't know."

Just then, Harry came into the bar.

"Hi Kat. Anything else happen to you last night?"

"No. After I talked with you at 3 am, I fell asleep and nothing else happened."

"Good." Harry turned to Dee and said, "Everything ok here Dee?"

"No problems boss. We're all set for the night."

Katherine thought for a minute. "Didn't Dee tell her Harry told her about last night?"

When Harry went back to his office, Kat said to Dee, "What time did you get out of here last night?"

"Around two."

"I don't know how you do it Dee. If I were up to two or two-thirty, I'd sleep the whole next day."

"I am tired, I didn't get to sleep until after four."

A couple had come through the door so Kat turned and walked back to the hostess station. As she did, she wondered if Dee had been at Harry's when she called. She knew he was there with someone.

Later that night, Harry stopped back into the bar. He made the rounds and then stopped at the hostess station.

"Kat, want to go kayaking again this weekend?"

"Sure. Why don't we go to Stage Harbor? I'd like to see the seals."

"Sounds good to me."

"I'll make us a lunch and we can make a day of it."

"I'll pick you up at 10 am."

"I'll be ready."

On Saturday, Harry drove to Katherine's house just before 10 am. Katherine came out dressed for the day in a jogging suit and light jacket. The weather was nice, sunny with no wind, temperature around sixty.

"How do you think it will be kayaking," she asked Harry.

"Should be nice and calm."

"Great. I packed a lunch. I can put this small cooler in my kayak and then we can stop somewhere and have a light lunch."

"Then, let's go get the kayaks."

They drove to Sundancers to pick up the gear. While there, Antonio was in the kitchen preparing things for the day. He saw Harry getting the life jackets and paddles out of his office. He came out into the lot as Harry was putting the things into the Jeep. Katherine was already in the front seat.

"Kayaking again Harry?"

"Yeah. I'll be back later this afternoon. If anyone needs me, have them call my cell."

"Will do."

Antonio walked around to the passenger side. He looked in the window and said, "Have fun Kat."

"We will," was her response.

Harry got in the drivers side. The drove away as Antonio looked on.

When they got to Stage Harbor in Chatham, Harry and Kat unloaded the kayaks, life vests, paddles and lunch cooler. Katherine stayed with the stuff by the launch while Harry parked the Jeep in the small lot by the bridge. When he came back, he looked out at the water.

"Look Kat, the seals are right here."

Katherine looked out onto the water. She could see two heads bobbing in the water to the south.

"Let's go," she said.

They launched the kayaks and paddled to where they had seen the seal heads.

"Where did they go?" she asked Harry.

"Over there," he said pointing to the south.

The seals were near the entrance to Stage Harbor. Harry and Katherine paddled quickly in that direction. As they got to the entrance to the harbor, the seals had disappeared again.

"Do you think they went out into Nantucket Sound?" Kat asked.

"No. There they are," said Harry pointing to the right up the Oyster Pond River.

"Let's follow them," exclaimed Kat.

The two followed the seals for the next hour. The seals didn't seem to mind the kayaks. They splashed around, diving and skimming the water surface. After about two hours, Harry said, "I'm getting a little hungry. Want to stop and have lunch?"

"Me too. Let's stop over there," Kat was pointing to a sandy beach off to her left.

"Ok."

The two beached their kayaks. Harry helped Kat get out of hers. She reached inside her kayak and took out the cooler. She had made ham and cheese on rye with yellow mustard. She had also brought along two beers to drink. They sat on a log eating lunch.

"This is a nice trip Harry."

"And tiring," he added.

"My arms are getting pretty weak," Kat said.

"Thankfully, the tide's going out so our trip back down the river should be pretty easy."

"Say Harry, when I called you the other night when someone was trying to break into my house, were you with someone?"

"Why do you ask?"

"Oh, no reason in particular. I just thought you were preoccupied when I called you at 3 am."

"Let's just say I was busy."

"By any chance was it busy with Dee?"

"No Kat, I don't pry into your personal life, why are you so interested in mine?"

"It's just a girl thing Harry."

"Then I'd rather not say."

"Ok, but I don't know why you're being so secretive?"

"Not secretive, just discrete."

"Is Dee seeing someone else?"

"I didn't say it was Dee, but nice try."

"Still being coy."

"Let's get going Kat. It's over an hour paddle back."

"Ok Harry."

The two got back into their kayaks and began to paddle in silence. They didn't say much more during the trip back. When they got back to the launch, they stowed the gear on Harry's Jeep and drove back to Sundancers. There, they put the kayaks back behind the bar, the life jackets and paddles in the office and went into the bar for a drink. As they took up stools by the door, Dee said, "Have a nice trip Harry?"

Katherine heard the comment and was then sure it had been Dee who was with Harry the other night.

"Did you see any seals Kat," Dee asked her as she sat.

"Yes. We saw a few and followed them up a river. What was the name of that river Harry?"

97

"The Oyster Pond River."

"If you go again, turn left out of the harbor entrance. There's a cut I told you about through the sand leading out to the Atlantic. Like I told you earlier in the week, we used to go through there with our boat a few years ago but it's filled in somewhat now. I think you can still get through in a small boat or kayak. There are lots of seals on the other side.

"No kidding," said Kat. "We'll have to go that way next time Harry."

"So now you want to kayak on the Atlantic Ocean?" he asked her.

"If it's a calm day, I don't see why not."

"Yeah, there are days when the water's like glass on the Atlantic side. Go out on one of those days and you'll see thousands of seals," Dee added as she placed drinks in front of the two.

"How about again next week?" Kat asked.

"Let' see how things go," was Harry's response.

Katherine wondered if he was talking about Harry's love life or the weather.

They sat and talked for another hour.

Finally, Harry said, "Why don't I take you home Kat. I have a few things to take care of here later tonight."

"Alright Harry. Can I see you after you've taken care of business?"

"Not tonight. I don't think I'll get out of here until after two."

"I can wait up for you."

"Maybe another time."

Katherine wondered if Dee was one of the things Harry had to take care of.

Dee came over to the two. "See you later Harry."

"Later." Harry said as he looked to Katherine. She had an unhappy look on her face that said it all.

They left in Harry's car. He dropped her off and walked her to the door. He attempted to give her a kiss but she turned her head and just said "Good night."

Then she closed the door behind her.

Chapter 14

The next few days at work were a little stressful. Katherine wouldn't socialize with anyone. She did her job but wasn't the cheerful person she normally was. At one point, Harry stopped at the hostess station and said, "What's wrong Kat?"

"Nothing's wrong Harry."

"You don't seem to be happy."

"I'm just a little moody these days."

"Anything I can help you out with?"

"No. I'll get over it."

"Let me know if I can help," said Harry as he walked to the kitchen.

Then, a man Katherine didn't know came into the bar. He walked over and took up a seat near the bar entrance. Dee came around and gave the man a big hug and kiss on the lips. Katherine's eyebrows rose upon seeing the two. She walked over to the corner of the bar.

"Kat, I want you to meet my boyfriend, Ted. Ted, this is Katherine. She's our new hostess."

"Hi Katherine. Nice to meet you."

"Same here Ted."

Katherine went back to the hostess station. She had that bounce back in her step.

When Harry came back out of the kitchen, Katherine was all smiles. She said, "Harry, got any plans tonight?"

"Nah. It should be pretty slow here. What did you have in mind?"

"Why don't you come to my place? Spend the night?"

"Hmm. That sounds like a plan."

"What time do you think you can be out of here Harry?"

"Oh, Dee can close up. I'll come over after your shift. Say tenish."

"I'll be waiting."

Harry went back to his office. Katherine went back to work. She was cheerful and smiling to everyone who came in for the rest of the night.

At 9:30, she cleaned up the hostess station, wiped down and put away the stack of menus and grabbed her purse. She said goodnight to Dee and left. Before she went to her car, she knocked on Harry's office door.

"Come in," Harry said from behind his desk.

Katherine opened the door. "I'm going home now Harry. I'll see you in a little while."

"I'll only be a few more minutes Kat. I just have to make sure things are all set inside."

"See you at my place."

"I'll see you there."

Katherine closed the door, and then went to her car. She drove home. When she got home, she lit a few candles, turned the lights down low and set her television to a soft music station. Then she went to her bedroom and changed into comfortable clothes. After changing, she went to the kitchen. She found a new unopened bottle of wine in the refrigerator. She opened it and poured herself a drink. She left another empty glass on the counter. Thinking everything was taken care of, she took her glass of wine into her living room and curled up on her couch waiting for Harry to arrive.

A little after ten, she heard a car pull into her driveway. A minute after hearing the car door close, there was a knock on her door. She opened it and let Harry in. She closed the door, locking the deadbolt. Then she turned off the outside and foyer lights.

"There's a bottle of wine in the fridge if you want a glass."

"Thanks. I think I'll have one. Can I get you one while I'm there?"

"I already have a glass."

Harry went into the kitchen emerging a minute later with a glass of wine. He sat next to her on the couch.

She picked up her glass and made a toast.

"To a relaxing night."

"Or what's left of it," said Harry.

"Oh, there's a lot left. Just wait and see."

Harry clinked her glass and took a drink. He reciprocated the toast and said, "To a beautiful woman."

She held her glass and took a sip. Then she put her glass on the table. She leaned into Harry and gave him a passionate kiss. As she did, Harry reached under her blouse to undo her bra. To his surprise, she didn't have one on. He caressed her.

Katherine undid Harry's shirt pushing it off his shoulders. Then she unbuckled his belt. She unhooked his pants and unzipped the fly. He lifted up slightly allowing her to remove his pants and underwear. Then she stood and shed her pants. Harry was aroused sitting on the couch. Katherine put her legs on Harry's sides straddling him.

As he kissed between her breasts, she lowered herself on him. She sighed welcoming his warmth. For the next few minutes, Katherine worked slowly and then increased the pace. She and Harry reached climax at the same time. They embraced in the same position for a few minutes until Harry relaxed.

Then she stood motioning Harry to follow. She turned off the rest of the lights and blew out the candles as they went to her bedroom.

"Let's take a hot shower together," she insisted.
"Lead the way."

The two went into the bathroom. She turned on the shower. Within a few minutes, the two were in a steamy shower enjoying each other's company.

As they were drying off, Harry thought he heard someone trying to break into the house. He motioned for Katherine to be quiet. Then he put on his pants and went down to the front door. Someone was trying to get in. Harry flipped on the inside and outside lights. He turned the deadbolt and opened the door.

As he opened the door, he caught a glimpse of someone running down the driveway. Harry took up chase. When he got to the end of the driveway, he jumped up in pain. It was then he realized he didn't have his shoes on and had stepped on something sharp. Fortunately, it was only a rock and didn't cut his foot. Looking in the direction the intruder went, he heard a car start up and saw it pull away. He recognized the car. It belonged to Ed Phillips.

When Harry came back in, Katherine said, "Did you see who it was?"

"No. It was too dark. Plus, I didn't have any shoes on so I couldn't go further than the driveway."

"I'm sure glad you were here Harry."

"Whoever it was is gone. I don't think there'll be any more trouble tonight."

"Then let's go to bed."

"If you don't mind Katherine, I'd like to go back to Sundancers and see if things are ok there."

"Do you think whoever it was might try to break in there?"

"I don't know. I just don't have a good feeling about this."

"Ok Harry. Why don't you come back after you have checked things out?"

"It might take a while. I'll see you tomorrow."

"Ok. But call me if there is any trouble."

"I will and you do the same."

He finished dressing and left. When he did, he went to Sundancers looking for Ed's car. It wasn't in the lot. He kept going. After he crossed the bridge, he looked at the cars in the Bridge Bar parking lot. Ed's was parked in the rear corner of the lot. Harry parked and went in. Harry knew the bartender working that night.

"Hi Joe."

"Hi Harry. What're you doing here?"

"Looking for someone."

"Anyone I know?"

"You know Ed Phillips?"

"Sure, he came in a few minutes ago. He must be in the men's room."

"Where's he sitting?"

"Over there at the end of the bar."

Harry walked over and took up the seat next to one that was empty but had a full bottle of Bud in front of it. A few minutes later, Ed came out of the men's room. He hesitated at first but then took the same seat with the beer in front of it.

"Hi Harry. Funny seeing you here."

"Oh, why's it funny Ed? Did you think I didn't see you at Katherine's?"

"I don't know what you're talking about," Ed said slurring his words a little.

"Look Ed. You ran right past my car in Katherine's driveway. I saw your car leave her street."

Ed took a long drink of his beer. Then he turned to Harry and said, "She's a bitch Harry. She leads you on, then doesn't even remember your name."

"Ed, your drunk. You need to be more careful what you do Ed. Your drinking's going to get you into big trouble."

"Harry, she's had sex with just about every guy I know, including me. She uses us, and then throws us away. I'm just trying to teach her a lesson."

He finished his beer and then asked Joe for another along with a shot of whisky. Harry motioned Joe to cut Ed off and Joe acknowledged Harry's instructions.

"Ed, why don't you go home," said Joe.

"Because that bitch needs to be taught another lesson," Ed said slurring his words almost to a non-understandable language.

"What do you mean another lesson, Ed?" questioned Harry.

"I thought she got the message when I knocked her out and spread those condoms around her bedroom the last time I visited her at her house," said Ed attempting to stand.

"So it was you who attacked her, took her pajamas and left them in my office," said Harry grabbing Ed's arm.

"Is that where I left them?" said Ed looking at Harry. "I took them. Left her there naked."

"Ed, you could be in a lot of trouble."

"No one had any proof it was me."

"Except, now I know it was you. And Joe heard you as well."

"Lots of luck making that stick," Ed said mumbling something else that neither Joe nor Harry understood.

Joe looked at Harry and said, "I don't know what he's talking about and I don't want to know. Why don't you take him home Harry. Deal with him tomorrow, when he's sober."

"I should call the police," said Harry. "I'm not sure if what he said is the truth or not, so I'll have to find out tomorrow. Give me a hand with him if you can Joe and I'll take him to his place."

"What was all that about teaching someone a lesson?" asked Joe.

"Oh, Ed's got it in his mind that one of the women at my place needs to be taught a lesson."

"And he thinks he's the one to teach it?"

"I guess."

"I don't know what gets into these guys," said Joe as he took Ed's left arm.

"It's the liquor."

"Probably."

Joe helped Harry walk Ed to Harry's Jeep and poured him into the passenger seat. Harry got in and they left. Harry took Ed to his house. It took a bit of effort to get Ed out of the Jeep and into the house. When they were inside, Ed passed out on the couch. Harry left, locking the door behind him.

"Tomorrow should be interesting," he said as he walked to his vehicle.

Harry left and went home for the night. He didn't want to have to tell Katherine about any of this.

Chapter 15

Harry drove back to Sundancers after dropping Ed off. When he got there, Dee was just closing up for the night. Harry used his key to let himself into the bar.

"What's going on Harry?"

"It's been one of those nights."

"Really? I thought you were going to Kat's."

"I did. Then when we had finished taking a shower, I heard someone trying to break into her house. I went to the door but the person ran away."

"Did you see who it was?"

"Not face to face, but I saw the car he used and I know who it was."

"You do? Who was it?"

"I'd rather not say. It gets complicated."

"How could someone trying to break into Katherine's house get any more complicated?"

"It was someone we know. But he was so drunk, I'm not sure he knew what he was doing."

"Someone we know? Who was drunk? Really Harry, that doesn't narrow it down at all."

"Yeah. Then, I was able to find him at the Bridge Bar. When I confronted him, he could hardly talk let alone stand up. I had to take him to his home so he could sleep it off."

"So you don't want to tell me who it was?"

"I'd rather not. That way you won't get yourself involved in any of this mess."

"Harry, some of the things that have happened were to some of my friends."

"Yeah, and it's possible one of your friends was the one causing the trouble."

"I see your point. Ok, I won't ask you who it was."

"Thanks Dee."

Harry walked behind the bar and poured himself a beer. He sat at the corner by the entrance to the bar drinking his beer in deep thought. When Dee was done, she got Harry another beer and one for herself. She joined him.

"Last time we sat here talking over a drink, you let me try on those silky pajamas I found in your office."

"I let you try them on?"

"That's how I remember it."

"Hmm, I seem to remember we had a few drinks and had a pretty good buzz going."

"You could be right."

"And then you wanted me to take you to my place."

"Where did you ever get that idea?"

"Right after you stripped naked and put on those pajamas."

"I did all that?"

"Yes you did."

"Well, you don't have to worry about anything like that tonight. Ted's coming to pick me up in a few minutes."

"That's good. I don't think I'd be any good again tonight anyway."

"So, Kat had her way with you, did she?"

"Let's just say I had a full night."

A vehicle pulled into the lot parking by the front door. The driver didn't turn the vehicle off. Then after a knock on the door, Dee let Ted in.

"Hey Ted," said Harry.

"Harry. Ready to go Dee?"

"Let me get my bag."

Dee retrieved her purse from under the bar. She gave Harry a kiss on the cheek and left. As they were walking out the door, Ted said, "What was that all about?"

"Harry had a bad day."

"Dee, you and Harry, is it more than just work?"

"Why would you ask?"

"Oh, I don't know. I just get the impression you two are close."

"We have been through a lot together. We're good friends."

"If you say so."

"Let's go home. I'm still a little wired from work and need to unwind."

Ted knew what that meant. He smiled, opened the door for her, and then drove her home.

The next afternoon, Katherine came to work at four. She got everything ready for the night. Then she went to Harry's office.

"Harry, everything work out last night?"

"Yeah, everything worked out."

"Did you find the car you were looking for?"

"Nah. I'm not sure whose car it was. I thought I did, but there was no one here with a vehicle like that when I got back here."

"I was hoping you'd find out."

"I'll put out the word to leave you alone. That might help."

"Only if it's someone you know."

"Or someone the people I give the word to know."

"I hope it works. I've got to get back in. My shift's starting."

"Ok. I'll stop in later."

Katherine walked back into the bar. She began her work. The night went along pretty smoothly. Around nine, Ed Phillips came in. Katherine saw him come in the door.

"Hi Ed, how are you doing?"

He ignored her and kept walking to the far end of the bar. He took up a stool as far away from the hostess station as possible.

"What will it be Ed?"

"Give me a beer Dee."

"Sure."

Dee got him the beer, and he drank it pretty quickly and asked for another.

"Might want to slow down Ed," said Dee placing a second beer in front of him.

"I have a terrible hangover. I'm hoping a few beers will make it go away."

"Hair of the dog huh?"

"Kind of."

Harry came walking through the kitchen. He stopped by the door and surveyed the bar. His eyes came to rest on Ed seated at the far end of the bar. Harry walked over to Ed.

"Ed, feeling better tonight?"

"Thanks Harry for getting me home last night. I don't know what came over me. I drank way too much."

"I'd say so Ed. Do you remember what you did last night?"

"Some of it's a little vague. I think I tried to break into someone's house. I remember someone chasing me but then I recall being at the Bridge Bar talking to you."

"Yeah, you tried to break into Katherine's house. I was there with her. I was the one who chased you. Then I found you at the Bridge Bar. You confessed to me about breaking into her house some time ago and attacking her. You told me about spreading condom contents on her you found in her freezer and about stealing her pajamas."

"I did?"

"Yes you did. I think you owe her an apology."

"Do you think I should tell her?"

"I do."

"Dee, can I have a shot and another beer? Then I'll talk to her."

"Ed, why don't you wait until her shift ends? She should be done in about a half hour. Then you can talk with her."

"Ok. Harry, can you ask her to listen to me. I feel embarrassed by my conduct."

"I'll talk to her."

Harry walked away. He approached Katherine at the hostess station.

"Kat, when you're done working, take a few minutes and talk with Ed. He has some things you need to hear."

"What could Ed want to talk to me about?"

"Just listen to him for a few minutes. He'll clear some things up for you that I know have been upsetting you."

Harry turned and walked back into the kitchen. When he left, Dee came over to Katherine at the hostess station and said, "I overheard Ed talking with Harry. I think Ed was the person trying to break into your house last night."

"Why would you think it was Ed?"

"Harry wouldn't say. But he said he found Ed at the Bridge Bar last night after he left your house and had to take him home he was so drunk."

"And you think it was Ed trying to break into my house?"

"Could be."

"Thanks Dee."

Katherine kept looking at Ed for the next half hour. When she neatened everything up for the night, she walked over to where Ed was seated.

"Harry said you want to speak to me?"

"Katherine, I'm sorry for what I did. I was drunk and did all those things to you."

"So it was you trying to break into my house last night?"

"Yes."

"And the other night?"

"Yes."

"Why Ed?"

"I've been carrying this grudge since you dropped me after our night on the beach."

"Ed, that was just sex."

"Sex to you, but I had feelings for you."

"Look Ed, you can't go around terrorizing people just because they don't see things the same way you do."

"I know."

"I'm willing to let it go if you promise not to do it again."

"I promise. And I promise not to break into your house again."

"You didn't get in."

"Well, not this time, but it was me who attacked you and spread around the condoms some time ago."

"Ed, how could you have done such a thing? We were intimate with each other."

"That was why. My emotions got the best of me."

"Look Ed. These recent things are one thing. Knocking me out in my own bedroom, doing what you did to me and taking my pajamas, that's a whole other issue."

"I'm really sorry Katherine. It'll never happen again."

"I don't know Ed. I'm going to have to think about it."

Katherine stood, turned and walked away. Dee stopped her at the end of the bar, "I'd press charges."

"I don't know. Now that I know, I don't think he'll be a problem anymore."

"Now that Harry knows, I'm sure he won't be a problem anymore. Harry takes it very personal when someone goes after his woman."

Katherine just looked at Dee. The words registered in her mind. She turned and walked away.

Chapter 16

Katherine retrieved her purse from under the hostess station and walked out. As she was crossing the parking lot, Harry came out of his office.

"Katherine, can you come in for a few minutes? I have something I'd like to talk with you about."

"Sure Harry. Want to get a drink and talk in the bar?"

"No. I'd rather talk in private."

The two walked into Harry's office. Instead of sitting behind his desk, Harry sat in one of the side chairs and offered the other one to Katherine.

"This might be difficult to talk about Kat, but I know who was trying to break into your house. Plus, I know who attacked you a few months ago. And I have a pretty good idea how those pajamas you asked me about ended up here at Sundancers."

Harry was straining to get out the whole story. Katherine could see he was having trouble finding the words.

"Harry, I already know."

"Know what?"

"I know who did all those things."

"How did you find out?"

"Ed confessed."

"I know he wanted to speak to you, but I didn't think he would talk to you about everything today."

"I listened. And he told me the whole thing."

"What do you want to do?"

"I don't know Harry. After talking with him, I can see how he was affected emotionally by me. I know I had sex with him up on the beach one night but I didn't think anything more of it. I guess he did. Then, combining alcohol with those strong emotions caused him to act. I didn't really get hurt so I'm inclined to let it go."

"I'm sure you could press charges if you wanted."

"That's what Dee said also, but Ed's really a nice guy."

Harry put his arms around her and hugged her. "You're really a nice person Katherine. I don't think some of the people around here understand you."

"Why thank you Harry."

"I'm sure Ed will be happy to hear you're not pursuing it any further. Do you plan on talking with him again about it?"

"I told him I'd think about it. After a few days, I'll talk to him."

"Kind of let him worry for a few days huh?"

"It'll keep him in check for a while."

"I guess. So where are you going now?"

"Home. I could use some rest. I have tomorrow off so I think I'll just take it easy."

"Ok. I'll call you tomorrow. Maybe we can do something."

"Maybe." She stood and walked to the door. "Till tomorrow."

After Katherine left, Harry walked back into the bar. He went over to Ed.

"So you talked to Katherine," Harry said to Ed as he took up the stool next to him.

"Yes. I couldn't tell from her reaction what she intends to do, but I hope my telling her helps."

"I think you've put her at ease with regard to who has been trying to break into her house, but other than that, I'm not sure. She's hard to figure out sometimes."

"You think she'll press charges?"

"Who knows? If I were you Ed, I'd be real nice to her. Maybe she'll feel sorry for you."

"I will."

Harry got up and walked away. He walked behind the bar and talked to Dee.

"What do you think Harry?" Dee said to him as she was making a drink for another patron.

"I think another mystery has come full circle. Maybe things can settle down now."

"What about Katherine? Do you think she'll press charges?"

"Nah. She'll let him stew for a few days and then let him off the hook."

"How can you be so sure?"

"I talked to her a little while ago and that's what she told me."

"You going to tell Ed?"

"No. It's up to her. So, don't say anything."

"Got it."

Harry walked through the kitchen and went back to his office. Dee went back to bartending. Ed finished his drink and left.

When Katherine got home, the message light on her phone was blinking. She picked up the phone and called in for messages.

"Katherine, it's Steven Kennedy. I have some information about Bowman's retrial. Call me in the morning."

She pressed delete. There were no more messages. She straightened things up around her house and went to bed around eleven.

She woke up around 7 am. She made coffee and an English muffin. Then she took a shower. When finished, she dressed in casual clothes, went to her mailbox, retrieved the newspaper and took up residence on her oversized chair to read. She read the headlines and the rest of the main section. As she began reading the local section, there was an article in the paper talking about upcoming legal matters in Barnstable Court. One case caught her attention.

"Retrial of Thomas Bowman is scheduled to begin on Tuesday."

Katherine read the underlying paragraph, which outlined the original charges against Tom Bowman having attacked women in the Cape Cod area in the past. The article finished with a statement that the defense had filed charges of improper conduct by the judge in seeking a retrial. Katherine's hairs went up on her arms.

Katherine picked up her phone to call Judge Bennet. She called the phone number she had in her book for him.

"Judge Carstens office," said the secretary who answered the phone.

"I'm calling for Judge Bennet," said Katherine.

"I'm sorry, this is Judge Carstens office. Judge Bennet retired a few months ago. Is there something I can help you with?" asked the secretary.

"Is Judge Carstens handling the Bowman retrial?"

"Yes. May I tell the Judge who's calling?"

"No, that's alright. I don't need to talk to the Judge."

Katherine hung up the phone. The secretary already knew where the call had originated. Katherine Sterns name was showing on the caller-id.

After disconnecting the call, Katherine called Steven Kennedy.

"Steven Kennedy."

"Steven, it's Katherine."

"Katherine. I'm glad you called."

"There was something in today's paper about Tom Bowman's retrial."

"That's what I wanted to talk to you about."

"The paper said the retrial starts on Tuesday."

"Yes. And it's being handled by Judge Carstens."

"I know. I tried to call Judge Bennet but he's retired. The secretary told me about Judge Carstens."

"It shouldn't matter who the Judge is."

"Maybe not, but the paper said something about improper conduct by Judge Bennet."

"I don't know what that's all about. Don't let it upset you."

"What kind of improper conduct could they be talking about?"

"The defense must think they have something that swayed the Judge in rendering the verdict he did."

"Like what?"

"We'll find out on Tuesday."

"Should I plan on attending?"

"You can if you want. You don't have to testify or anything. The retrial will probably use what has already been introduced."

"I think I'll attend anyway."

119

"Ok. Then plan on meeting me at the courthouse at 9 am."

"Ok. I'll see you on Tuesday. Bye."

Katherine wondered what was going on. Could the defense have come up with something that would get Tom Bowman off? She became a little nervous.

Chapter 17

Katherine was clearly rattled. She had hoped Tom Bowman would just go away. Now, the defense had something. She'd have to wait until Tuesday. She went to her kitchen to make a drink. She wanted a vodka and Sprite but didn't have any Sprite in the refrigerator. She went into her garage to retrieve a bottle she had in her garage refrigerator. As she walked back into the house, she could hear her phone ringing. It stopped before she could answer it. She looked at the caller-id. It read "Private Number". Then the message waiting light illuminated. She called for messages.

"Katherine, it's Charles. I'm in transit. I'm boarding a plane in a few minutes for Boston. I should be on Cape Cod tomorrow. I'd like to get together with you. I'll call you in the morning."

Katherine deleted the message. The call got her to thinking. It might be time to settle up with Mr. Chamberlin. She called Carol Tindle.

"Carol, it's Katherine Sterns."

"Katherine, how are you?"

"Fine. Listen, I'm calling to tell you I think things will start happening this week."

"Really. Do you think we'll be able to get our money back?"

"That's my plan."

"What should I do?"

"Nothing. I'll get you details as soon as I can. Chamberlin's coming back to Cape Cod this week so I'm pretty sure you'll see action."

"Thanks Katherine. I really appreciate what you're doing."

"He got me as well Carol. I'm just settling the score."

"Let me know if there's anything I can do."

"Will do."

Katherine hung up. She called the other women on the Chamberlin Victims list and gave them a similar message. When finished, she sat back satisfied things would start to happen soon.

When Carol Tindle finished talking to Katherine, she called the Dennis Police station. She asked for Captain Trudy.

"Captain Trudy."

"Captain, it's Carol Tindle. I just got off the phone with Katherine Sterns. She said Chamberlin's coming back to Cape Cod and things should start to happen."

"Did she say exactly when Mr. Chamberlin was coming back?"

"She just said this week."

"Ok. If you get anymore information, please call."

"I will."

When Captain Trudy hung up the phone, she went to the detective office and spoke with Detective Simpson.

"Detective Simpson. Remember the case last year Jenkins had worked where a number of widows were taken for large sums of money?"

"Yeah."

"Well, the main suspect Jenkins focused on disappeared. I just found out he may be making an appearance here on Cape Cod sometime this week."

"What would you like me to do?"

"It seems that the suspect, a Charles Chamberlin, has been in contact with one of his victims, a Katherine Sterns. I found out from one of the other victims, Carol Tindle, that Mr. Chamberlin told Ms. Sterns he's coming back to Cape Cod. Ms. Sterns had contacted all of the other victims in the case and informed them that they'll all be getting their money back sometime soon. I'd like you to see what you can find out about Ms. Sterns and the mysterious return of the missing funds."

"Ok Captain. Let me look into it."

"Let me know what you find out."

"Will do."

Simpson had his marching orders. His first order of business was to talk with Katherine Sterns. He got her phone number from the file and called.

"Katherine Sterns."

"Ms. Sterns. This is Detective Simpson from Dennis PD. I'd like to talk to you about Mr. Charles Chamberlin for a few minutes if I can."

"Charles Chamberlin, there's a name from the past."

"It's come to our attention Mr. Chamberlin has recently contacted you and is coming back to Cape Cod."

"Where did you hear that?"

"An interested party has provided the information."

"I don't know what you're talking about."

"Are you sure Ms. Sterns?"

"Yes."

"Listen Ms. Sterns. If there's something going on, you don't want to be taking matters into your own hands."

"Detective, I have no idea what you're talking about."

"Ok for now Ms. Sterns. I'll be watching."

"Look Detective. I have nothing to tell you."

"Have it your way Ms. Sterns. I'll be around."

He hung up. Katherine sat back wondering who called the police. It didn't matter anyway. She already knew how to get the money back and didn't feel at risk in carrying out her plans.

Detective Simpson called Carol Tindle.

"Ms. Tindle, this is Detective Simpson from Dennis PD. Captain Trudy assigned me to follow up on the information you provided. I tried to talk with Ms. Sterns regarding the situation but she was uncooperative. Is there anything more you can tell me?"

"There's one more thing. Katherine sent me and the other women an e-mail saying things would be happening soon."

"Do you have any idea what might be happening or what soon means?"

"Only that she said we would all be getting our missing money back. I don't know how she's going to do it, but she seemed confident in her ability to get our money back from Chamberlin."

"Thanks for the info, Ms. Tindle. If you hear anything more please call the station and ask for me or Captain Trudy."

"I will Detective."

Detective Simpson decided he might want to have a face-to-face talk with Katherine Sterns. He looked up her address in the file and drove to her house. When he got there, her car was in the driveway so he walked up to the door and knocked. She opened it. She was dressed in workout pants with a halter-top. Her hair was pulled back into a ponytail. She looked terrific. Simpson didn't say anything for a second, staring at her beauty.

"Can I help you?"

"I'm Detective Simpson."

"I told you on the phone I have nothing to say Detective."

"I know Ms. Sterns. But my investigation tells me something's about to happen and you're at the center of it all."

"You sound just like my former fiancé, Frank Jenkins."

"I knew Frank. I'm sorry for your loss."

"Thanks Detective. It took a long time but now I'm past it."

"If you're acting out some solution to the crimes Frank had been working on, you're way out of your league and should leave the police business to us."

"Where did you ever get an idea like that?"

"I've talked with some of the other victims. They have provided some insight into what's going on."

"There isn't anything going on."

"That's not what you said in the e-mail you sent them."

"I just told them what Mr. Chamberlin has told me. He intends to return the supposedly missing funds to each of the women."

"Supposedly missing funds, I thought he took you for over two million?"

"I've gotten it back. He intends to give me the rest of the gains he was able to make on the funds when he gets back."

"Is that what he told you?"

"I already have the principal back in my account. I expect to get the rest when he comes back this week."

"So you're saying this guy stole two million from you, then gave it back to you recently and now intends to give you the gains he made while he had use of your funds?"

"That's about it."

"He's a thief. He stole the money from you."

"Well, there are some things none of us picked up on when we thought the funds were stolen."

"Like what?"

"As it turns out, Mr. Chamberlin had each of us sign a document when he provided us with the information he said he had been working on for our husbands before they passed away. One of the clauses in the document we signed authorized him to continue to represent us as a financial consultant, including investing funds in accordance with the materials he gave each of us. I thought I was just signing a receipt for the materials he turned over to me but when he brought the representation clause to my attention, I was surprised. I showed it to my attorney and he says the agreement was legal. So I don't think there's anything for you to be pursuing."

"Can I take a look at the so called agreement?"

"Sure."

"You know Ms. Sterns, for somebody who knew nothing, you have a lot of information."

Katherine walked to another room and came back a minute later with the document. It looked official. When Simpson checked the last page, it had her signature, Chamberlin's signature and was dated. He flipped through the pages.

"There it is," said Katherine pointing to a paragraph with a title of Continued Financial Consulting. Sure enough, the paragraph gave Chamberlin the authorization to access accounts, invest funds and provide financial consulting on an as-needed basis.

"I'd like to get a copy of this if I may."

"I have a copier. I'll make one."

It took about five minutes to copy the entire document. Katherine came back and handed Simpson the copied document.

"Here you go Detective."

"I'll be getting back to you Ms. Sterns."

"Anytime." She closed the door as Detective Simpson left.

After Detective Simpson drove away, Katherine picked up her phone calling the police station. She asked for Captain Trudy.

"Captain Trudy."

"Captain, this is Katherine Sterns. I just had a visit from your Detective Simpson. I'd appreciate it if you would have your personnel stop bothering me. I gave him a copy of my agreement with Charles Chamberlin. It'll explain what he's been doing for me with the funds I thought he stole from me. I'm pretty sure he had a similar agreement with the other women whom he represented. This matter should be closed, now."

"Ms. Sterns. I'll see what Detective Simpson has to say, but as of right now, we still have an open case. Until the DA instructs us to stop pursuing it, we are bound to follow up."

"Then talk to your DA because there was never any crime."

"As I said, I'll follow-up with Detective Simpson and we will determine what to do from there. Is there anything else I can do for you today, Ms. Sterns?"

Trudy didn't like Katherine when Frank was alive and didn't like her even more now that he's dead she was in charge.

"No," was all Katherine said and then she hung the phone up. Hard.

When Detective Simpson got back to the station, he showed the document to Captain Trudy.

"What do you make of it, Simpson?"

"Looks like it might be legit."

"Show it to the DA and see what he says."

"Will do."

"Simpson, keep an eye on Ms. Sterns for the next week or two. I think she's up to something."

"How close do you want me to get, Captain?"

"Not in-your-face style, but from a distance."

"I understand."

Detective Simpson left the Captain's office and drove to Hyannis. He went to visit the DA at the courthouse. He showed the document to the DA.

"This is interesting Detective. Looks real."

"It is. I got it from Ms. Sterns."

"I wonder if the other women signed something similar?"

"I can find out."

"Contact the other victims Detective and find out. If they all signed the same thing, then our Mr. Chamberlin might not have committed any crimes after all."

"I'll let you know what I find out."

Detective Simpson left the courthouse. When he got back to the station, he called each of the women. He told them what he was looking for and each one, except Sharon Kelly, provided him with the same answer. Except for Sharon, they all had signed a document with Chamberlin.

Simpson thought about it for a minute. Even if the widows had continued with Chamberlin's services, Sharon

Kelly was an exception. He would have to come up with hard evidence tying Chamberlin to Sharon Kelly's missing money. If he could, then Chamberlin might still be guilty of the crimes against Sharon Kelly. He made a note to visit Sharon Kelly in the next few days in order to pursue her situation apart from the others.

Chapter 18

The day before the initial hearing regarding Tom Bowman's retrial, Steven Kennedy called Katherine.

"Katherine, it's Steven Kennedy."

"Hello Steven. Is something up?"

"Not really. I just wanted to speak with you for a few minutes before the retrial hearings start."

"Couldn't it wait until tomorrow?"

"No. That's why I'm calling you tonight. I would prefer if you not attend the initial hearing."

"Why?"

"I have it from a reliable source that the defense has come into possession of pretty damning evidence to support their case."

"What does that mean?"

"A friend of a friend, who works at the courthouse, told my friend the defense has a video in their possession which they will use to show Judge Bennet should have removed himself from the case."

"What could they have?"

"I'd rather not get into it."

"Steven, this means a lot to me. What is it?"

"Well, apparently, the defense has a video showing you kissing Judge Bennet in his chambers during Tom Bowman's trial."

"Where did it come from?"

"The courthouse has surveillance cameras mounted all around the building. Apparently, someone reviewing video looking for a fender bender in the parking lot came across pictures of you kissing the judge. The picture is supposedly very clear having been taken from atop a light pole in the parking lot looking into the Judge's chambers."

"I remember it. It was just a friendship kiss."

"There's more."

"Like what?"

"The video shows you kissing him passionately on the lips for more than a second or two. Plus, the defense has a witness who works at the Route 28 motel who's prepared to testify you and Judge Bennet got a room at the hotel around the time of the trial. Can any of this be true?"

"How do you know all of this?"

"The defense team had to submit documents detailing what they intended to present as reasons for retrial consideration."

Katherine was silent.

"Katherine?"

"Steven, I'll have to think about all of this. Can I call you back?"

"Look Katherine, don't come tomorrow. If something comes up requiring your attendance, I'll call you."

"Ok Steven. If you insist."

"I do. I'll call after the hearing and let you know how it went."

"Please do."

Katherine hung up the phone.   She became very agitated. She went to the refrigerator and got herself a glass of wine. For the next hour, she sat on her couch drinking until all the wine was gone. When it was all gone, she wanted more. She got her purse and keys. Then she drove to Sundancers.

Walking into the bar, Dee said, "I thought it was your day off?"

"It is. I wanted another drink but I'm all out of wine at home."

"Want another glass of wine?"

"No. Make it a martini."

"Ok."

Dee went off and made a martini. She brought it to Katherine and put it on the bar. As she was about to drink it, Kenny Brown came over and sat next to her.

"Hey Kat, how's it going?"

"Not tonight Kenny, I'd prefer to be alone."

"Trouble with Harry huh?"

"No."

"Some other guy?"

"Yeah, Tom Bowman."

"Harry should have let me put a hurt on that guy."

"Thanks Kenny. But you can't solve this problem."

"You sure? Let me at him. I'm sure he'll leave you alone."

"It's not like that Kenny. Tom's going for a retrial and he might get off."

"I thought they had him?"

"They did. But something came up that might get him a retrial."

"How could that be?"

"Some procedural errors or something."

"I don't get it. He was already sentenced."

"Yes, but the appeals court has agreed with the defense. There's a hearing in the morning. We'll know after that if he gets the retrial."

"Well, if he bothers you, let me know. I'll take care of it."

"Thanks Kenny, but my attorney's handling it."

"If it doesn't work out, let me know."

"I will."

Kenny got up and left her alone. She drank two more martinis and Dee finally said, "Kat, you might want to go a little easy. Something must be really bothering you."

"I did some stupid things to ensure Tom Bowman got what he deserved at the first trial."

"Like what?"

"As it turned out, I went to college with the Judge who heard Tom's case. I had some things on the Judge and I think he sided with the prosecution as a result of my leverage."

"What could you have had on the Judge?"

"Naked pictures of me and him the night of his bachelor party."

"You're kidding?"

"No. I was so young then and I got along with all the guys."

"But that was so long ago."

"Yeah, but there was more."

"So you blackmailed the Judge with this stuff?"

"I just told him he would get all of the stuff back over time if he did the right thing."

"I think that's blackmail, Kat."

"Plus, I slept with the Judge."

"Yeah, you said you did. But that was after his bachelor party."

"No. I slept with him during Tom's trial."

"You're kidding?" Dee rolled her eyes, and then listened intently for more.

"No."

"Kat, that's serious stuff. Tom's lawyers are probably trying to get the whole thing thrown out. The Judge should have stepped aside."

"He couldn't. I left him samples of pictures just to make sure he followed though."

"Oh, Katherine."

"Dee, I'm going home. Drinking isn't solving the problem for me."

"I hope it all works out for you."

"So do I."

"See you tomorrow Katherine. Drive carefully."

Katherine picked up her purse and keys. She walked out, got into her car and drove home.

After Katherine had left, Harry came into the bar. He took up a stool next to Kenny.

"You just missed Katherine, Harry."

"Oh really?"

Dee added, "She was here for about an hour."

"Something's really bothering her," commented Kenny.

"There's a hearing tomorrow for Tom Bowman's retrial. She's worried it isn't going to go the way she wants it to go."

"I don't know why it's bothering her," said Kenny as he picked up his beer having seen Tina Fletcher come into the bar and taking up a stool across from them.

After he had left, Dee said, "Harry, Kat did some things during the time of the trial that might have an affect on the hearing tomorrow."

"What could she have done?" asked Harry.

"For one, she slept with the Judge. Plus, she has pictures of the Judge and her naked."

"You're kidding?"

"That's what she said."

"Oh boy. A dark cloud just keeps following her."

"You said it."

"I guess we'll have to wait till tomorrow to see how this all turns out."

"That's what she said."

Harry got up and went to his office. He wanted to call Katherine but decided it might be best to leave her alone for the time being.

Chapter 19

Attorney Steven Kennedy arrived at the courthouse a few minutes after nine. He looked around outside the courtroom and didn't see Katherine. As he entered the courtroom, he surveyed the gallery. He let out a sigh of relief not seeing her, and took up a seat behind the prosecution bench.

The prosecutor was Ann Levine. She had prosecuted Tom Bowman at the original trial. Tom Bowman sat at the defense table with his attorney, Harold White. The door behind the bench opened.

The bailiff announced, "All rise, Barnstable Court is now in session, the honorable Judge Alan Carstens presiding."

Everyone stood. The judge took his seat and instructed everyone to do the same, and then he spoke.

"I understand the appeals court has granted Mr. Bowman this hearing to determine if a retrial should be granted. Are you ready to proceed Mr. White?"

"Yes your Honor."

"Is the Prosecution ready?" the Judge asked Ms. Levine.

"Yes your Honor."

"All right, Mr. White, your petition states you feel your client had been wrongly prosecuted in the initial trial and that the defense has evidence that will clearly show this to be the case. Is this a true statement?"

Everyone looked at Attorney White. He rose holding a folder and what looked like a CD.

"Yes your Honor. I hold here evidence showing Judge Bennet in compromising video during the trial with one of the victims. I also have documentation and witnesses prepared to testify as to the Judge having sexual relations with said witness during the same time period. Judge Bennet should have excused himself from the trial and should have never entered the judgment."

"Approach the bench Mr. White."

Attorney White stepped forward, with Attorney Levine following.

"Is this some form of circus Mr. White? You are accusing an honorable Judge of the court with inappropriate conduct. You better have convincing evidence."

"Your Honor, the evidence will stand on it's own merit."

"Ms. Levine, have you looked at this material?" the Judge asked pointing to the folder and CD.

"My office is aware of the information about to be presented." She turned to the prosecution bench to look at her associate as she made the statement. It looked like she wasn't really sure if her office knew what was about to be presented or not.

"Ok. Step back and proceed," ordered Judge Carstens.

Attorney White started out by putting the CD into a player. In a minute, the projection on a large screen came to life.

"What you are seeing here your Honor is video from the surveillance camera outside the courthouse. If you'll take note of the date-time stamp in the lower left hand corner, you'll notice it was taken on one of the days my client was in court."

"I object, your Honor," said Attorney Levine. "Mr. White is showing a video which could have been altered."

"Your Honor, I'm prepared to have the court security personnel testify as to the authenticity of the video."

"I'll allow the video for now."

"If I may continue, your Honor."

"Please do."

"You'll notice the video shows a very clear view of the offices on the side of the building where the camera is recording."

As the video played, people could be seen in the various offices within the view of the camera.

"If you look at the fourth window from the right, you will be able to see right in to Judge Bennet's chambers."

"Are you sure Judge Bennet's office is the fourth window?"

"Yes your Honor."

Attorney White pressed pause on the remote controller he held in his hand.

"Next you'll see some of the evidence as to why we think Judge Bennet should have excused himself."

Attorney White pressed play. The video continued. Judge Bennet could be seen coming into his office. He was standing next to his desk having just taken his robe off. A woman could be seen entering his office. They talked for a minute and then she approached him, put her arms around him and kissed him rather passionately for a fairly long period of time. At no time did the Judge try to repel the woman. In fact, he seemed to be very involved with her. After kissing, they both could be seen looking out the window at vehicles moving about the parking lot below. Their faces were clearly identifiable. The Judge on the left, Katherine Sterns was on the right.

Attorney Levine stood. "I object."

Judge Carstens said, "So do I."

"Your Honor, this video should be examined by a professional to ascertain its validity," said Ms. Levine.

"Ms. Levine, you indicated your office was aware of the materials being presented. I would have thought your office would have presented written arguments prior to this hearing if you questioned the validity of the video."

Attorney White turned to Tom Bowman and smiled. Then he stood. He turned off the video. He walked to the bench and handed the court recorder the folder.

"I'd like to introduce as evidence the ledger from the Route 28 Motel recorded during the time period of Mr. Bowman's original trial."

"I object your Honor. This document is hearsay."

"Your Honor, the Route 28 Motel manager, Ms. Helen Venice, is here today and is prepared to testify as to the validity and accuracy of the ledger."

Attorney White held up the folder and pointed into the courtroom where Ms. Venice was seated. She raised her hand so the Judge could identify who she was.

"Overruled, please proceed Mr. White."

Attorney White asked for Ms. Venice to take the stand. She did and was sworn in. He approached her and handed her the folder containing the ledger.

"Ms. Venice, is this the ledger for the Route 28 Motel for last year?"

"Yes."

"Can you open the ledger to the page with the tag on it?"

She opened the ledger and quickly flipped to a page containing a tag. "Please tell the court what the ledger contains."

"On this date, a room was rented to a Mr. Michael Bennet at 5 pm. The rental was for one night. The cost of the room was sixty dollars."

"Can you tell from the reservation or booking who used the room?"

"Not normally, but the reservation was made by Katherine Sterns. See the note here next to Mr. Bennet's name. I made that note when Mr. Bennet paid for the room."

"Why did you make that note?"

"Ms. Sterns comes to our place from time to time. We are in the habit of making note of returning customers."

"Is this for a frequent renter program or something?"

"No. We just try to keep track of the same people coming and going."

"Is there an issue with some of these people?"

"Well, we figured if something bad happened, we had better know who was at our business. Some of the women who make reservations at our place are there frequently."

"Are you saying they might be prostitutes?"

"I object, your Honor," said Attorney Levine. "This is pure speculation."

"I'll allow it. But, please move on Mr. White."

"So your note in the ledger indicated Ms. Katherine Sterns spent a night with Judge Michael Bennet."

"Not just the note, I was on duty that night and I saw Ms. Sterns and Mr. Bennet go into the room. A short time

140

later the lights went out. I didn't see her leave so I'm pretty sure she was there for a while."

Attorney White continued, "What time did Mr. Bennet check out?"

"I wasn't on duty when he checked out, but the ledger shows him checking out at around midnight."

"The same day?"

"That's what it indicated."

"So he didn't spend the whole night there with her?"

"I guess not."

Attorney White faced the Judge. "Your Honor, as you can see, Judge Bennet should have excused himself from the trial. It's clear he was involved with one of the victims and possibly even influenced by Ms. Sterns. Based on what we have presented already, I move for vacating the sentence and freeing Mr. Bowman."

"Attorney Levine," Judge Carstens looked at her for a response.

"Your Honor. Based on what has been presented the prosecution feels Mr. Bowman's verdict should be set aside."

"Your Honor," Attorney White interrupted. "We are asking that Mr. Bowman not be retried. An injustice has been done and my client has served time in jail."

Judge Carstens thought about it for a minute. He asked to look at the folder Attorney White had submitted into evidence and then he said, "I agree with Mr. White. Mr. Bowman, I am ordering you be released and the verdict from your original trial set aside. The prosecution may at it's discretion resubmit for retrial although I would strongly suggest the Prosecution make sure of it's evidence prior to attempting any retrial."

Judge Carstens looked at Attorney Levine as he made the statement.

"We understand," said Attorney Levine.

"Then Court is dismissed," said Judge Carstens hitting his gavel on the bench.

Attorney White turned to Tom Bowman and shook his hand.

"You're free to go Tom. I don't think the DA will re-file the case based on what we presented today. The Judge has warned them. Unless something new comes up, there's no way you'll have to deal with this any further."

"Thanks Harold. I appreciate all you did."

"You're welcome Tom. Now go get your life back together."

Tom Bowman stood and walked out the courtroom a free man.

Tom felt good about the decision. He wanted to have a celebratory drink. He decided to have it at Sundancers so he drove from Hyannis east on Route 28 eventually crossing the Bass River and then turning left into Sundancers parking lot. He parked and went in.

Harry saw him get out of his car from his office. He went out of his office and into the bar passing through the kitchen. As he entered the bar, he saw Tom taking up a stool. He walked right over to him.

"Bowman, I thought I told you not to come in here."

"You did. But that was before I was vindicated."

"What are you talking about?"

"I just came from court. The verdict from my first trial was set aside. The court recognized the injustice that was done and has set me free."

"I think you might owe me an apology," Tom said to Harry.

"I don't owe you anything. Get out of my place."

Harry was getting loud, something he rarely did. Kenny Brown, who had been seated on the opposite side of the bar, saw this as his cue. He rushed around the end of the bar and with one punch knocked Tom Bowman right off the stool. Tom hit the floor like a ton of bricks being dropped. Tom got up slowly, rubbing his face where Kenny had struck him.

He turned to Harry and said, "This isn't over Harry. You know who was responsible for everything that happened and it wasn't me."

"Look Bowman, I want you out of my place and don't ever come back."

"You heard him Bowman," said Kenny ready to strike again.

"You all saw it. Kenny struck me. I'm going to press charges."

"We didn't see anything," said Harry. "Just get out of my place."

Tom Bowman brushed past Kenny and kept walking. As he left, he said, "This isn't over."

He left the bar.

Chapter 20

Katherine worked around her house that morning waiting for Steven Kennedy to call her. She was visibly agitated and couldn't sit still. She tried cleaning, then reading, then tried to watch TV but nothing could get her mind off the court hearing regarding Tom Bowman.

After lunch, she decided to take a walk on the beach before getting ready to go to work. She got into her car and drove to the West Dennis beach.

It was a sunny day, temperatures in the low 60's with no wind. There were a few other cars in the parking lot spread out a good distance from each other. She got out of her car, donned a baseball cap and started to walk to the west. After going about a quarter mile, she stopped to look out at the water.

For some reason, she glanced back to where her car was parked. She noticed a pickup truck pulling in right next to her car. She didn't recognize the truck and continued to watch for a few more minutes. The driver of the truck, a man, got out and went around to the front of Katherine's car. It looked like he was looking at her license plate or something. Then he had his foot up on the seawall and was tying his sneaker.

"I must be getting paranoid," she said out loud.
She turned and continued walking.

She made the turn at the end of the lot in about fifteen minutes then started her return trip. When she got back to her car, the truck was still there but the driver was nowhere to be found. She hadn't passed a man while walking back to her car and didn't know where he had gone. She looked both ways but only saw two women off in the distance by their cars talking. Then she got into her car and drove home.

An hour after taking the walk, she had just finished getting ready to go to work. She went outside to get her mail before leaving. When she took her mail out of the mailbox, she looked down the street. Parked a few houses away was the same pickup truck she had seen at the beach. She couldn't see anyone in the truck and became nervous. She quickly went back into her house.

After she closed her door behind her, she looked out her window just barely being able to see the truck. She heard it start up. It began to come in the direction of her house. She ran to her door, opened it and ran down the driveway trying to get a look at the driver. The truck passed her house before she could get to the end of the driveway and sped off. She didn't see who it was.

At three, she got into her car and drove to work at Sundancers. Walking in the door, Dee said, "Hey Kat. Ready for another night?"
"I don't know Dee. I think I'm getting paranoid or something. I was hoping to hear something about Tom Bowman's retrial hearing, but my attorney hasn't called yet."

Dee had been there when Harry and Kenny had the run-in with Bowman but she didn't say anything to Katherine about the incident.

"Anxious huh?"

"No, I'm really paranoid. I went for a walk on the beach today and I swear someone was following me. Then after I went home, I saw the same vehicle I saw at the beach on my street. When it drove off, I ran to the end of my driveway to catch a glimpse of the driver but I was too late."

"What kind of vehicle was it?"

"A pickup truck."

"I'm not sure I can help you there. Most of the guys who come in here drive pickups."

"Yeah, I know. This one was black. The only thing I remember unique about it was a confederate flag sticker on the front bumper."

"Well, that shouldn't be hard to see. I doubt there are many pickups around here with a sticker like that on the bumper. I'll keep an eye out."

"Thanks Dee. Now, I've got to get ready for the night."

Katherine went to the hostess station, read the reservation book for the night and made notes to herself on the seating chart. She got the copies of the daily specials and put them into the menu folder stack on the hostess podium. She was ready for work physically, maybe not mentally.

Harry came out of the kitchen to check and make sure everyone was ready for the night's business. He talked to the waitress staff, to Dee and then turned his attention to Katherine.

"All set Katherine?"

"I think so. Say Harry, I told you Ed apologized to me for the things he did. How do you think I should handle it?"

"Like you said, you didn't get hurt, I'd let it go. After all, Ed was considerably drunk when he did those things. I don't think he really meant to harm you."

"You're probably right. I just can't believe he would come after me after he and I had been intimate."

"Think about what you just said Katherine. That's exactly why he did what he did. He was hurt and jealous. Those emotions can be very powerful. Mix them with alcohol and who knows what will happen."

"It was just sex, that's all."

"Maybe to you, but I think it was much more to Ed."

"So you don't think I should do anything?"

"Hey, it's your decision. But do you really want any more trouble?"

"You have a point."

"I have a few more things to check up on before we get busy. I'll check back with you later."

"Thanks for your advice Harry."

"You're welcome."

Harry went back into the kitchen to talk with Antonio. Katherine returned to the hostess station to greet the first couple that had just come in for dinner. After seating the couple, she returned to the hostess station. Her cell phone vibrated in her pocket. She took it out to look at the caller-id. It was Steven Kennedy.

"Steven, I was hoping you would call."

"It took most of the day for the hearing. Judge Carstens has made a decision with regard to Mr. Bowman."

"What was the decision?"

"You're not going to like it."

"Why not?"

"The Judge heard the evidence as did everyone in the courtroom. Then after a brief sidebar with the DA, the Judge announced that the court would not be proceeding with a retrial."

"So they sent him back to jail?"

"No."

"How can that be?"

"If you saw the evidence presented, you would know why the Judge did what he did."

"What evidence?"

"Bowman's attorney showed a surveillance video from the courthouse taken during Mr. Bowman's original trial. In the video, Judge Bennet can be seen in the window kissing a woman."

"Can you tell who was with the Judge?"

"Yes. It was you."

"I told you it was only a greeting kiss."

"I saw the video and it sure looked like more than that." Judge Carstens thought so also.

Then Bowman's attorney produced a witness and documentation from the Route 28 Motel who testified you and Judge Bennet got a room there one night during the trial. I think the motel ledger and testimony of the motel manager sealed the decision."

"Judge Carstens released Tom Bowman and set aside the original judgment. Tom Bowman's a free man."

"Can he be retried?"

"The Judge was pretty specific. He said the DA had better come up with a much better case if he wanted to file for retrial. So the door's open for a retrial but I wouldn't put much faith in it."

"Wow. It couldn't get any worse."

"I also found out who bailed Tom Bowman out. It was someone named Ed Phillips."

"That shit head."

"So you know Mr. Phillips?"

"I know him."

"Well, he's the one who bailed Bowman out."

"I'll have to talk to Ed about this. I should have pressed charges."

"For what?"

"He's the same person who attacked me a few months ago in my home. I only recently found out."

"Be careful Katherine. I'd call the police if you think you can prove what you've told me."

"I'm not sure how I can prove it. Ed confessed his actions to me, but the police had not identified him as the perpetrator."

"Then they probably don't have sufficient evidence on him. Otherwise, the police would have brought him in."

"What should I do?"

"Does he come into the place where you work?"

"That's where I am now and yes, he comes in here all the time."

"Then I'd be careful."

"Ok. Thanks for calling me Steven."

She hung up the phone. As she turned around, Harry was standing behind her.

"What was that all about?"

"I just talked with my attorney. He said Judge Carstens set Tom Bowman free today. There was evidence shown in court showing Judge Bennet should have excused himself from the original trial."

"Like what?"

149

"It doesn't matter what, Judge Carstens said the evidence clearly showed Judge Bennet was wrongly influenced and should have stepped down."

"Who would have tried to influence a Judge?"

Harry looked her in the eyes. She couldn't look directly at him and said, "I did."

"What did you do Katherine?"

"I had some things on the Judge and I coerced him into giving Tom Bowman the maximum sentence."

"What could you have on a Judge that would make him do such a thing? Pictures or something?"

"Yes. Pictures from when I knew the Judge back in college."

"Just how compelling were these pictures?"

"They showed me and the Judge naked the night of his bachelor party."

"So you blackmailed a Judge."

"I wouldn't call it blackmail, just nudged him in a certain direction."

"Katherine, it's called blackmail. I've got a few things to do. I'll talk to you later."

Harry left via the kitchen for his office. Katherine went back to her hostess duties.

Chapter 21

About a half hour later, Ed Phillips came into the bar. Katherine had been seating a family and was walking back to the hostess station. When she saw Ed coming in, she lingered near the waitress station trying to avoid Ed. He walked along the windows and took up a bar stool midway down the bar. He ordered a beer and took a look at a menu.

Dee walked over to the hostess station.

"Katherine, Ed just came in. I've been watching the vehicles as they come into the lot and Ed's driving a pickup truck with a confederate flag sticker on the front bumper."

"Oh really."

"Yeah. See that black pickup over there. Ed came here in that truck."

"I'll have to talk to him."

Katherine was trying to avoid talking with Ed, now she had to confront him. She walked over to where Ed was seated and stood behind him.

"Ed, is that your black pickup truck over there?"

She pointed to the truck parked on the opposite side of the lot.

"Yeah, that's my truck."

"I see it has a confederate flag sticker on the bumper."

"So, what of it?"

"I saw the same truck parked at the beach and then on my street. When I tried to approach it, the driver sped away."

"If it was yesterday or today, it wasn't me."

"I thought you said it's your truck?"

"It is. I lent it to Tom Bowman for a few days so he could take care of a few things now that he's out of jail."

"So you admit helping Tom?"

"Why wouldn't I help him? I'd help any friend."

"Why did you bail him out of jail? I think that goes a little beyond being just a friend."

"Hey, I don't ask you what you do with your money. And I don't ask you what you do with your friends."

"Ed, why do you sound so bitter?"

"I'm not bitter."

"You still have a thing for me, don't you?"

"I…"

He didn't get a change to respond.

"So that's what this has all been about. Your coming to my house and breaking in. Spreading that stuff around. Taking my pajamas. Then trying to get into my house again. Then bailing Tom out. It's all to get my attention."

Ed turned around to face Katherine.

"Look Katherine. I thought we had something more than you did. I think I get the picture. You'll not have any more trouble from me."

"I hope not Ed. I'd hate to have to press charges."

152

Kenny Brown had come in while Katherine was talking to Ed and had taken up a stool two away from Ed and behind Katherine. She didn't know he was there.

"Kenny here can be my witness. Kenny, did you hear our conversation?"

"Pretty much."

"Then will you tell Katherine you witnessed my saying she will not have any further problems with me?"

Kenny looked at Katherine and was about to speak.

"Ok, Ok. I heard him. Just make sure you keep your word Ed."

"I will."

A couple had come into Sundancers and was standing at the hostess station. "I have to get back to work."

She turned to greet the couple. Katherine seated them then returned to the hostess station. Tom Bowman pulled into the parking lot and got out of his car. Katherine walked out the door and confronted Tom in the parking lot.

"Tom, did you have Ed's truck and park next to my car at the West Dennis Beach?"

"When?"

"Earlier."

"Well."

"And did you then follow me home and park down the street from my house in Ed's truck?"

"No, no."

"Come on Tom. Ed told me he lent you his truck and how many black pickups do you know around here that have confederate flag stickers on the bumpers?"

"It could have been anyone."

"But it was Ed's truck. That one over there was the one parked on my street."

"So I parked on your street."

"And at the West Dennis Beach?"

"So?"

"Tom, what do you want? The Judge set you free. Now, why don't you stay out of my life?"

"I'm not in your life Katherine. I just stopped in to buy Ed a beer and thank him for letting me use his truck."

"So you're not here to keep tabs on me?"

"Why would I want to?"

"I don't know. Revenge?"

"Look Katherine. I did some stupid things and I spent some time in jail for them. You tried to influence the Judge to make sure I got the maximum time the Judge could give me even for some things I didn't do. The courts saw through the errors in the trial and have let me go. I'm willing to drop the whole thing."

"What do you mean drop the whole thing? You're stalking me."

"No I'm not. I thought about it but my attorney gave me some good advice and I intend to take it."

"What did he say?"

"He said I should accept things for what they are. I might have gotten out sooner than I would have for the actual things I did, but a retrial would tie me up probably for the same amount of time as the sentence. I should consider myself fortunate for Judge Bennet's mistakes and move on. So that's what I'm doing. Moving on."

Harry interrupted the two from their heated discussion in his parking lot. He saw Tom get out of his truck and then saw Katherine fly out of Sundancers shouting at him. They didn't know Harry was witness to most of the confrontation.

"Look you two, I'm trying to run a business here. Your shouting in the parking lot isn't good for business. Can you two put this off until another time?"

"I'm sorry Harry. I should get back to work."

Katherine turned and walked back inside.

"Did I understand you right Bowman, you've been released?"

"Yes. Like I said, I had a hearing today and a new Judge set me free. There were issues with the first trial where Judge Bennet should have excused himself and didn't. Judge Carstens has set aside most of Judge Bennet's sentences and has released me from the minor charges with time served."

"And that stuff your attorney told you about moving on?"

"That's what I was trying to tell Katherine. It's time to move on and leave things from the past in the past."

"Well, I still don't want you in my place. Bad things seem to happen when you're around."

"So you're telling me to leave?"

"Yes. Go in and have your beer with Ed. Then move on."

"Ok Harry. Thanks for understanding."

Harry stood and watched Tom walk in. Tom walked over to where Ed was seated. He shook Ed's hand and took up the stool on the other side of Ed, away from Kenny. Harry walked back into his office.

"Have a shot with us Tom. Kenny and I were just making a toast."

Kenny shot Bowman a nasty look.

"You can drink with him Ed if you want, but not me."

Kenny stood and walked out onto the deck.

There were three empty shot glasses in front of Ed and a half full beer when Tom walked over. After Kenny had walked away, Ed said, "Dee, give Tom a beer and shot of Jack. Make it two."

"Ed, you've had three shots already and a number of beers. You can't drive home." Dee said as she got Tom a beer and shot.

She set Ed up with another shot anyway.

"Tom can drive me home," said Ed slurring his words a little.

"I agree with her Ed, you might want to tone it down."

"Just one more," said Ed picking up the shot glass and downing it.

Katherine walked by on the opposite side of the bar with two elderly ladies. She had menus in her hand and directed them to a table in the dining room.

"Wouldn't you like to have that," Ed slurred pointing at Katherine.

"Who wouldn't," Tom said.

"I've been with her Tom. She's terrific."

"I know."

"You slept with her too?"

"If you mean did I have sex with her, I did."

"Me too." Ed said as he slopped some of his beer on the floor. "And I'd love to do it again."

"Look Ed. I'm not looking for any trouble. Why don't we get out of here? I'll take you home."

"What trouble? I just want to have sex with her again."

Ed tried to get up off the stool and knocked it over. He stumbled a little and half fell over.

"Come on Ed, I'll take you home."

"Ok Tom."

Tom threw a fifty on the bar. "Will that take care of his tab?"

Dee picked up a slip from the register and said, "Sure will."

"Then we'll be going."

Tom took Ed's arm and walked him to the door. They both got into Tom's vehicle and left. As they did, Katherine walked back to the hostess station. Dee had been standing by the door watching Tom get Ed into his car.

"Ed sure got drunk pretty quickly," said Dee.

"I just talked to him a half hour ago," said Katherine.

"He had a few shots with Kenny and another one with Tom. Plus he had a few beers. It hits some people kind of quick."

"I guess."

"I'm glad Bowman took him home. I wouldn't want to see Ed driving in that condition."

"So much for the two of them for tonight. Maybe now things will settle down?"

"Maybe," said Dee turning and going back to the bar.

Chapter 22

Detective Simpson had contacted all of the widows who had funds stolen. All but Sharon Kelly did indeed sign a document with Mr. Chamberlin authorizing him to continue to act as a financial consultant. When Detective Simpson tried to get the women to cooperate in pressing the matter with Mr. Chamberlin, they were unanimous in their response. They wanted to wait a little while before doing anything. Even Sharon Kelly, who lost money as a result from a different set of circumstances, wanted to put Detective Simpson off for a few weeks. She anticipated getting her situation resolved to her satisfaction in the near future.

Simpson couldn't get anywhere with any of the women. He went to see Captain Trudy.

"Captain, I've tried to get any one of the women to cooperate with us regarding Chamberlin. They all believe things are going to be resolved soon for each and every one of them."

"I know. I talked with Carol Tindle. She's convinced Katherine Sterns has the whole situation under control."

Simpson responded, "I talked with Ms. Sterns. She got her money back. Why would she want to help the others?"

"I don't know. Maybe she wants to get even with Chamberlin somehow."

"I wonder what she has planned?"

"Don't make it too obvious, but keep an eye on her."

"Ok Captain. Anything else?"

"No, that's it for now."

Detective Simpson went back to his office to formulate a plan. He would frequent the place where Ms. Sterns was working and see who she talks to, and what gets said. That should be a start.

Captain Trudy called the DA, Ann Levine.

"Ann, I'm not sure we still have a case against Charles Chamberlin. The women all had agreements with him allowing him to act as their financial advisor. Only Sharon Kelly didn't have the arrangement and she isn't cooperating. According to one of the women, Carol Tindle, Katherine Sterns has been in contact with Mr. Chamberlin and he plans on returning their money."

"Including Ms. Kelly?"

"Her funds are unclear. He only represented to Ms. Sterns that he intended to return the principal he invested for the women he had agreements with, plus a nice profit."

"If he delivers on his promise, I don't see how we proceed."

"I agree. That will only leave us with Ms. Kelly."

"Yeah, and if she gets her missing funds back somehow, I'm sure she won't want to cooperate."

"Can you really blame her?"

"I guess not. But how's Ms. Sterns going to make all this happen?"

"According to Ms. Tindle, Mr. Chamberlin plans on giving the funds back himself."

"But that didn't include Ms. Kelly. Sterns must have something up her sleeve."

"We might end up having a case against her instead of him if somehow she commits a crime against him."

"Wouldn't that be unexpected?"

"Sure would."

"Look Pam, I'm not going to push this matter unless something changes."

"I understand. Ann, I'll call you if anything changes."

"Please do."

They hung up and went about their business. Chamberlin was temporarily off the hook.

The next night at Sundancers, Katherine showed up for work dressed in style. She had on a yellow silk low cut blouse and a black skirt. She wore a pair of black flats since she had to be on her feet for hours. She had her blond hair done that day allowing it to hang past her shoulders. She looked good.

Harry and Kenny were seated at the bar having a discussion about baseball.

"Harry, are you going to sponsor the baseball team again this year?"

"I plan on it."

"Do you have a manager yet?"

"You'll have to ask Ron. He did it last year and I think he plans on doing it again this year."

Katherine walked behind the two with a couple she was seating. Kenny got a whiff of her perfume.

"Harry, do you smell that?"

Harry was focused on the baseball team and said, "Smell what?"

"Katherine. She sure smells good."

160

"What are you talking about?"

"Here she comes. You've got to smell her."

"Hey Kat," said Kenny. "How are things?"

"Kenny, Harry."

She stopped between the two. Kenny leaned into her neck and sniffed the air.

"Katherine, you smell great. What is that?"

"A new perfume I picked up today. Like it Harry?"

"I like it," said Kenny.

"What about you, Harry?"

Katherine leaned in to Harry. Harry pretended to smell the perfume.

"Smells nice," was his response. He has a sinus problem and couldn't smell it at all so he faked it.

"What do you have planned after work Kat?" asked Kenny.

"Kenny, I'm working. Go after the other women and leave me alone."

She walked back to the hostess station.

When she had walked away, Kenny said to Harry, "I'd sure like to hook up with her tonight."

"Kenny, like she said, she's working."

"Yeah, but she'll be done around ten. You know she's fantastic in bed."

"So you say."

"Come on Harry, wouldn't you like to take her home?"

"I'm her boss."

"So what. Did you get a look at her? Did you smell her?"

Harry had already enjoyed the pleasures of Katherine Sterns but he didn't want to brag to Kenny.

"Kenny, like Katherine said, why don't you focus on the other women?"

"Oh, I get it Harry. You've already got something in the works with her."

"Think what you want Kenny."

"Ok Harry. But you let me know if you're not going after her."

"Right."

Harry got up and went to his office via the kitchen. Later, when Katherine was finished for the night, she hung around talking with some of the other patrons. Around one, only Harry, Katherine and Dee were left in the bar.

"Dee, why don't you go home? I'll close up tonight."

"Thanks Harry, Ted's home waiting up for me."

"Say hello to him for me."

"Ok. See you tomorrow."

"Bye."

Dee got her purse and left. When Harry saw the taillights on her car exit the parking lot, he turned the lights down at the bar and all the other lights off. The light blue glow coming from the bar had a romantic feel to it. Harry went to the DJ station and turned on some soft music. He went behind the bar and made Katherine her favorite martini. Then he went to where Katherine was sitting, set her martini down and extended his hand asking her to dance. They embraced and slow danced. Frank Sinatra was his favorite, and the song was just finishing.

"Harry, are you trying to seduce me?"

"No. I just thought it would be nice to spend a quiet moment together. You know, turn the lights down low, put on some nice music."

Katherine looked out on the river. The lights from across the river glistened on the water. She turned her head back to Harry and put it on his shoulder. Then she leaned back giving him a passionate kiss.

"So you agree," Harry said kissing her again.

"It's nice to be able to just relax. I just wish all these problems would go away."

"I think things are starting to settle down. You'll have to let your obsession with Tom Bowman go if you want that problem to subside."

"You're right."

"Now about the other things, I think some of those issues will solve themselves as well."

"Like what?"

"Like your troubles with some of the men in your past."

"And just how will those problems go away?"

Harry stepped back holding her hands. He looked her in the face and said sincerely, "I'd like for you to focus exclusively on one guy."

"Just one?"

"Yeah."

"Care to tell me who?"

"Me."

"What are you asking me Harry?"

"Let's just say I'd like us to do more things together and see where it goes."

"Harry, are you having trouble committing?"

"Katherine, it's taken me a long time to come to terms with focusing on just one woman."

"Oh, is that what you're doing?"

"Yes."

"So, you want us to be an item?"

"That sounds so formal. I just want to get closer to you and see how things progress."

"Harry, if things work out to your satisfaction, are you going to be able to make a deeper commitment?"

"I don't know. I just know that I'm ready to take the next step."

She leaned in and kissed him again. They danced slowly to the music of Ann Murray singing, "Can I Have This Dance for the Rest of My Life."

Katherine said, "Did you plan the music Harry?"

"Not really. This an all music station on the radio."

"Uh Huh."

They danced a few more minutes until the song was over. As it finished, he held her tight and kissed her.

"Want to come with me to my place?" she said after returning the kiss.

"I'd like to but I have a few things to do before I go home tonight."

"Like what?"

"I have to finish payroll for the week and get the bank reconciliation done."

"Tonight?"

"Yea. If I don't do it now, you and everyone else won't get paid tomorrow."

"Then why not come over when you are done?"

"It might take an hour or two. By then it'll be 3 am."

"I can wait up."

"Tell you what. Let's plan on doing something this weekend. I'm taking off the whole weekend and I've checked your schedule. You're off as well."

"Ok. Sounds good to me. Don't work too late."

"I'll call you tomorrow."

He kissed her again and walked her to the door.

When she had gone, Harry walked over to the DJ station and turned off the system. He went back to the bar, pickup up their glasses and put them in the bus tray. Then, he turned the lights off. The place looked reasonably cleaned up. He locked the door and then went through the kitchen, locking the kitchen door behind him on his way to the office. He sat at his computer for the next hour processing the payroll checks, signing them and putting them in envelopes for the employees. When he was done, he made the necessary entries on his computer into his bookkeeping software, then he put them all in the safe. When he looked at his watch, it was 3:15 am.

Harry thought about Katherine, then rubbed his eyes, yawned and walked out to his car. Tomorrow would be another day.

Chapter 23

Around eleven the next morning, Harry got himself a cup of coffee. Then he picked up his phone and called Katherine.

"Morning Katherine."

"Hi Harry. Did you work much more last night after I left?"

"Another hour or so, but I got everything done I wanted to do. Now I'm all set to take the weekend off. Do you want to do something on Sunday?"

"What about Saturday?"

"I'm going to Boston to meet up with a few friends. We have tickets to see the Sox on Saturday night. I expect to get back here around nine Sunday morning."

"Then why don't we plan on going kayaking Sunday? I'd like to go to Stage Harbor again to see the seals."

"That works for me. When you come to work later today, we can put the kayaks on my Jeep and I'll drop them at your house before I go to Boston. That way I can pick you and the gear up at your house Sunday morning."

"Works for me. I'll see you around 3 pm at work."

"See you then."

Katherine went about her day doing her chores. She stopped in at Joey's Pizza around noon to pick up a pizza. After lunch, she got herself ready for work. She dressed in a pair of dark gray slacks and black flats. She put on a gold-colored cashmere sweater. She allowed her hair to flow long. After putting on some makeup, she declared herself ready for another day of work.

When she got to Sundancers, she went into Harry's office. He came out with her and they loaded the kayaks onto Harry's Jeep. They put the paddles and life vests in his trunk. Antonio who had been standing in the kitchen back door saw them load everything into Harry's vehicle. As an order came in to the kitchen, he went back to work. After putting everything into Harry's Jeep, Harry said, "I'll drop this stuff off on my way to Boston."

He gave her a kiss on the cheek.

"I'll plan on seeing you Sunday morning at my house."

"If anything comes up, I'll call you."

"Harry, what could come up?"

"I don't know, but I'm meeting a few old friends in Boston and one never knows."

"Ok. I'll do the same."

"Any of these friends female?"

"Why Katherine, are you jealous?"

"Just asking."

"Well, I'm meeting with the guys I used to hang around with when I was much younger."

"All guys, huh?"

"What do you have planned for tomorrow, Katherine?"

"Oh, I don't know. I'm sure I'll find something."

"Well, enjoy your day off. I'll see you Sunday."

"See you then."

Harry got into his vehicle and headed to Katherine's to drop the stuff off. Katherine went into work. A little while after she started her shift, Antonio came out of the kitchen. He approached the hostess station to talk with Katherine who was sitting on a stool looking at the reservation log.

"Hey Katherine. I saw you and Harry putting your kayaks on his Jeep. Going kayaking after work?"

"Maybe Sunday."

"Oh, Sunday."

"Yeah. We're both taking the weekend off for some relaxation. We plan to go kayaking on Sunday."

"So what are you doing tomorrow?"

"I'm off. I have a few things I need to tend to."

"Say, I'm off tomorrow as well. Want to do something together?"

Katherine looked at Antonio with a puzzled look. "Antonio, what do you have in mind?"

"Nothing really. I just thought if you and I were both off tomorrow with nothing planned, we might do it together."

"Thanks for the offer Antonio but actually, I have a matter I need to get resolved."

"Anything I can help with?"

"No. I have to do this one myself."

"Does it involve Harry?"

"That's really none of your business Antonio."

A couple came into the bar and stood at the hostess station. "Can we have a table for two? Outside?"

"Sure, right this way," said Katherine picking up two menus and leading the couple into the restaurant and onto the back deck.   When she came back to the hostess station, Antonio had returned to the kitchen.

At a little after eight, Tom Bowman came into the bar. He had a young woman with him. He saw Katherine standing behind the hostess station and said, "Katherine, this is Helen. Can we have a table in the corner of the restaurant where we might have some privacy?"

Katherine looked at Helen and extended her hand. "Nice to meet you."
Helen returned the greeting.   Then Katherine led the two to the back of the restaurant giving them a table in the corner.
"This is about as private as it gets Tom."
"Thanks Katherine."

As Katherine walked away, Helen said to Tom, "I sense there's something more than a casual acquaintance between you and her."
"We have a past," was all he said.
Then he put his arms around her and gave her a sweet kiss.   Katherine watched from behind the plant barrier separating the bar from the dining room. When she saw Tom embracing the young woman, she turned and walked back to the hostess station.

Dee saw Katherine watching and said, "What's that all about Katherine?"
"Who knows? She could be his daughter."
"You're not jealous are you?"
"Tom? Hell no. I just think he looks ridiculous."
"You think he's trying to get under your skin?"
"I don't know."
"I wouldn't let him get to you."
"Oh, he's not."

Katherine kept walking back to the hostess station. There was a family of four waiting for her to return. The family consisted of a mother, father, young boy and a baby. Katherine picked up two menus, coloring book and crayons.

"Right this way folks, I have a nice table for you right by the windows."

She put the family at the table next to Tom and Helen. As she walked away, the baby began to cry. She thought to herself, "Serves you right."

Dee heard the baby start to cry and looked back into the dining room. As Katherine walked by again, she said, "Nice move."

Katherine just smiled. She went back to the hostess station. As she sat on the stool, Charles Chamberlin walked in. He approached the hostess station.

"Hi Katherine. I just got in."
"Charles."
"When can we get together?"
"What did you have in mind?"
"What time do you get off work?"
"In a couple of hours. But I have plans for the weekend."
"Oh, that's too bad. I was hoping we could get everything straightened out and start over."

"Are you ready to return all the funds?"
"I am."
"And the gains?"
"That too."
"Let me think about it for a while. Are you going to be here for an hour or two?"

"I've got all night."

"I'll come see you at the bar later."

"I'll be here."

Katherine went about her business. Charles took up a stool near the windows so he could have a good view of the hostess station and the rest of the bar. He had a few drinks, played a little keno and ordered an appetizer. Around 10 pm, Katherine had finished up her work when she approached Charles.

"I'm finished for the night Charles, want to come over to my place so we can talk?"

"I'll be there in about twenty minutes."

"See you there."

Katherine went back to the hostess station, picked up her purse and then said goodnight to Dee. She left by herself in her car.

After finishing his drink, Charles asked for his check. He paid it and then left. Dee did not hear what Katherine had said to Charles when she got off work so she didn't think anything about the two leaving around the same time.

Katherine got to her place first. She turned on most of the lights in the house including those in her study. She put on a pot of coffee and took out two mugs. As the coffee finished percolating, she heard a car door close in her driveway followed by footsteps on the porch. Then, the doorbell rang. She opened the door for Charles.

"Come in. I've just put on a fresh pot of coffee."

"Thanks. I could use a cup."

"So Charles, you said you wanted to straighten things out. As I recall, that means I should be getting the rest of the returns on the funds you invested for me."

"That's right. I've wrapped things up in Rio. I'm in a position to reconcile everything back here now."

"When do you think you'll send me my portion of the gains?"

"I can do it right now if I can use your computer."

"You know where my study is, go ahead and use the computer. I'll get you a cup of coffee. Black and one sugar?

"You remembered, thanks."

Charles walked into her study. He sat at her computer typing a few keystrokes from time to time. Katherine went to the kitchen and made two cups of coffee. She felt confident the software she had experimented with was doing its job. When she walked into the study, she handed him a cup.

"Black, one sugar."

He took the cup and said, "Thanks."

He sipped the coffee, put it down on the desk, "Your transfer is completed. If you want to check your account, you'll find a very nice deposit."

"I'll check it tomorrow Charles. Why don't we go into the other room?"

He stood. As he exited the study, he turned to go into the living room. She stopped him and said, "No, this way."

She led him to the bedroom.

Chapter 24

The two rose around 8 am. Katherine went to the kitchen and made a nice breakfast. She shredded two sweet potatoes and made home fries, then cooked bacon and scrambled eggs. She made a few pieces of rye toast, buttered them and put everything on the table. She took orange juice and jelly out of the refrigerator and called Charles for breakfast. He came to the table dressed in his underwear.

"Looks great," he said taking a seat at the table.
"Me or the breakfast?"
"Both."

"So what do you have planned for the day, Charles?"
"I should probably start contacting the other women."
"Can it wait until next week?"
"I guess. Why? Did you want to do something?"
"Kind of."
"What did you have in mind?"
"You saw the kayaks outside when you came in last night, didn't you?"

"Yes."

"Want to go kayaking?"

"Can't say I ever did that before. Is it hard?"

"Nah. It's real easy."

"Do I need anything special?"

"I have everything you'll need right here."

"Where would we go?"

"I have a place in mind. We might even get to see some seals."

"Seals?"

"Yeah. We can go to Stage Harbor. It's nearby and kayaking is real easy there."

"What about boats?"

"It's not very busy. And the boats all go slow in the harbor anyway."

"I guess I'm interested."

"Charles, you shower, get dressed and load the kayaks onto the rack on my car. I'll get things cleaned up. We should be ready to go in about an hour."

"Ok."

They ate their breakfast, reminiscing about the night before. Charles seemed at ease with Katherine's renewed interest in him. If Katherine was nervous about anything, it didn't show.

Charles showered and got dressed. Then he went outside, loaded the kayaks on her car, and tied them down. It had taken him about forty-five minutes to get everything done. When he came back into the house, he called out for Katherine.

"In here."

He walked into the study. She was seated at her computer typing something.

"Looks like a nice day," he declared.

"Supposed to be mid-60's," she said.

"Will it be cold kayaking?"

"Not really. You'll heat up once we start paddling. Mid-60's should be nice."

"Then we're all loaded up and ready to go."

"Just one more thing and I'm ready," she said continuing to type.

"Did you check your account for the transfer?"

"Yes I did. Thank you for making good on your word."

"I know I could've provided more information sooner but I wasn't sure how the investments would work out at first."

"That's all in the past Charles. Time to move forward."

"I like your thinking, Katherine."

"Then let's get going."

Katherine retrieved a couple bottles of water from the refrigerator and four energy bars. She put the bars in a zip-lock bag along with her cell phone. The water bottles were put into a soft cooler. She handed the cooler to Charles.

"What's this stuff for?"

"We'll get thirsty and probably hungry kayaking. Bring these things along for later."

"Why don't we just stop somewhere for a bite when we get hungry?"

"Charles, we'll be on the water. There's no place to stop where we are going."

"I thought you said it was a harbor?"

"It is. But there's nothing like that there."

"Ok."

"That should do it," she said pressing the enter key. She stood and walked out of her study with Charles following her. As they left the room, the computer continued to run. A few messages flashed across her screen indicating completion of the tasks Katherine had initiated. One said "Messages Sent."

A few others said, "Transfer Complete."

They arrived at Stage Harbor about a half hour later and Katherine stopped the car at the launch ramp.

"We'll unload here and then I'll park in that lot over there," she said pointing to a small parking lot across the street.

They took everything out of her vehicle including the soft cooler and zip-lock containing the energy bars. Katherine put the paddles together and put one in her kayak and the other in the kayak Charles would use. She handed Charles a life vest.

As he put it on, he said, "It says Adams on this life vest. Who does it belong to?"

"A friend of mine."

Then he realized the kayak had the same name written on the outside of it. "So I'm Adams for the day?"

"Yeah, I guess so. You know my boss, Harry Adams, don't you?"

"Yes."

"They belong to him."

"Do you two do this often?"

"I got into kayaking with Harry. He bought me a kayak."

"So, are you seeing Harry?"

"Charles, I don't ask you about your relationships, why are you prying into mine?"

"Just asking."

"Well, don't. You stay with the kayaks, I'll be right back."

She got into the car and parked it in the lot. She came back over and pushed her kayak into the water. She got in and instructed Charles to do the same. He did. Then, she gave him a few instructions about paddling. They were moving away from the launch.

The water was like glass. The only ripple they could see occurred when they approached a few geese that took off. They paddled around the east side of the harbor looking for seals but didn't see any.

"Who lives over there?" Charles said pointing to a few houses on the east side of the harbor.

"That's Morris Island road. It leads to Quitnesset. It's a little community of very expensive real estate."

"Oh, can you drive down there?"

"Only if you know how to get there. The streets are a little confusing when you get over by the lighthouse."

"Can we paddle by the lighthouse?"

"Maybe. If the ocean side is calm, we could try to paddle up there. Better yet, next time we come kayaking, we can launch out of Riders Cove. Then we'll see all of Pleasant Bay, including the lighthouse."

Charles thought to himself, "So there's going to be another kayaking trip." He smiled and continued paddling.

When they reached the mouth of the harbor, Katherine said, "Since it's so nice, maybe we should look outside the harbor for the seals."

"Do you think it's safe?"

"The water's calm even down there by Monomoy," Katherine said pointing south at the barren land strip extending south and just east of the harbor mouth.

"Dee said there should be a cut to our left. She said it leads to the other side of Monomoy and that there are large rooks of seals on the eastern shore. Follow me."

Before Charles could say anything, Katherine was paddling out of the harbor heading east towards Monomoy Island. Charles paddled faster and eventually caught up to her.

"What's this body of water we're in right now?"

"It's Nantucket Sound. On Sunday, I'm going with Harry kayaking around Monomoy."

"All the way around?"

"Yeah."

"It looks like a long way," he said looking at Monomoy Island.

"We can kayak about five miles per hour so it's really not that far."

"How long do you think it will take to make a trip like that?"

"It's about eight miles to the tip. I think we planned three hours to go down and back."

"I think that's a little more than I'm prepared to do."

"Not to worry Charles. We are only going through a cut just up in front of us. As soon as we see the seals on the other side, we can paddle back."

"Ok."

The two paddled for another fifteen minutes. Then Katherine said, "There to the right, around that bend looks like the cut Dee was talking about."

They paddled further. Sure enough, there was a cut in the sand winding eastward. The water was only a foot or so deep.

178

"I can see the bottom clearly," exclaimed Charles.

"Dee said it used to be deep enough to take a boat through but storms have filled it in."

"They used to take boats through here?"

"That's what she said."

They paddled further and eventually rounded a bend where they could hear waves breaking. Then they could see the ocean.

"We made it," said Katherine cheerily.

"That wasn't so bad," Charles commented.

"Look over there," said Katherine pointing to the south along the shoreline. They could see quite a few seals sunning themselves on the sandy beach. The waves in the Atlantic were very gradual, less than a foot in size. As they exited the cut, their kayaks barely rocked as they paddled along the shoreline.

"Let's check them out," declared Charles.

"I want to get a picture," said Katherine reaching inside her kayak for the zip-lock bag.

She took it out, turned the cell phone on and selected the camera option, then took a few pictures. Then she stowed the cell phone back in the zip-lock bag and put it back inside the kayak.

"I can't get over how many seals there are," said Charles.

"Me either. When Harry and I saw seals over by Stage Harbor, there were only a few. There have to be a thousand over there on the beach."

"What's that?" said Charles pointing a little further south and just off the beach.

"It looks like seals in the water," said Katherine. "Let's paddle over there and see them up close."

"Is it safe to get close to them?"

"I don't see why not. We're a lot bigger than they are," Katherine said confidently.

"I'll follow you," Charles said.

They kayaked south for about a half hour following the seals swimming. As each one came up for air, Charles would say, "Look there."

The two didn't pay much attention to the time or where they were going. They were just enjoying the day.

Chapter 25

After two hours, they could see the tip of Monomoy. Charles was getting a cramp in his left arm from paddling.

"Think we can stop and rest for a little while?" he asked.

"Sure. Let's paddle up to the beach and see if we can easily get out."

They headed towards the beach. As they approached the shoreline, they rode a small wave in until their kayaks made landfall. Katherine got out, pulling her kayak up onto the sand. Charles did the same.

"I'm whipped," was all Charles could say as he sat on the sand.

"We still have to paddle back."

"Can't we walk along the beach?"

"It's quite a way and would take us much longer. Plus, do you really want to have to carry these kayaks?"

"You're right. Let's just rest a little."

"Have some water and an energy bar. You'll feel better in a few minutes."

They both took off their life vests and stowed them inside their kayaks. Katherine took the soft cooler and zip-lock out of her kayak. She handed him a bottle of water and energy bar. Charles opened the water and drank half of the bottle.

"I'd go easy if I were you Charles. You'll get cramps if you drink too fast."

"I'm really thirsty."

He took another drink.

"Eat a little of the energy bar and then sip the water," Katherine said demonstrating herself how it should be done.

"You've done this before. I'm out of shape."

"Take your time, you'll be fine."

He took the energy bar and finished it off in three bites.

Katherine looked up the beach and saw something move.

"Look, it's a seal on the beach," she said pointing to the north at the seal. "I want to take a picture of it to send to Harry."

She got her cell phone out, again and turned it on. She selected the camera option.

"Charles, go stand next to the seal."

"I don't want it to attack me."

"Look at it. It can hardly move around out of the water."

"Just the same, take the picture without me in it."

"Ok."

She snapped the picture and then sent it to Harry. Then she turned the phone off and put it back into the kayak.

They sat on the beach for about twenty minutes. As they sat there, a slight breeze picked up coming from the north. It had a chill to it.

Charles was looking to the northeast and said, "Why does it look like the water and sky blend together out that way?"

He pointed to the northeast.

"I don't know."

"When we came out, I could easily see a few miles and the horizon was easily distinguishable. Plus, the sun was out."

"Maybe it's clouds or something."

"Do you think the weather is changing?"

"I'd say it is. I think we should get going."

They went to their kayaks putting them back into the water. In their haste, they didn't put their life vests back on. Katherine got into her kayak first and pushed off. What was once pretty calm water, now possessed waves now some having white caps. The breeze turned her kayak south before she could start paddling. A wave broadsided her kayak almost knocking it over. Charles followed and had difficulty getting into his kayak due to the waves and wind. They both began to paddle rapidly and turned back north. The two were side-by-side making their way away from the shoreline.

Charles realized they had forgotten to put the life vests back on and yelled to Katherine, "I forgot to put my life vest back on. Should we go back to shore and put them on?"

Katherine looked back towards the shore. Seeing the waves breaking on the beach and having seen the trouble Charles had getting restarted, said, "Too late now. Let's keep going."

There was more than just a little chop on the water and Charles noticed a few big rollers starting to form a little ways offshore.

"Look at those waves out there," he was pointing out about a half mile.

"Must be shallow water or something out there because it's still calm enough for us to paddle."

The water slapped the side of the kayaks a little but not enough to cause any alarm. When they had left Stage Harbor, they had quite good visibility looking out on the water and when looking south at Monomoy. Now heading back, they couldn't see very far out on the water and worse, they couldn't see half of Monomoy.

"Why can't we see Chatham?" asked Charles as they continued to paddle.

"I'm not sure. This never happened to me before."

"I think we need to paddle faster."

Katherine could hear the nervousness in his voice.

"Remember, it's a few miles back. We don't want to get so exhausted we can't make it back," she said as she slowly moved her paddles from side to side.

The fog was coming in their direction. At first, the air seemed to get damp very quickly. Then it got cold. It looked like smoke traveling at them at considerable speed.

"Looks like fog," said Katherine as she started to pick up speed paddling.

"You can feel it. It's getting colder."

"Just keep paddling at a steady pace," she said to him.

Within the next few minutes, the fog surrounded them. They were only ten or fifteen feet apart and could barely see each other. Monomoy isn't exactly a straight island and Katherine and Charles had been traveling in a straight line trying to minimize the amount of time it would take them to get back to Stage Harbor.

"I'm getting cramps," said Charles as he stopped paddling and pressed his hands against his stomach.

"I told you not to drink the water so fast."

"I know. Let's rest for a minute or so."

They stopped paddling and drifted for a minute or two. The breeze picked up a bit more slowly turning their kayaks to the east. The two didn't detect the change in direction.

"I hear the waves breaking on the shoreline," said Katherine pointing ahead.

"I hear them also. Maybe we should head back to the beach and wait it out," Charles said in a shaky voice.

"If we keep the sound of the waves on our left side, we should be able to keep moving north back to the harbor."

"Sounds right."

Charles sounded a bit calmer.

They continued to paddle keeping the sound of the waves to their left side. After about twenty minutes, he said, "I can't hear the waves anymore."

"Stop paddling and listen."

They both stopped paddling and drifted.

"They seem to be coming from over there," he pointed in front of them to the left.

"Yeah, I hear it."

"Let's keep going. Keep the beach on our left."

She continued to paddle. He did as well.

"I can't see a thing," exclaimed Charles.

"Me either."

"Katherine, I think it's time to call for help."

"How could anyone find us in this fog?"

"Use your cell phone. They can zero in on the signal."

"I've never heard of anyone doing that."

"The phone works under GPS. In fact, you might be able to get our location from your phone."

"You mean like when I use it for directions?"

"Yes."

"Ok, I'll try it."

Katherine took the zip-lock out. She opened it and removed the phone. She flipped the phone open and pressed the power button. The phone illuminated and after a few seconds was ready for use.

"I don't have any bars. I don't understand. I sent Harry the picture I took of the seal. I should still have a signal. We haven't traveled that far since I sent it."

"Leave it on for a few minutes and let's paddle to see if you can get a signal."

"Ok, but my battery's low."

"You didn't charge your phone?"

"There was too much going on last night. I must have forgot."

"Well, watch it and turn it off before the battery goes dead."

"I'll try."

They paddled for another ten minutes. She kept looking at the phone from time to time but it never picked up a signal. Finally, she stopped paddling and turned the phone off. She put it back into the zip-lock bag.

"What are you doing?"

Charles had paddled over to her kayak. He saw her put the zip-lock bag back inside her kayak.

"I can't get a signal and the battery is almost dead. We need to save it for a while. When we get a little further north, I'll try again."

"Ok. Let's continue paddling."

They continued at a moderate pace. Charles was sweating from so much paddling. Katherine was as well. They had left the beach over an hour ago. By Charles's estimate, they should now have been almost half way back to the harbor. They stayed a few feet apart while paddling but couldn't see more than a hundred feet or so in front of them. The fog was very thick.

They kept up the pace for another hour. Charles followed a little behind Katherine. She stopped paddling to rest for a few minutes. She took out a bottle of water and finished what was left in it. Then she ate the remaining half of the energy bar she had started when they were on the beach.

"Katherine, we should be pretty close, don't you think?"

"Look up Charles. I can see blue sky."

He looked up and through the fog he could see blue sky.

"I think it's starting to clear."

"Good. Then we should be able to get back before it gets dark."

"It's getting dark already. Yeah, I can see some blue sky but it's starting to darken."

They paddled a little more and eventually the fog lifted for a few minutes. It didn't rise far, but it was enough that they could see for a mile or so.

"I don't see any land," said Charles in a very concerned tone.

"Me either."

"I thought we were paddling along the shore?"

Just then, they could hear a wave breaking over a sandbar not too far in front of them and to their left.

"Could we have been chasing waves?" he asked in a condescending tone.

"Somehow we must have gotten turned around. I don't know how that happened."

"I thought you knew what you were doing, Katherine?"

"I can't control the fog, Charles. Let's think about this for a minute."

"What's to think about? We're lost."

"We're not lost, we're just a little further offshore than we had planned to be."

"I don't see any land, anywhere."

"If only I could get a signal on the phone."

"Try again," he implored her.

"Ok."

She took the cell phone out again and turned it on.

"No signal. Plus, it's almost dead."

"I don't have a good feeling about this," said Charles looking at her.

"What if something happens to us out here?"

"Well, you don't have to worry about any money problems. I took care of it before we left."

"What do you mean?"

"Do you remember the last time when you transferred my funds to my account?"

"Yeah."

"Well, I had one of those software programs running on my computer that traps keystrokes."

"Really?"

"Really. And after you left, I got the information from the software identifying your bank, account and password. Then I checked your account. I could see the account had quite a bit of money in it, but I remembered you telling me all the transactions hadn't settled yet so I waited for you to come back. When you transferred the gains last night, I checked

188

your account again. Everyone's money seemed to be in your account so I transferred everyone their money before we left this morning."

Charles became very angry.

"How could you? I told you everyone would get their money back plus a nice return."

"Yeah, but what about the money you made? You planned on keeping a few million for yourself."

"I earned it."

"That's not how I see it. And I think the rest of the women agree with me."

"I got you a fifty percent return."

"From what I could see, you made a lot more than fifty percent."

"That was my part of the deal."

"Charles, I don't think I or any of the other women would agree with you. Somehow you got us to sign that agreement. None of us thought you were continuing to represent us, let alone take us for the money you did."

"So you took it all?"

"All of it."

"You bitch."

"Call me what you want Charles but you had it coming. I used a software package I bought from Staples. You know, the kind of software that parents buy to keep tabs on what their children are doing on their computers. Isn't that the same kind of software you used to gain access to my funds when Sam died?"

He didn't say anything for a few minutes. He knew he had fallen into victim status.

"Well, I made money for everyone."

"And I took it all," she said laughing.

He tried to swing at her with his paddle but missed. His kayak turned over when he tried to hit her. He fell out into the water. She quickly paddled away from him. When she did, she dropped the phone into the bottom of the kayak. It didn't take long and she couldn't see him anymore as the fog had settled on the water again. She had disappeared into the fog.

"Katherine, where the hell are you?"

She could hear him yelling and swearing at her from behind her. She continued to paddle.

Chapter 26

It didn't take long and she could no longer hear Charles. She stopped paddling and listened. Nothing. She could only hear the sounds of the ocean. She decided to call out to him.

"Charles. Where are you?"

There was no response. She called out again and again. But he didn't answer. Now she was alone and it was getting dark. She took out the phone and turned it on. Nothing. She noticed it was a little after six pm. Even if she could get a signal, who could she call? Harry was in Boston. Maybe she could call Andrew Dunn. He had helped her in the past. Or maybe she could call Sundancers and see if someone from there could help. She didn't want to call 911 because there would be a lot of questions she would have to answer regarding Charles. It didn't matter. There was no signal. She put the phone back into the zip-lock and stowed inside the kayak.

She paddled for twenty minutes and then would rest for a few minutes. This continued for what seemed like hours. Nighttime came and the temperature dropped into the forties. She didn't get very cold as paddling kept her warm. Every now and then, a wave would rock her kayak and one almost turned it over. She used the paddle to compensate for the wave action and became pretty good at keeping the kayak stable. The fog finally lifted and she thought she could see lights off in the distance. She didn't know if the lights were from a boat or from land but she decided to paddle in the direction of the lights.

The paddling continued for hours. It didn't seem like she was making any progress. She wondered if her mind was playing games with her or if the object was moving. She rationalized that if it were a boat, it could be headed anywhere, maybe even out to sea. She decided to break off the pursuit. Being in a kayak, she didn't have much of a vantage point from which to decide on a direction. Eventually, she came across a high-flyer marker used by lobstermen to mark the beginning or end of a string of lobster pots. She reasoned that a string of lobster pots meant someone put them there. If they were still in sight in the morning, she might hang around to see if someone came to tend the pots.

She stopped paddling and took out her cell phone. When she turned it on, it had one bar of signal strength. She had Sundancers on speed dial one and she pressed it. To her amazement, Dee answered on the second ring.

"Dee, it's Katherine. I'm in trouble."
Katherine could hear a loud band playing in the background.
"Is that you Katherine? I can't hear you very well. The band is playing and it's real loud in here."

"Listen Dee, I went kayaking today with," the phone crackled and Katherine thought she had lost the connection.

"I didn't hear you Katherine. I thought you said you were kayaking?"

"I did. We went out of Stage Harbor earlier today." Then the phone seemed to go dead. Katherine looked at it and the phone had dropped the call. No signal.

Ron Jessup had been working with Dee at Sundancers when Dee hung up the phone.

"Who was that?" he asked.

"Katherine. She said she was kayaking and something about trouble. I couldn't get the whole story."

"What did she want?"

"I didn't get that far. We'll have to wait for her to call back."

Ron looked at the full bar around them, "I hope she doesn't need anything from us. We're real busy."

"We'll have to wait for her to call back to find out."

They went back to bartending, not thinking anymore about the call.

Katherine didn't call back. The bar was so busy, Dee completely forgot about the call until later on that night.

Antonio had finished cleaning up the kitchen and was seated at the end of the bar by the kitchen having a drink with his girlfriend, Dana. Dee made herself a drink and came around to the outside of the bar letting Ron wait on the two guys who were still at the bar. She sat next to Antonio and took a sip of her drink.

"Ron, did Katherine ever call back?"

"I don't think so."

"I wonder what was up with her?"

Antonio looked at Dee, "When did she call?"

"Earlier, around nine," Dee answered.

"Was Harry with her?"

"I don't know. She said something about kayaking and having some kind of trouble. Maybe it was car trouble or something."

"I saw her and Harry loading their kayaks onto Harry's Jeep yesterday. They were talking about going kayaking this weekend but I thought they were going on Sunday," Antonio said to Dee.

"Yeah, Harry and Katherine were talking about it in here the other day and I told them about the seals by Stage Harbor. I think she said something about Stage Harbor when she called earlier."

"Try to call Harry on his cell and see if they are having some kind of car trouble or something," Dee said to Antonio.

"Ok."

Antonio took out his cell phone and called Harry. It went right through to voice mail. Antonio closed his phone.

"I got his voice mail," Antonio said.

"Anyone have Katherine's cell number?" Ron asked.

"Since she called earlier, Ron, it should be on caller id."

Ron picked up the bar phone. He tabbed through caller-id until he found Katherine's cell number. He pressed talk. It went to voice mail as well.

"I got her voice mail," was his response.

"Maybe they solved whatever problem they were having," said Antonio.

"Or maybe they didn't," said Dee. "Do you think someone should go and look for them?"

"Where would we start?" asked Antonio.

"I thought she said something about Stage Harbor when I talked with her earlier and if they went kayaking, then I'm pretty sure they were going to Stage Harbor. So, their car should be parked by the ramp on Bridge Street."

"Dana, we're not doing anything. You want to take a ride down to Stage Harbor?"

"Can we stop at the Inn and have a drink?"

"They'll probably be closed at this time of the night. But, if they're open we'll stop."

"Ok. Then let's go."

"Dee, will you be here for another half hour or so?"

"Sure. We have some cleanup to do."

"I'll call you if we find them."

"Ok."

Antonio and Dana finished their drinks and left. They got into his car traveling east on Route 28. In twenty minutes, they arrived in Chatham. At the rotary, Antonio made the first right towards Stage Harbor. They were at the boat ramp in a few minutes.

"I don't see anyone," Dana said to Antonio.

"Me either."

Antonio stopped the car on the ramp pointed towards the water. He opened the door and got out. He looked around but no one was there. Then he looked back across the street to the small parking lot and saw Katherine's car. "There's Katherine's car over there in the parking lot."

"Is anyone in it?"

"I don't see them. Let me walk over and take a closer look."

Antonio walked over to her car. No one was there. Neither were the kayaks or any of the equipment. He walked back to his car.

"That's strange."

"What?"

"There's no one there, not even the kayaks."

"Maybe they left them somewhere or had someone pick them up and they took them with them."

"Maybe."

"Anyhow, there's no one here. I'm going to call Dee and let her know what we found."

He opened his cell phone and called Sundancers. Dee answered.

"Dee, it's Antonio. I found Katherine's car down here at Stage Harbor. There's no one here. They must have had car trouble and someone picked them up. Their kayaks aren't here either."

"Ok Antonio. I'll try to call her at home."

"I'll see you tomorrow. Me and Dana are going to stop somewhere and get a drink."

"Ok. See you tomorrow."

Antonio and Dana went into town looking for someplace open. Everything was closed so they headed back west on Route 28. When they got to Harwich, Jake Rooney's was still open so they stopped in there for a drink.

Dee finished up her night. She and Ron cleaned everything up and closed Sundancers for the night. As they were locking the door behind them, she said, "I'll try to call Katherine when I get home."

"Ok. Call me if they need any help."

"I will."

"Night."

"See ya."

They both got into their vehicles and went home.

Between the time Dee left the bar and before she got home, Katherine had tried to use her cell phone again. When she tried to call Dee back at Sundancers, the call went through to voice mail. Katherine knew that meant the bar was closed. She called Dee's house but got the voice mail there as well.

"Dee, it's Katherine. We're lost kayaking in the Atlantic. It's dark, cold and foggy. Get us help."

When Dee got to her house, she put her things away, got her mail. Sorted through the mail and then turned on her TV. She was about to doze when she noticed her phone blinking. She picked it up and called in for messages. She got the panic message from Katherine.

"Ron, it's Dee."
"What's up?"
"I had a message on my phone from Katherine when I got home."
"What did she say?"
"She said they are still kayaking and lost on the ocean in a fog."
"What?"
"I don't believe it. Where did she say they were?"
"The call cut out before she could say anything more. What should we do?"
"Call the police."
"You think so?"
"I do. Look Dee, if you don't want to call them, I will."
"No, Ted will be home shortly so I will call them when he gets here."
"Do you think you should wait?"
"I called him from my cell when I was on my way home. He's meeting me here soon."

"Keep me in the loop Dee. I can come over if you want?"

"No, that's ok. Ted will help if I need it."

"Ok."

"I'll call you Ron."

They hung up. Ten minutes later, Ted came in. Dee told him the whole story as she understood it. They both listened to the voice mail.

"Ron thinks we should call the police."

"Katherine, I think he's right. Want me to call?"

"No, I'll do it. You just be here if the police come over."

"I live here. Where else would I be going?"

"You know what I mean. I need some support."

"You're really bothered by this aren't you?"

"I am. It's not just Katherine I'm worried about, but Harry was with her."

"Ok, Ok. I'm here for you."

She picked up the phone and pressed 911.

Chapter 27

Saturday afternoon, Carol Tindle went to her bank to get some cash. She put her debit card into the ATM machine taking $400.00. She requested a receipt and when she looked at it, she was surprised.

"Wow. She actually did it."

The receipt showed her checking account had a balance of $3,302,176.12. She knew she only had a little over two thousand in her checking account. Katherine had delivered. She took out her cell phone and called Theresa Lee.

"Theresa, I just checked my checking account. Katherine did it. I got back all the money Charles had plus a nice return."
"You're kidding?"
"No. Check your account."
"Can you hold on a minute? I'll go check my account right now on my computer."
"I'll hold on."

Carol could hear Theresa walking, and then typing.
"Holy cow."
Then "WooHoo."

She was looking at her computer screen. It showed the current balance in her account of just under ten million dollars She looked at the activity list. It showed a transfer of $9,348,250.

Theresa came back on the phone, "My account has a large deposit in it today as well. You're right. She did come through and the gains Charles was able to achieve were excellent. I can't believe she made this happen."

"Or Charles returned the money himself," said Carol in an excited voice.
"Who cares? I'm going to move the money to a safer place right away. I don't want to take any chances on losing it again."
"That's a good idea. I'm going to do the same," added Carol.
"I wonder if the other women got their funds back?" Theresa asked.

"Theresa, you call Sharon Kelly and Ann Pierce. I'll call Sarah Jacobs and Katherine. Let's all get together at that place Katherine works, Sundancers, to celebrate tomorrow around two."
"That's a great idea Carol."
"Call me if you can't reach either Sharon or Ann."
"Ok. Otherwise, we'll see you at Sundancers tomorrow at two."
"See you then."

Theresa called Sharon Kelly.

"Sharon, this is Theresa Lee. I'm not sure you remember me, but we met at Katherine's last week."

"Sure I do. You were taken by Charles Chamberlin just like the rest of us."

"That's right. Listen, I just got off the phone with Carol Tindle. Both her and I got a deposit this morning returning our funds Charles had invested. While I know you didn't invest with him, he did take money from you. Katherine had said she was going to get everyone's money back. Check your account today and see if you got your funds back."

"Can you hold on? I can check it right now."

"Please do."

Sharon put Theresa on hold. She made a call to her bank asking for the balance in her account. The teller taking the call had her answer two security questions and then provided the balance. It was $2,359,600.78. She thanked the teller, pressed flash, then returned to talking to Theresa.

"I just called my bank. They confirmed a sizeable transfer into my account this morning. It looks like I got back all the money I was missing plus a fifty percent return. I guess Katherine did come through."

"She sure did. Carol's calling both Katherine and Sarah Jacobs. We're going to try to get together where Katherine works at Sundancers in West Dennis tomorrow around two to celebrate. Care to join us?"

"I'd love to. Where's Sundancers located?"

"On Route 28 just after the Bass River Bridge on the east side. If you're traveling east, it will be on your left. They have a big sign out front. They're located in a building on the river behind a retail business on Route 28."

"I think I can find it. I'll see you tomorrow at 2 pm."

"See you then."

Next, Theresa called Ann Pierce.

"Ann, it's Theresa Lee."

"Hi Theresa, how are you?"

"Just great."

"I meant to tell you, you looked great when I saw you at Katherine's."

"Oh, thank you. I've been trying to keep in shape since my husband died."

"I know what you mean. If I'm ever to get another man, I'll have to keep my figure."

"Well, Katherine came through for us. You should check your account today. We all received deposits into our accounts we provided to Katherine. She got all our money back including a nice gain."

"Really?"

"Yes. Do you have a home computer?"

"I do."

"Then go check. I'll wait."

"Ok."

Ann Pierce went to her computer and logged into her banking account. She had a balance of $3,994,231.45. Theresa could hear her shouting with joy in the background. Then Ann came back on the phone. She was excited.

"I got my funds today as well. I can't believe it."

"Katherine said she was going to make it happen."

"And she did."

"Listen Ann, we're all getting together tomorrow at Sundancers at 2 pm for a little celebration. Care to join us?"

"I still can't believe it and yes, I'll be there."

"Ok, we'll see you then. Bye."

"Alright. See you tomorrow."

Ann hung up the phone. She jumped for joy. She was having a good day.

When Carol Tindle had hung up, she called Sarah Jacobs.

"Sarah, it's Carol Tindle. How are you doing today?"

"I've had better days."

"Your day's about to get better."

"Why? What's going on?"

"Well, we got our money back today."

"Who got their money back?"

"All of us. Katherine was able to get our funds back for us just like she said she would."

"You're kidding?"

"No. I just talked to Theresa Lee and she got her funds back as well."

"I don't know if she got my funds back or not. I'll have to check my account."

"Check it now, if you can."

"Ok."

Sarah used her laptop to access her bank account. When she logged in, it showed a balance of $376,885.29. She looked at the transaction register. It showed a deposit into her account that morning of $375,922.33. Then she went back to the phone.

"Looks like she was able to get my funds back as well. And it looks like there was another fifty percent added."

"She said Charles told her we were getting a nice return."

"I can't believe it."

"Believe it. Sarah, we're all getting together at Sundancers tomorrow at 2 pm to have a little celebration. Can you make it?"

"Absolutely. I want to personally thank Katherine for making this happen."

"We all do. I'm going to call her after I hang up."

"Ok. I'll see you there tomorrow at 2."

The last thing Carol had to do was talk with Katherine. She called Katherine's house but only got her voice mail.

"Katherine, it's Carol. I got the funds you promised. So did the other women. We'd all like to get together at Sundancers at two on Sunday to celebrate. We hope you can make it. See you there."

She hung up the phone and smiled.

Chapter 28

Katherine had been paddling throughout the night. She would hear waves breaking from time to time and thought she was near a shoreline. Each time, she would alter her course to follow the breaking wave sounds only to find another shoal. She had not seen nor heard from Charles in hours. She had no idea if he could survive in the cold water or not.

She would stop to rest from paddling from time to time and this would give her time to think. She started talking to herself.

"I hope all the money transfers went through."
"Everyone's going to be happy, except Charles."
"Maybe he won't make it."
"That would solve a lot of problems."
"What if he does make it? Would he go to the police?"
"Nah, he won't. He's already had enough troubles with them."
"Maybe he didn't have all his money in the account he used when he sent me my funds?"

"He's pretty smart. I'll bet he has other accounts."
"He'll be fine."

She started paddling again. As she looked up, she could see stars in the sky. There was no moon, but the heavens were lit up with little white dots. A wave hit the side of her kayak listing it nearly sideways. She corrected with her paddle in time and righted the kayak.

"That was close."
She wasn't in a rip or it didn't seem like one. The seas were starting to get much rougher.
"If I align the kayak to go with the waves, I should be all right."
When the next wave came, she turned the kayak slightly and surfed the wave a little. As she did, she thought she might be able to travel easier working with the waves as opposed to against them. The only trouble was, she had no idea where the waves would take her, or whether the tide was coming in, or going out.

For the next hour, she paddled little. She rode the waves as best she could. A few times, she had to use the paddles to keep the kayak straight. At one point, the waves got a little rougher and then seemed to calm down. As she looked back, she realized she had gone over another shoal. She took the time in the calm water to rest.

She reached for the water bottle. As she tipped it up, she drank the last few drops that were left in it. Looking to the sky, she saw blinking lights moving from her left to right. She wondered where the plane was going.

"Are you going west or east?" She said out loud.
"If it's east, I'm going the other way. If its west and I follow, I should hit land eventually."

This would be a tough decision. She knew many planes traveled overnight to Europe, regularly in sight of Cape Cod. She had seen them before from the beach or when she would sit on her deck having a drink. She longed to be back home instead of kayaking at night on the Atlantic Ocean.

The waves were working from left to right. She reasoned that the plane she saw was an overnighter coming from Europe going somewhere in the States. She decided to keep riding the waves. She was pretty sure she was headed west.

Chapter 29

Dee made the call to the police station. Her call was immediately answered.

"911 please state your emergency."

"Yes, my name is Darlene Crowe. I work at Sundancers in West Dennis. I'd like to report a missing person."

"Let me get some info, like name, and known circumstances. My name is Officer Percy."

"Officer Percy, one of the women who works with me, Katherine Sterns, called during the night. She said she was in trouble."

"What kind of trouble?"

"I think she was kayaking and was lost."

"What time did she call?"

"It must have been between nine and ten."

"It's after midnight now Ms. Crowe. Did you hear from her again?"

"No. And that's what's bothering me."

"Is it possible Ms. Sterns found her way back and just didn't contact you?"

"I guess, but one of our other employees, chef Antonio, went down to Stage Harbor to see if Katherine was having car trouble. Her car was there but she wasn't."

"So someone else might have picked her up?"

"That could be but she didn't answer her cell phone nor her home phone."

"Was she kayaking with anyone?"

"Yes. Harry Adams. He owns Sundancers."

"Might she be at Mr. Adams house?"

"I tried there also. No one answered."

"Ms. Crowe. We'll contact Chatham Police and have the car checked out. If you still can't get ahold of Ms. Sterns in the morning, call the station back."

"Ok Officer Percy. If you find either of them, have them call me."

"Ok."

Dee hung up the phone. She walked into the living room to speak with Ted.

"They're going to have Chatham Police check out Katherine's car and see if they can find her."

"You did the right thing Dee. Let's get some sleep. You can try to find them in the morning."

"I'm too wound up to sleep right now Ted. You go ahead in. I'll be in shortly."

"Ok. Goodnight."

Ted gave her a kiss. He went to the bedroom to sleep. She sat up for another half hour. She tried Harry's place again. Still, there was no answer. She tried Katherine's again and got the same.

Officer Percy got up and went into his Sergeant's office.

"Sarge, we had a call from a Darlene Crowe at Sundancers. She said one of their employees is missing."

"What does she know?"

"She said Katherine Sterns, that's the person missing, called her and told her she was kayaking and lost in a fog."

"Who would be kayaking at night? Is she crazy?"

"I don't know. But she said another employee of theirs went down to Stage Harbor where the Sterns woman had gone kayaking from and found her car. But she wasn't there."

"Did you ask if she was there with anyone else?"

"Yes."

"And?"

"Ms. Crowe said the Sterns woman was kayaking with their boss, Harry Adams."

"And did she try contacting Mr. Adams?"

"She said she did but got no answer."

"Sounds like the boss might be doing something with one of his employees. I'll bet he took her home to shack up with her and turned his phone off."

"Maybe. What do you want me to do?"

"Call Chatham Police and have them verify that the Sterns woman's car is where Ms. Crowe said it is. If it is, have someone go by her house. If it looks like someone's there, have the patrol officer knock and find out. If no one's at her house, have someone check out Mr. Adams place. After that, we'll have to involve the Coast Guard."

"Ok. I'll get right on it."

Officer Percy went back to the main desk. He called one of the patrol officers who had been sitting at the corner of

Route 28 and Route 134 observing the little traffic there was at that time of the night.

"Sloan, come in."

"Sloan here. What can I do for you Percy?"

"Sarge wants you to take a ride to a few places and see if anyone is home. We had a report of a missing person. He thinks the woman either went home with her boss or took the boss to her house for the night. Anyway, no one's answering the phones at either place so he wants you to check it out."

"Ok. Give me the addresses."

Officer Percy provided Patrolman Sloan with Katherine and Harry's addresses. Sloan wrote them down. Then he put the cruiser in gear heading to Katherine's house first.

Sloan pulled into Katherine's driveway. He parked behind a Toyota Camry already parked in the driveway. He got out and went up to the door. He rang the doorbell. No one answered. He rang it again. Again, there was no answer. He went back to his cruiser.

Next, he went to the address Percy had given him for Harry's house. When he pulled in the driveway, there were no cars there. The house was completely dark. He got out and went up to the door anyway. When no one answered the knock for the second time, he got back into his cruiser and called Percy.

"Percy, it's Sloan. I checked out the Sterns woman's place and Mr. Adams place. There was no one home at either place. There was a car in the driveway at Ms. Sterns house, a Toyota Camry."

"Did you get the plate number?"

"Sure."

He gave Percy the plate number.

"I'll give Sarge the plate and tell him what you found."

"Ok. I'm going back on patrol. Sloan out."

Officer Percy walked into Sergeant Edgar's office.

"Sarge, Sloan checked out the Sterns and Adams places. No one was home. There was a car parked in the Sterns driveway. Here's the plate number."

Percy handed a piece of paper to Sergeant Edgars. Edgars turned to his computer, clicked a few keys and then looked at the screen.

"The car's a rental car belonging to Avis. Says here it's based out of Logan."

"Do you think the Sterns woman had recently rented a car up at Logan for some reason?"

"Who knows? But if they haven't been found by this time tomorrow, contact Avis and see if you can find out who rented the car. And Percy, did you call Chatham police yet?"

"I'll do it right now."

"Let me know if anything comes up."

"Ok Sarge. And, I'll leave a note on the desk for the day shift."

"Thanks Percy."

Sergeant Edgars went back to what he was doing. Percy went back to the main duty desk.

Chapter 30

Officer Percy called Chatham Police in the wee hours of the morning.

"This is Sergeant Olsen. How can I help you?"

"Sergeant, this is Officer Percy at Dennis PD. We had a call a little while ago from a Ms. Darlene Crowe reporting a friend, Katherine Sterns, missing. She says her friend went kayaking with her boss, Harry Adams, out at Stage Harbor. She said another friend went to Stage Harbor and found Ms. Sterns car there but no Ms. Sterns. Can you have someone check it out?"

"Sure. That area down by Stage Harbor is kind of isolated. There isn't much down there. If her friend's car broke down, they might have had to walk a few miles to get help."

"She said both Ms. Sterns and Mr. Adams have cell phones so one of them should have been able to call for help."

"They might have cell phones but that area sits pretty low. There might not be a signal down there."

"I hadn't thought of that possibility."

"I'll have it checked out anyway and call you back."

"Thanks Sergeant."

Sergeant Olsen called one of his patrol cars and asked to have a look around Stage Harbor. Twenty minutes later, he got a response.

"Sergeant Olsen, this is Officer Morley. I'm down here at Stage Harbor. There's a car parked in the lot across the street from the boat launch but there's no one here."

"Does the car have a kayak rack on the roof?"

"Yes."

"That's the one. Give me the plate number."

Officer Morley read the plate number. Sergeant Olsen typed it into his computer and confirmed the car belonged to Katherine Sterns.

"Morley, do you see any kayaking equipment anywhere around there?"

"No."

"Maybe whoever picked them up picked up the equipment as well," said Sergeant Olsen.

"Maybe."

"Go ahead and continue your patrol Morley. Keep and eye out for kayak stuff or two adults walking. I'll follow-up on this from here."

"Got it Sergeant."

When Sergeant Olsen got off the police radio, he picked up the telephone and called the Coast Guard station in Chatham. Olsen explained the situation to the Coast Guard station chief indicating that they might need help from the Coast Guard in the morning. The station chief said there wasn't much they could do until sunrise especially given the heavy fog he could see outside the station window.

Sergeant Olsen called the Dennis Police Station. Officer Percy answered.

"Percy, it's Sergeant Olsen from Chatham PD. I had one of our patrolmen check out the Stage Harbor area. He found a car where you said it was. So I guess your caller has reason to be concerned."

"I'll pass that info along to Sergeant Edgars. He's on duty here tonight."

"And another thing Percy. I called the Coast Guard. They said there isn't anything they can do until tomorrow. They don't like to start a search at night unless they have exact coordinates and there's a dense fog out on the water tonight."

"Did the Coast Guard say they would start first thing in the morning?"

"Yes. But they can only send out boats. Their helicopter isn't much good in the fog. They said when the fog lifts, they'll send out a helicopter."

"Ok. I'll pass that information along as well."

"Percy, did anyone go to the homes of the people who are supposedly missing yet?"

"Yes. I had a patrol car go to both places and no one was at either place."

"Looks like you might have two missing people."

"Looks that way."

"I'll call your station if we get any more information."

"Thanks Sergeant Olsen.

Officer Percy went back into see Sergeant Edgars.

"Sarge, I talked with a Sergeant Olsen at Chatham PD. They verified the Sterns woman's car is parked down at Stage Harbor."

"Did their patrolman see anything out of the ordinary?"

"Other than a car being there all night, he said everything seemed to be ok."

"What else did Olsen say?"

"He said he contacted the Coast Guard. They told him they couldn't do anything until daylight. There's a dense fog on the water tonight so the Coast Guard isn't going to begin a search until tomorrow."

"Don't they have a helicopter?"

"Yes. But the Coast Guard told Sergeant Olsen it couldn't go up until the fog lifts. They'll start a search using boats in the morning."

"Too bad. It would go a lot faster if they could use the helicopter."

"Sergeant Olsen said the Coast Guard told him they would use the helicopter as soon as the fog lifts."

"Ok. Make a note for the day shift. Let me know if anything else develops."

Sergeant Edgars went back to working on the same report he had started working on three hours before. He said, "I'll never get this report done with all the interruptions."

Percy went back to the duty desk. He wrote up a report and put it in the in-basket for the day shift.

Chapter 31

The night seemed to go on forever for Katherine. She paddled a few minutes, and then would coast for a few minutes. Her arms felt like putty. She was exhausted.

Sometime during the night, she had finished off the last bottle of water and wanted to drink seawater. Something in the back of her mind told her not to, so she didn't.

At just before 5 am, the sky to the east started to show signs of light. She had endured a difficult night alone on the Atlantic Ocean in a kayak.

At first, she couldn't see anything other than swells that seemed to be eight to ten feet in height. Her kayak would rise up and down. At the bottom of a swell, all she could see was water all around her. At the top of a swell, she would look all around trying to get a fix on something other than water.

After an hour, the sun peeked above the waterline. It looked like the water itself was on fire. She had a difficult time looking directly to the east and when she turned away, her vision became blurred due to looking into the brightness.

As her kayak rose up one more time, she thought she could see something when looking away from the sun. Then the kayak went down again into another trough. As it rose again, she looked in the same direction as before and thought she could finally see land.

She began to paddle in the direction of the sighting. Every time the kayak reached the top of a swell, she looked up. After about twenty times, she was sure she could see land. What troubled her was that the land seemed to be to her northwest.

As she kept paddling, the landmass came more into focus. She thought it looked like an island but then rationalized that if she had been traveling north along the national seashore of Cape Cod, there are no islands once you get past the tip of Cape Cod. She was stumped.

Having been to Chatham before, she knew there was a lighthouse at Chatham harbor and other lighthouses along the coast at Nauset and Truro.

She also remembered a smokestack tower in Provincetown had been pointed out to her by Ed Phillips one afternoon when she and Ed had gone to Chapin beach. None of these landmarks were visible. The island looked isolated. She couldn't see any lights, streets or houses. Maybe she was just too far away to see such details.

She kept paddling now that she was sure land was within reach. After another hour, she looked at the landmass ahead of her again realizing it was now positioned more north of her. The currents were taking her past the island to the southwest. She swore to herself and tried to paddle faster. She didn't realize her efforts were weak at best. Fatigue had taken all her strength from her. Her efforts were mostly in her mind, as her body wasn't responding.

She stopped paddling. She reached down inside her kayak and pulled out the zip-lock bag containing her cell phone. She turned it on. When the phone lit up, it had two bar signal strength. She thought her luck had finally changed. Then she thought of who she might be able to call. She remembered she was supposed to go kayaking with Harry that morning so she called his home phone. The phone rang twice and then switched over to voice mail. She started to cry.

In a shaky voice, she said, "Harry, its Katherine. I went kayaking with Charles Chamberlin yesterday out of Stage Harbor. We saw seals on the Atlantic side and tried to get close to them. We didn't pay attention to the weather and ended up getting trapped in fog. Charles fell in the water when a wave knocked your kayak over. I lost track of him in the fog. I don't know where he is and I don't know where I am. I can see land near me but I can't seem to get there. I need help."

She wanted to say more but her phone went dead. She looked at it. The battery had no more life to it. She closed the phone and put it in the zip-lock bag. Then she put the zip-lock into her pants pocket.

When she looked up, her kayak had been turned all the way south. The sun was to her left. She used her paddles to turn back around pointing the kayak at the landmass far off in the distance. She began to paddle again.

Her mind seemed to settle into a blank state. She seemed to be hallucinating. She willed her arms to paddle more. The kayak moved forward at a crawl. Another two hours went by. When she looked to the left, she could see the landmass that had been ever elusive on the horizon. The current was now taking her north. As she continued along, the seas became choppy. What were once large swells spaced out fifty or sixty feet apart now consisted of smaller whitecap waves a foot or two high but right on top of one another.

She tried to change her kayak direction to head west toward the landmass but the waves almost knocked her kayak over. She feared falling into the ocean so she righted her course back to the north. The sun seemed to be nearly overhead telling her it must be near mid-day on Sunday. She spoke out loud, "Harry, where are you?"

As her kayak continued along, she finally saw a red marker buoy in the water to her left. A short time later, she saw another one, then a black one and then a green one. When she looked further up to her left, she could see land again. She had no idea where she was. She willed herself to paddle in the direction of the land.

A wave broadsided her kayak tipping it over. She lost her grip on her kayak paddle and ended falling out of the kayak. The water felt very cold. It must have been sixty degrees maybe less. At first, she held on to the kayak but another wave hit it and almost pulled her arm out of the socket. She let the kayak go. She found herself treading water in the middle of a rip south of Monomoy. At one point, her feet touched the sand under the water.

She tried to stand but the next wave knocked her over. She was being washed over a sandbar. Every time she tried to stand, another wave knocked her down. This happened a few times and then she couldn't feel the sand under her feet anymore. She had been washed clear of the sandbar.

Katherine tried to swim. Her arm strength had been so consumed from the kayaking she had nothing left. She tried to float on her back but the waves kept breaking over her causing her to ingest seawater. She became mad at herself for not putting the life jacket on when she and Charles had gotten back into their kayaks.

Being in the water, she couldn't see the landmass anymore. The waves turned her around and she became disoriented. At some point, the exhaustion got the best of her and she passed out.

Chapter 32

On Sunday morning, the Dream Catcher II had been fishing for cod southeast of Nantucket. They had just pulled their net for the last time on this trip. Like the other pulls, this one was full of nice size cod. The boat hold was overflowing with fish having completed a successful four-day fishing trip. Captain John Adams, no relation to the historical John Adams nor Harry, got on the boat intercom.

"Let's head home guys. We're full.
The crew was all smiles. They would have a nice payday.
Captain Adams yelled down to crewman George Fox.
"Fox, put the fish wherever you can find a place. Then stow the gear. We can be in port in a few hours."
"Got it Captain."

Captain Adams turned his attention to the return trip. He brought up the menu on the GPS and selected Chatham as his next destination. Then he engaged the autopilot. The boat slowly turned heading northeast back to Chatham.

Over the next two hours, the crew worked to pack the fish in ice and stow the gear. By early afternoon, they were done with the cleanup. Dream Catcher II had a crew of four on this trip. The crew went to the galley to make some lunch. Fox made a sandwich and cup of soup for the Captain, and then took it to the bridge.

"Got you some lunch, Captain."

"Thanks Fox."

"We've got a nice haul. Had to leave some of the fish in the transfer bins."

"Hope you put ice on them."

"That's done. They should hold until we reach port."

"Good job, Fox. Watch the helm while I visit the head."

"Got it."

Captain Adams went to the bathroom, and was gone for about ten minutes. When he came back, Fox said, "What's that over there, Captain?"

"Where?"

"Over there," Fox was pointing at something bright green bobbing in the water.

The Captain disengaged the autopilot. He put his hands on the throttle pulling the lever back. The boat engines cut back to an idle.

"Go forward Fox and see if you can hook it."

"Will do."

Fox went forward grabbing a long pole with a hook on the end. He reached over the side of the boat snagging the hook on the kayak. A minute later, he pulled the kayak on board. When he looked inside, he found a life vest and pulled it out. He left the kayak on the deck but took the life vest to the bridge.

"I found this inside the kayak," Fox said to Captain Adams holding the life vest up.

"Anything else?"

"Nope. Look here, there's a name on the life jacket," he turned the life jacked so they could both read the back. "Adams. Just like your name, Captain. Weird, huh?"

"Think it drifted away from some weekender on Cape Cod?"

"Could be. Think we should report it?" Fox said as he set the life vest down on the console.

"Probably. You call it in. I'll get us back on course."

Fox picked up the mike and selected a channel on the marine radio.

"Coast Guard Station, this is Dream Catcher II."

A crackle could be heard over the speaker and then, "Go ahead Dream Catcher, this is Coast Guard Station at Chatham."

"We are returning from a fishing trip and are a few miles southeast of Nantucket. We came across a kayak adrift in the ocean."

"Were you able to retrieve it?"

"Yes. We have it on board."

"Are there any identifiable markings on the kayak?"

"Yes. It has a name Adams inscribed on the hull and we found a life vest inside the kayak with the same name written on it."

"You say the I.D. is Adams?"

"Yes."

"We have had a report of two missing people kayaking out of Stage Harbor yesterday. Please keep an eye out for another kayaker."

"Will do."

"I'll have someone pick up the kayak and life vest from you when you dock. Please contact me again when you enter the harbor."

"Understood. Dream Catcher II over and out."

Commander Collins of the Chatham Coast Guard Station was notified of the call from Dream Catcher II. She called the Chatham Police. After reporting the finding, she was given the name of Detective Simpson at Dennis PD. She called Simpson.

"Detective Simpson, this is Commander Collins at Chatham Coast Guard Station. We just took a call from a fishing boat that found a kayak adrift in the Atlantic. They're bringing the kayak to the dock in Chatham. Could you send someone down who might take a look at the kayak and determine if it is one of the two you're looking for?"

"Sure Commander. What's the name of the boat?"

"Dream Catcher II. It should be in port in about an hour or so."

"I'll have someone there to meet them."

"Thanks Detective."

When Detective Simpson hung up, he called Sundancers. Dee answered the phone.

"Sundancers."

"This is Officer Simpson of Dennis P.D. Is Darlene Crowe available?"

"This is Darlene Crowe. How can I help you?"

"A boat has picked up a kayak off Nantucket and is bringing it to port. Can we get someone to go to Chatham Harbor to ID the kayak?"

"Did they find them?"

"Only one kayak has been found."

"And the people?"

"Not yet. As I said, a kayak has been found and we'd like to see if it belonged to your friends."

"Ok Detective. We'll have someone go there. What's the name of the boat and when should we be there?"

"The boat is Dream Catcher II and it is due in a little over an hour from now."

"Thanks Detective."

"Someone from the department will be there as well."

"Got it."

Dee hung up the phone. Ron and Antonio were both standing at her side waiting to get any information they could.

"That was Dennis PD. A fishing boat has found a kayak in the Atlantic and is bringing it back to Chatham with them."

"Did they say which one it is?" Antonio asked.

"No. The police want someone to go there and see if the kayak can be identified."

"That should be easy," said Antonio. "Their names are written on the outside of the kayaks."

"I should have asked them that," said Dee.

"I'll go down and see if it belonged to Harry or Katherine," said Antonio taking his apron off and putting it on the bar.

"Call us as soon as you know," said Ron.

"I will."

"I don't have a good feeling about this," said Dee in a shaky voice.

"Don't assume, Dee. We don't know anything yet," said Ron putting his arm around her shoulder.

"We know they're missing," said Dee as she went back to work.

Antonio took the next half hour to instruct his assistant in handling the kitchen while he went to Chatham. Forty-five minutes later, he was on his way to the dock. When he arrived at Chatham Harbor, he parked next to the Dennis Police cruiser. He got out and approached the officer who was standing on the dock.

"Officer, I'm Antonio Davies. I'm the chef at Sundancers. I'm here to ID the kayak being brought in on the fishing boat."

"Officer Trent," he extended his hand to Antonio.

"Look Officer Trent, it should be easy to identify the kayaks. They have my friends names written on the outside of them."

"That's good to know. Here comes the Dream Catcher now," Officer Trent pointed to a boat just coming around the bend into the harbor.

Dream Catcher II pulled up to the main dock by the fish house. They tied the boat up. Officer Trent walked over to the boat and spoke with the Captain.

"Officer Trent from Dennis PD."

"Captain Adams."

"So you found the kayak a few miles southeast of Nantucket?"

"Yeah. We were returning from a fishing trip and spotted the kayak."

"See anything else?"

"No."

"Ok. Mr. Davies, please take a look. Is this your friend's kayak?"

Antonio looked at the kayak as crewman Fox leaned it against the rail.

"That's one of them. See the name written on the back side."

They all looked at the name, Adams.

"That one belongs to my boss, Harry Adams. The other one has the name Sterns on it. It belongs to Katherine Sterns. She works at Sundancers, too."

"Sterns. Isn't that the same name as one of those two guys we saw on the ice a year or two ago?" asked crewman Fox.

"Yeah. Sterns. What was the other guys name?" Captain Adams asked.

Antonio said, "You mean Tom Bowman?"

"Yeah. That's the name," said Fox. "Hey, didn't the Sterns guy die?"

"He did," replied Antonio.

"Wow. What are the odds of one of the people kayaking being related to one of the guys we found on the ice floe?" asked Captain Adams.

"Related? She was his wife," exclaimed Antonio.

"No kidding?" said Fox.

"Where's that life vest, Fox?" Captain Adams asked.

"It's on the bridge," Fox said to Captain Adams.

Captain Adams went inside the cabin and emerged with the life vest. He turned it so they could all see the name.

"That's his as well," said Antonio.

"Do you know if he wore this regularly when he kayaked?" Trent asked Antonio.

"He couldn't swim very well so he always wore it," said Antonio in a confident voice.

"Well, it looks like he didn't and should have," said Trent.

"Ok. Captain, can you have your man put that stuff by my cruiser. I'll take it from here."

"Will do."

Captain Adams supervised getting the stuff off the boat. He shook hands with Officer Trent and said a few things to him when they were done. Then the boat crew went to work on unloading their catch.

"Mr. Davies. I'm going to have this stuff taken back to the police station. After I get this stuff back to the station, Detective Simpson will probably come by to talk with some of the people at Sundancers if you don't mind?"

"Please, anything we can do to help. I'll be at Sundancers. Your department can call there anytime from 8 am until 2 am. They'll know how to get a hold of me if I'm not there."

"Thanks," said Officer Trent.

They shook hands and went their separate ways.

Antonio took out his cell phone. He called Sundancers.

Ron answered the phone.

"Ron, it's Antonio. I'm down here at Chatham. I just finished talking with the police. The kayak's Harry's."

"Oh no," was all Ron could say.

"I'm on my way back. I'll be there in a half hour and then I'll tell you the details."

"Thanks Antonio."

He hung up. As Ron turned, he had a blank look on his face.

Dee said, "What is it, Ron?"

"Antonio will be here in a half hour. He says he'll fill us in when he gets here."

"Is it bad news?"

"All he said is the kayak belonged to Harry."

Chapter 33

Antonio got back to Sundancers about a half hour after talking with Ron on the phone. When he came in, everyone at the bar quieted down. Antonio went behind the bar. He asked Dee for a drink. She got him a shot and beer. He downed the shot and half the beer. Then, he turned to face everyone.

"Here's what we've got," Antonio started saying.

"A boat picked up Harry's kayak somewhere out in the Atlantic southeast of Nantucket. His life vest was found inside the kayak so it doesn't look like he had one on. The Captain and crew of the Dream Catcher II didn't find a body. They called the Coast Guard and were instructed to bring the equipment to the dock in Chatham. I met Officer Trent of Dennis PD at the dock. We both examined the kayak and vest when the Dream Catcher came into port. I identified the stuff as belonging to Harry. Trent said Detective Simpson would be coming by in a little while to talk with some of you to see what you might know. That's about it."

Kenny Brown had listened intently to all Antonio had said. "Didn't they find Katherine's kayak?"

"You know all I know Kenny," said Antonio.

"Did the Captain say what the water conditions were when they found the kayak?" Ed Phillips asked.

"He said there was a good chop on the water and fog overnight."

"Anything else?" Tina Fletcher asked.

"A crewman, named Fox, said he didn't think anyone could survive in the water for long out there. The water temperature was around sixty degrees."

Tommy Anderson asked, "How long could Harry survive in 60 degree water?"

"Not long," replied Antonio. "Detective Simpson said hypothermia would set in within an hour at that temperature."

Dee started to cry. "Poor Harry."

Sue Kent and Linda Sage also began to cry.

"Hold on everyone, we don't know any more than what I've told you. Let's wait and see what develops," Antonio implored.

"I can't believe Kat and Harry are both missing," said Ann Benard hysterically.

"Calm down Ann. I'm sure they'll be found safe," added Ed Phillips.

"How would you know Ed?" commented Kenny.

"Hey everyone. Let's calm down," said Antonio. "Dee and Ron, get everyone a drink on the house."

Ron and Dee did as instructed. Things settled down a little over the next few minutes.

The door opened and Detective Simpson walked in. Everyone turned to look at him. Antonio got up and walked over to the detective.

Extending his hand, Antonio said, "I talked with everyone when I got back Detective. Everyone's a little shaken up. Is there any more news?"

"Not yet."

"Well, how can we help you?"

"I'd like to speak with each of you individually to ask a few questions that might help us locate your friends."

"Ok. Who would you like to start with?" Antonio asked.

Everyone was quiet now.

"Who took the call when Katherine called last night?"

"I did," Dee raised her hand.

"Can we speak for a few minutes?"

"Sure."

Dee came out from behind the bar and led Detective Simpson to a table in the dining room.

"What can you tell me about the call you got last night?"

"It must have been around nine or ten. The band was playing. The music was loud and we were crowded. When I answered the phone, I could hardly hear Katherine."

"Are you sure it was her?"

"Yes. I know her voice plus she said something about kayaking."

"What did she say?"

"Something about being lost and in a fog, I think."

"Did she say where they were?"

"No, but I know they went out of Stage Harbor. I had talked with her and Harry about going out of Stage Harbor a few days ago to see the seals. I'm sure they were going there. Plus, Antonio went down to the boat launch at Stage Harbor and saw her car there."

"Yes, its there. Why didn't you report it last night?"

"We thought they had car trouble. It wasn't until later on when we couldn't get in touch with either Harry or Katherine that we became concerned."

"So you're sure they didn't get picked up by someone else?"

"I've asked everyone I know. No one has seen either of them since Friday."

"Ok. Thanks for the information."

"Say Detective, can't you trace the phone call Katherine made from her cell phone to determine where she was when she made it?"

"Its not that easy. We can trace the call through the nearest cell tower the call went through but that's about it."

"Wouldn't information like that at least put you in the area she is in?"

"It might. We have someone following up on her cell number already. Antonio provided me with Katherine and Harry's cell numbers when we were in Chatham."

"Let us know if you find anything out, will you?"

"I'll try to keep you informed."

"Thank you."

Dee went back to the bar and told Antonio Detective Simpson wanted to speak with him next. Antonio walked back to the table where Detective Simpson was seated.

"She seems pretty sure it was your boss who was kayaking with Ms. Sterns."

"I saw the two of the loading the kayaks on his car on Friday. Then he put the life vests and paddles in the trunk. I think he was dropping them off at Katherine's house on Friday."

"Why didn't they just take his car?" Detective Simpson asked.

"Who knows? Harry has a thing about leaving his expensive car in a remote lot. He probably talked Katherine into using her car so his wouldn't be a target for someone."

"What do you make of the boat finding the kayak so far out to sea?"

"I'm not that familiar with the area they were kayaking in Detective, but I would think the currents might have played a role in the location."

"That and the fog," said Detective Simpson.

"Yeah. Dee said Katherine mentioned something about a fog on the phone during the short call last night. I can't imagine being on the Atlantic in a fog, and at night."

"I may need you to assist me again Antonio."

"Her kayak is pink. It has Sterns written on it just like Harry's green one had his name written."

"I was thinking of help with something other than a kayak," said Detective Simpson looking Antonio in the face with a very serious expression on his.

"You mean like a body?"

"It's a possibility."

"Oh shit."

"Can you send anyone else back who might have something to add to the situation?" Detective Simpson asked Antonio.

"Sure."

Antonio walked back to the bar. He addressed the group.

"Anyone think you might have anything to tell the Detective that might help to find Harry or Katherine?"

No one said a thing.

Detective Simpson was standing at the end of the bar. He stepped forward and said, "If any of you think of anything else, please call the station."

He walked up to Antonio and said, "I'll call when I need you."

"Ok."

Then Detective Simpson left.

After he walked out the door, Dee asked Antonio, "What did he mean, when he needs you?"

"I think he expects to find a body or two and wants me to come identify them."

"Oh no."

"They haven't found one. He's just thinking ahead."

"I don't like it at all," said Dee.

"Let's keep working, Dee. It should take our mind off all this."

"Ron, how can you work? We're talking about Harry."

"And Katherine," said Kenny.

Dee and Ron went back to work. They didn't say much more for the rest of the afternoon. Every time the phone rang, Dee jumped and the bar would go quiet. None of the calls were about Harry or Katherine.

Chapter 34

Captain Trudy had a phone conversation with Detective Simpson while Simpson was returning from Chatham.

"What did you find Detective?"

"A fishing boat, the Dream Catcher II, picked up a kayak a few miles off Nantucket. It had the name Adams written on the outside. I had one of the employees from Sundancers come down and identify the equipment. He confirmed it belonging to Harry Adams, the owner of Sundancers."

"Anything on the other person?"

"Not yet. The Coast Guard is conducting a search by boat right now in the Stage Harbor area. As soon as their chopper is ready to go, they plan on conducting an aerial search of the region."

"If the fishing boat found one kayak out in the Atlantic, why search around Stage Harbor?"

"From what I gather, there's access to the Atlantic from the Stage Harbor area. The Coast Guard likes to start with as much as they know. And right now, they know the people kayaking started out at Stage Harbor."

"Do they expect to expand the search out into the Atlantic?"

"Yes. The Station Commander said the search team would lay out the conditions since the missing people went on the water looking at wind, currents, tides and potential progress for two people in a kayak."

"That's quite a few variables to have to consider."

"That's what the Commander said also. But when they charted out the location of where the fishing boat found the kayak, it was within the area the Coast Guard had identified. The Adams kayak seemed to be following the north to south current along the east side of Monomoy and then affected by the gulf stream. Hopefully, the other person followed a similar pattern."

"Is there anything you'd like us to do from the station at this time?"

"Yes. If you could have someone contact the phone company, I'd like to see if we can get a fix on the cell phone call made by Ms. Sterns to Sundancers last night between nine and ten?"

"I'll have Officer Ryan make a few calls and see what we can find out."

"Thanks Captain. In the meanwhile, I'm going over to Sundancers to talk with some of the people there again. I have a few more questions. Maybe we've been overlooking something."

"Ok. Keep me informed."

"Will do."

Captain Trudy walked out of her office down the hall to the operations room. A small office off the operations room belonged to Officer Ryan. He was the resident technical geek of the force.

"Ryan, Simpson's working a case and needs your assistance."

"Sure Captain. What does he want me to do?"

"Contact the phone company and see if they can trace a call from this cell phone number to this number last night sometime between nine and ten."

She handed him a piece of paper with two phone numbers written on it.

"No problem. It should only take an hour or two."

Tony Ryan had done this kind of search numerous times for the department. He had all the right contacts at the phone company. He made a call. He provided his contact and friend Kelly Lane with the information and hung up. Twenty minutes later, his contact from the phone company called back.

"Tony, it's Kelly. I've got the information you requested."

"Great."

"The call was made at nine-eighteen last night from the cell phone to Sundancers."

"Were you able to trace the transmission of the call?"

"Yeah. It went through a cell tower on Nantucket."

"Any other places?"

"No. So I'd say your caller's either on Nantucket or within 15 miles of the relay tower. That's about the maximum range for a relay tower like the one on Nantucket."

"Do you happen to know the exact location of the tower the call came through?"

"Yeah, its on the eastern side of the island. If you're going there, I can provide the exact GPS coordinates if you like."

"This is probably enough for now. I appreciate your help."

"Another thing Tony, There was another call a few hours later from the same cell to another number. It came through the same tower."

"Do you have the number of the other call?"

"Sure do."

She gave him the other number.

"Thanks Kelly. I'll call back if I need the exact tower location."

"You're welcome. I hope this information's what you were looking for."

"It is and thanks again."

Officer Ryan went to dispatch. He spoke to the dispatcher.

"Do you know where Detective Simpson is?"

"Yes. He reported in a few minutes ago and said he's just left Sundancers. He's on his way to the station."

"Can I have his cell number?"

"Sure." The dispatcher handed Ryan a sticky note with Simpson's cell number written on it.

Ryan went back to his office and called.

"Detective, it's Tony Ryan."

"Hey Ryan, what's up?"

"Captain asked me to trace a call for you. I have some info."

"Go ahead."

"The call from Ms. Sterns cell phone took place last night nine-eighteen. It came through a relay tower on Nantucket's east side. My contact says the caller had to be within fifteen miles of the tower for it to pick it up. Hope the info helps you. I can get you the exact coordinates of the tower if you need them."

"Thanks Ryan. I think knowing the tower's on Nantucket will be enough for right now. I'll pass the info along to the Coast Guard. This should help narrow their search."

"Listen, when I had the call traced, the phone company said another call was made from the same cell number a few hours later. I looked up the second number. It was to a Harry Adams's residence phone."

"Are you sure?"

"That's what my contact told me."

"I wonder why a call would be placed to Mr. Adams home if he was out kayaking with Ms. Sterns?"

"Beats me," was all Ryan could say."

"Thanks Tony."

"Let me know if I can help with anything else."

"Will do."

Detective Simpson hung up. He called the Coast Guard station.

"This is Detective Simpson of Dennis PD, can I speak with Commander Collins?"

"Sure Detective. Please hold."

"Detective Simpson, this is Commander Collins."

"Commander, I have some information that might help narrow the search criteria."

"What do you have?"

"We were able to trace a call one of the missing persons made last night. The call was made within fifteen miles of Nantucket. It came from Ms. Sterns cell phone."

"Could the call have been made from the island?"

"It could have, but since we found one kayak, I am assuming the other one was out on the water as well."

"Another thing. There was another call from Ms. Sterns cell phone overnight. This one took place early Sunday morning."

"Did it go through the same tower?"

"Yes. My guess is that the caller is somewhere near or on Nantucket Island."

"Ok. We'll look at the conditions again and take the information you provided into consideration."

"Thanks Commander. Let me know if you find anything."

"Will do."

Commander Collins took the information she had to the operations room. There, a technician used the information to plot out the possible area to be searched. It included the eastern end of Nantucket Sound, Monomoy Island, Nantucket Island and quite a bit of the open Atlantic Ocean.

The search team had started by boat at Stage Harbor. It took most of the morning to check the Mill Pond, the Oyster Pond River and Oyster Pond itself. The theory being utilized by the Coast Guard was that most incidents on the water occur within a few miles of the point of embarkation.

Around noon, the team had worked its way back to the mouth of the harbor. Their next area to search would be outside of the Stage Harbor area. Out of the harbor, they first searched south along the western side of Monomoy Island. This search included some of the northeastern end of Nantucket Sound. Then, the search boat returned to the mouth of Stage Harbor and went east looking along the inside of the National Seashore of North Monomoy.

At one point, the search team came across a cut, which went all the way through to the Atlantic. They didn't pursue it right away as their search still included a large amount of shoreline between Stage Harbor and the north inside of Monomoy.

A little after noon, the Coast Guard operations center contacted the search team informing them of a change in the search grid based on the information Detective Simpson had obtained. They turned their boat around and headed back into Nantucket Sound. They would begin their new search on the eastern end of Nantucket Sound further south than had been previously searched.

For the next two hours, they methodically went back and forth traversing Nantucket Sound, including Handkerchief Shoal, looking for any signs of a pink kayak. When the search pattern had been completed, a member of the search team called operations informing operations of their progress. Nothing had been found on the eastern end of Nantucket Sound.

The boat search team was instructed to begin a search of the Nantucket Island shoreline next. They were informed that a Coast Guard chopper was joining the search and would focus on Monomoy Island.

Chapter 35

Back at Sundancers, everyone was worried. Antonio was so nervous, he burned most of what he was cooking for patrons because he spent more time by the door waiting for the next phone call than he did attending to cooking. At one point, a burger on the grill caught fire sending quite a bit of smoke into the kitchen. He had to open the back door and all the windows to vent the smoke. Some of the smoke made its way into the bar area. When Antonio came out of the kitchen, Dee said, "What's going on Antonio?"

"I can't cook. I'm too nervous worrying about Harry and Katherine."

"They'll be ok. You'll see."

"Before, you were a basket case. Now, how can you be so positive, Dee? They found Harry's kayak out in the Atlantic. They found his life vest as well. He must have fallen in."

"I just know they will be found."

"Oh, I don't know. Things have a way of disappearing in the ocean."

"Calm down Antonio. Put your focus on running the kitchen and you'll feel better," said Ron trying to calm things."

"Ok Ron. I know I'm probably making more out of this that I need to. But someone might have to go with Detective Simpson to identify the body if one's found."

"Cross that bridge if and when the call comes Antonio. Now here, have a drink and see if you can focus on our customers."

Antonio downed the shot and beer. He turned and went back to work. After a half hour, Dee said, "Looks like he took your advice." She motioned with her head at two waitresses coming from the kitchen carrying dinners for customers seated in the restaurant section.

"Well, at least he stopped burning things," Ron replied.

Ed Phillps, who was an avid fisherman and boater, was seated in the middle of the bar. He along with everyone else had heard everything going on at Sundancers. Dee was serving him another beer. Ed took the opportunity to add his two cents on the situation.

"You know Dee, I've been out fishing in the area they found Harry's kayak many times."

"How do you know where they found it?" was her response rather sarcastically.

"I heard Antonio say they found it a few miles southeast of Monomoy, off Nantucket. I fish there a lot in the spring and fall for striped bass. There are a number of shoals and rips down there that are very productive."

"And what's your point?"

"Just that the waters there can be tricky. There's a pretty strong tidal flow along the southern end of Monomoy and out by Nantucket. If Harry and Katherine were kayaking out there, they could be anywhere by now."

"So you think you know more than the Coast Guard, Ed?"

"No, I'm just saying it might take quite a long time for the Coast Guard to search the area."

"And why are you telling me this?"

"Just that it might take a while, that's all I'm saying."

"Look Ed, I don't think your comments would help the situation any. Why don't you keep your thoughts to yourself?"

"Hey, I'm just trying to help."

"Well, don't."

Dee walked away to wait on Tommy Anderson at the other end of the bar. When she did, Ron came over to Ed.

"Ed, don't let her comments get to you. Everyone's stressed out over Harry missing."

"I know Ron. I was just trying to help. She shouldn't get her hopes up. This whole thing may not turn out with a happy ending."

"Finding Harry's kayak definitely was not a good thing. Maybe he was picked up by a fishing boat or something."

"Yeah, maybe," said Ed taking a sip of his beer.

"Like you said Ed, the area they found the kayak in is a good fishing area. I'd bet someone was out there fishing when they went kayaking."

"I hope," was all Ed added.

Ron turned and went to the end of the bar. Tina Fletcher was signaling him for another drink.

Tommy Anderson ordered a burger, fries and beer from Dee, and then he said, "Dee, Ed doesn't mean anything. You should go easier on him."

"I know. I'm just getting a little stressed."

"If you want someone to talk to, I'm here."

"Tommy, you talk?"

"Yeah, Dee. I can talk."

"I thought you were the strong and silent type," and she looked down at his crotch.

"Well, that's how I do my best work."

"Oh Tommy, what will we do with you?"

Sue Kent had been seated next to Tommy. She reached over and rubbed his thigh, "Want to talk to me Tommy?"

"Sure Sue. What do you have in mind?"

Dee turned away, "Oh Please."

She walked to the register to make an entry into Tommy's tab for his dinner and drink. Tommy and Sue had turned their attentions to each other, forgetting about Harry or anyone else for that matter.

Tina Fletcher ordered another round of drinks for her, Ann Benard and Linda Sage. When Dee brought their martinis over to their high table in the corner of the bar area, Paul Bremmer followed her.

"Here are your drinks, ladies," Dee said.

"Mine's the one with the onions," said Ann.

Dee placed the drinks in front of the appropriate woman.

"Hey ladies," said Paul as Dee walked away.

"Hi Paul," said Linda.

"Everyone got plans for the night?" he asked.

"Paulie, you're getting a little forward, aren't you?" asked Tina.

"Just trying to take my mind off things," Paul said.

"I don't have any plans for the night yet, Paulie," was a response from Linda. "What'cha got in mind?"

"Can I buy you a drink?"

"Sure, I'll come see you when I've finished this one."

Paul smiled and turned away. He went back to the bar where he had been seated. He ordered another beer and waited for Linda to come over. About twenty minutes later, she did.

"Gonna buy me that drink Paulie?"

"Sure."

He asked Ron to get Linda another martini.

As Paul touched his beer to her glass, she said, "After we finish these drinks, why don't we go to my place, Paulie?"

She put her hand down below the bar and in his direction. He smiled and said, "I'm ready when you are."

She looked up at him and said, "So you are."

They finished their drinks quickly, got up and left.

Ron seeing the two leave said, "Doesn't seem like those two are too worried?"

Dee added, "It has nothing to do with worry. When a cougar strikes, the prey have no options."

"Ha, Ha," was all Ron could muster.

At around two pm, a group of women came into Sundancers taking up a high table next to the bar. Dee walked over to take their order.

"Can I get you ladies menus?" she asked.

"I don't think so," said Sharon Kelly. "We're here to have a few drinks to celebrate."

"Ok, what will it be?" asked Dee of each of the women.

"Can I have a margarita?" asked Ann Pierce.

"Me too," said Sarah Jacobs.

"I'll have a dirty martini," said Sharon Kelly.

"Do you have Guinness?" asked Carol Tindle.

"Yes, draft or bottle," asked Dee.

"Bottle," replied Carol.

"I'll have a Chardonnay," said Theresa Lee.

"What are you ladies celebrating anyway?" asked Dee.

"We each just came into a nice sum of money," said Theresa Lee. "Is Katherine Sterns working today?"

Dee stopped writing in her pad. It fell to her side. She had a blank expression on her face. She looked up at the group and said, "Haven't you heard?"

"Heard what?" asked Sharon Kelly.

"Katherine and our boss Harry went kayaking yesterday and didn't return. Harry's kayak was found out in the Atlantic Ocean miles from shore. He wasn't in it."

"What about Katherine?"

"She tried to call here last night. I talked to her for a minute or so before the call dropped. She said she was in trouble, kayaking in the fog."

"Oh, my God," Carol Tindle said in a hushed voice.

"Don't tell us something had happened to her?" said Ann Pierce.

"We don't know anything more at this time. The authorities are looking for them."

"So you're saying Katherine and your boss Harry have been missing since yesterday morning?"

"Yes."

The ladies all looked at each other.

Then Carol said, "We got an e-mail from Katherine yesterday morning. That was when she said we should all check our accounts."

"And our funds all showed up yesterday. What's this all about?" asked Sarah.

Dee looked at Carol and said, "Katherine sent you an e-mail yesterday morning?"

"Yes."

"Do you know what time she sent it to you?"

"It was early in the day. I'm sure it was before noon," Carol said.

"I got my e-mail from her in the morning as well," added Ann.

"Why are you asking?" said Sharon to Dee.

"You're all saying you got e-mails from Katherine yesterday morning and that she told each of you to check your accounts?"

They all shook their heads in a yes motion.

"What could she have been up to?" Dee said out loud.

"We were all involved with a financial consultant named Charles Chamberlin some time ago when our husbands passed away. Mr. Chamberlin did some investing for us and we each got our investment funds back yesterday," said Theresa Lee.

"Except me," Sharon Kelly said. "I was involved with Mr. Chamberlin as a result of an automobile accident. Somehow he stole money from me, but thanks to Katherine, I got my money back yesterday."

"I know who Charles Chamberlin is," replied Dee. "I've seen him in here with some of the other patrons from time to time."

She looked over at the other high table where the Cougars were sitting. "I wonder what Katherine was up to," was all she said as she turned to go back to the bar to get their drinks.

Dee asked Ron to help her make the drinks. As they did, Dee conveyed the conversation she had with the women to Ron.

"Do you think there's something more going on here than Harry and Katherine kayaking?" Ron asked.

"I don't know. But something sure sounds fishy," was all Dee added.

She took the drinks back to the table for the ladies and then returned to the bar as the phone was ringing. When she picked up the receiver, everyone in the bar stopped talking.

"Sundancers, how can I help you?" Dee asked answering the call.

"I'm sorry, Harry isn't here right now. Can I take a message for him?"

There was a minute of silence, and then Dee hung up the phone. Ron walked over to her.

"Harry's buddy, Don, from Boston. He said to tell Harry he left a few things there and that he'd set them aside for him."

"When was Harry in Boston?"

"He didn't say."

Dee went back to waiting on patrons at the bar. Everyone started talking again. The noise level went back to normal.

Chapter 36

By mid-afternoon, the Coast Guard had searched all of Stage Harbor, eastern Nantucket Sound and the northern end of Monomoy Island by boat. A Coast Guard helicopter had joined the search. It was assigned the task of covering Monomoy Island from north to south in case the two missing persons had somehow made it to land. Captain John Wagner was the pilot of the chopper joined by co-pilot Captain Mark Hess and seaman Tom Martin attending to winch and observation duties.

As the chopper lifted off from the Coast Guard Station in Chatham after having met with Commander Collins, Captain Hess spoke on the intercom.

"Martin, be on the lookout for two people on the island. They might be injured or walking to the north trying to get off Monomoy Island."

"Got it Captain Hess. You want me to look out on the water as well?"

Captain Wagner came on the intercom, "We'll watch the water Martin. I'd like to make one pass on the west and

251

another back north on the east. We'll need a set of eyes on those dunes to make sure they aren't behind one of them."

"Ok Captain."

Co-pilot Hess said, "What do you think John, could they have survived in kayaks in that chop?"

He was looking at the waters to the east of the island as Wagner swung the chopper to the west side of the island.

"I don't see how. There's a pretty good chop out there. Let's make this run a few hundred feet off the west shore. Keep your eyes open for a pink kayak or two people."

Hess said, "A pink kayak huh?"

"That's what Commander Collins said. A boat picked one of the kayaks, a green one, up earlier today. Supposedly the other one is a pink one. We're looking for a man and a woman."

"Since we were delayed in joining the search due to fog conditions Captain, what are the chances they made it to land?"

"Mark, your guess is as good as mine. A lot depends on how far out they were and what skills they possessed."

"Where was the first kayak found?" Hess asked.

"Collins said it was a little southeast of Monomoy."

"Think we should look down that way?"

"First we have to look up and down Monomoy. Then, we'll see."

"Got it."

Wagner turned the chopper south along the western side of Monomoy. They moved along at a good pace but not so fast that Martin couldn't examine each and every dune and valley. As they approached three-quarters of a way down the island, Martin came on the intercom.

"Captain Wagner, what's that chimney over there to the east in the middle of the island?"

Wagner looked out his window to the left. "It looks like an old homestead."

There was a chimney but no building.

Martin said, "I don't see anyone in the area."

Wagner said, "Keep looking."

The chopper continued south. As it neared the tip of the island, Hess said, "That was a clean sweep Captain."

"Ok, let's do the other side."

Wagner turned the chopper around. They started north along the east side of Monomoy. They rounded the first big curve. Martin could see the same chimney he had seen from the other side. As he looked ahead, he said, "Look, there on the beach."

Wagner said, "I see it."

Hess said, "Looks like we found the pink kayak."

"See any people Martin?" asked Captain Wagner.

"Not yet."

Hess asked, "Should we land and check it out?"

Captain Wagner called the Coast Guard Station. Commander Collins came on the radio.

"Commander, I think we've found the other kayak. We're about three-quarters of the way down Monomoy on the east side. We're looking at a pink kayak on the beach. What would you like me to do?" Wagner asked.

"Captain, can you land near the kayak?" asked Commander Collins.

"Sure."

"Be careful not to disturb anything around the kayak in case we need it for evidence."

"Ok Commander. I'll call you back after we have touched down and checked the kayak out."

"Ok."

Wagner said, "Hess, land over there away from the kayak. Then Martin and I will check out the kayak."

"Got it," Hess said.

He guided the helicopter past the kayak to a flat spot on the beach. Gently, the chopper set down about twenty feet from the rolling surf. Wagner and Martin got out.

"Be careful where you walk Martin. The Coast Guard said this might be a crime scene."

"Got it Captain."

The two walked over to the kayak. Wagner leaned in and looked forward in the kayak. Then he leaned the seat back forward, looking to the back of the kayak. He could see a life vest inside and an empty water bottle on the floor. There was nothing else.

"There's nothing here Captain," said Martin.

"There's a life vest and empty water bottle. That's it."

"And look Captain, no footprints in the sand. How could this kayak have gotten this far up on the beach if someone didn't drag it here? The high-tide water line is way back there."

The two looked back to a clear line of seaweed running all along the beach about fifteen feet behind the kayak.

"I see what you mean Martin. This is strange."

Captain Wagner walked back to the chopper. He put his helmet back on and called the Coast Guard Station.

"Captain Collins, we checked out the kayak. We found a life vest inside it and an empty water bottle but that's it. The kayak has the name Sterns written on the outside. Looks like it was written with a magic marker."

"Captain Wagner, pull the life vest out and see if it has the name Sterns written on it as well."

"Will do."

Captain Wagner walked back over to the kayak and picked up the life vest. He carried it back to the chopper with him.

"Commander Collins, the vest has the name Sterns written on it as well."

"Thanks Captain. Can you bring the equipment back with you?"

"Sure. Commander, there's something else."

"What is it Captain?"

"Well, Martin noticed there are no tracks in the sand anywhere near the kayak. The kayak itself is about fifteen feet above the high-water line on the beach. If it came ashore in the last day or so, someone must have put it there but we see no signs of any human activity anywhere near the kayak."

"Captain, could a rogue wave deposited the kayak up that far on the beach?"

"I guess, but the kayak looks to be perfectly positioned like someone dragged it there. Plus, there's the high-water line from the tide."

Commander Collins could be heard speaking with someone at the Coast Guard Station.

"Wagner, there was a high tide earlier today. Maybe the tide washed away all the tracks?"

"I guess. Well, we'll bring the stuff back to the Coast Guard Station Commander."

"Thank you Captain. I'll meet you when you land."

"Wagner over and out."

Captain Wagner walked back to Martin.
"Get one of those orange weighted marker cones out of the chopper and leave it where we found the kayak. Than, let's take the kayak back to the station."
"Yes Sir."

Martin got the cone and put it on the sand at the top of the kayak. He grabbed one end of the kayak and Captain Wagner the other. They put the kayak in the back of the chopper. Martin secured it with a tie-down. Captain Wagner got back into the pilots seat.

"We going back to the station, Captain?" asked Hess.
"Yes. On the way, let's keep checking the island in case they made it to land and are walking back."
"Got it."
"Martin, keep looking," was all Captain Wagner said over the intercom as they lifted off.

They continued the search back along the eastern side of Monomoy. Along the way, they saw two colonies of seals on the beach but that was about it.
As they approached the Chatham Coast Guard Station, Captain Wagner said, "Hess, you stay with the chopper. I'll help Martin offload the kayak and meet with Commander Collins. We should be back underway in about fifteen minutes."
"Ok Captain."

Captain Wagner and Martin unloaded the kayak. Wagner grabbed the life vest and walked over to Commander Collins.
"This is all we found."
"Any other signs?"

"No. That's really puzzling us."

"I'll send someone down there if we need to have the area checked out again."

"Ok. We left an orange marker cone where we found the kayak. On the way back, I had my crewman looking at all the dunes and valleys along the way but he didn't spot anything."

"Ok. Then I doubt anyone's down there."

"Yeah, I don't think so. We could see pretty much the whole island as a result of the two passes."

"Say Captain, could it have been possible for a person to hide from you when you went down the west side and then hide from you again when you came back up the east side?"

"I guess it's possible but we didn't see any tracks at all."

"Ok. Thanks for your help bringing this stuff back."

"Commander, we're going to resume our aerial search a little further out east of Monomoy. Maybe we'll find something out there."

"Ok Captain. Call the station if you find anything."

"Will do."

Captain Wagner and Martin returned to the chopper. It lifted off a few minutes later starting another search pattern, this time about a half mile off shore.

Commander Collins called Detective Simpson at Dennis PD.

"Detective, we were able to have a helicopter join the search today after the fog lifted. They found a pink kayak on Monomoy Island with the name Sterns written on the outside. Plus, a life vest was found with the same name on it. Could you have someone come down and pick the stuff up?

"Sure Commander. I'll be there in a half hour."

Detective Simpson called Sundancers. When the phone rang, Dee picked it up. Everyone in the bar stopped talking.

"Yes, Detective, Antonio's here."

Dee called out to Antonio. "Antonio, Detective Simpson wants to speak with you."

Antonio came out of the kitchen, his face white, and took the phone from Dee.

"I can be there in about twenty five minutes. I'll see you there."

Antonio hung up the phone.

"Detective Simpson says they found the other kayak. He wants me to meet him at the Coast Guard station to positively identify it."

Tina Fletcher asked, "Anything else?"

"He didn't say. I'll be back."

Antonio left in his car.

Chapter 37

As Antonio pulled out of the parking lot, everyone started to speculate at the bar. Ron kept trying to settle everyone down by talking to each person quietly. There was so much speculation going on that Dee finally yelled at the top of her voice, "Enough already. This kind of talk isn't helping anybody."

The ladies who had come in for a celebration drink sat quietly away from the bar watching the commotion. Sharon Kelly was the first one to speak.

"Well ladies, it doesn't look good for Katherine now does it?"

"I hope nothing bad happened to her," said Carol Tindle. "Katherine delivered everything she had promised. I want to stay so I can personally thank her for getting my money back."

"We all do," said Ann Pierce.

"Why don't we all get another drink," said Theresa Lee.

"Sounds good to me," replied Sarah Jacobs.

Theresa motioned to Dee to come over to their table. When Dee did, Theresa said, "Can we have another round?"

"Sure. Everyone want the same thing?"

They all said yes.

Ann Pierce added, "Can we get some appetizers as well. I don't want to keep drinking on an empty stomach."

"Sure, what would you like?"

Theresa said, "How about some nachos, some chicken tenders and stuffed mushrooms?"

"Sure," Dee said as she picked up the empty glasses on the table and went back to the bar.

She entered their order into the computer and then made them a round of drinks. She brought them to the table. Setting the drinks down, Dee said, "I'm sorry your celebration didn't go as planned. But we still haven't found Harry or Katherine."

"We heard," said Theresa taking her drink.

Carol Tindle added, "We want to stay for a while longer to see if Katherine comes in. We're really thankful to her for all she did for us."

"So she helped each of you out with your situations?" Dee asked.

"That's an understatement," said Sarah Jacobs. "Chamberlin had millions of our money. Katherine got it all back for us yesterday."

Dee looked at Carol. "So this is the group you were talking about yesterday?"

"Yeah. We each had an E-mail from her telling us to check our accounts. The funds plus interest had been transferred to each one of us," said Carol Tindle.

"Carol, we probably shouldn't say anymore about our situation. Katherine isn't here to say what actually happened and we don't want to get her into any trouble," said Theresa Lee in a parenting tone.

"I guess," said Carol and she put her head down, and then reached for her drink.

"Well, you ladies don't have to worry about me saying anything," said Dee. "I've been friends with Kat for a while and I'm not going to bring up her name with anyone."

"Thanks Dee. We appreciate it," said Sharon Kelly.

"Your appetizers should be ready soon. I'll bring them over when they come out of the kitchen."

They all said thanks.

Dee went back to the bar. Ron had watched Dee talking to the ladies. He said to Dee, "What was that all about?"

"Oh, nothing, just girl talk."

"I thought I heard someone say something about Katherine?"

"Yeah, they were waiting for Katherine to come in to have a drink with them. They're all celebrating something."

"Oh, like an engagement or something?" he asked.

"Yeah, something like that, I guess." She didn't want to elaborate.

Dee went back to work. She went around the bar asking every one of they were all set with drinks and food.

"How about you Ed, want another drink?"
"Sure Dee, I'll have another beer."
"Coming right up."

She got him a fresh mug from the freezer and poured another beer. Then she moved down the bar to Kenny Brown and Tommy Anderson.

"Another, guys?"

"I'll have a beer," said Tommy.

"Give me a shot also," said Kenny.

Dee poured two beers and a shot of Jager for Kenny.

Then she moved around to where the regular girls were seated.

"Ladies, another?" she asked.

"Not me said Ann, I've got to get going. I've got a date with Paulie."

"He just left with Linda," said Dee.

The other women all said "aww."

"Paulie, Linda. When did this all happen?" asked Sue.

"Come on girls. Some of you have been out with Paulie. You know what he's got," Ann said.

"We're just teasing you Ann. Don't take it so personally."

"Oh, I'm not. You're all just jealous anyway."

"I can't believe you're not hanging around to see what happened to Harry and Kat," said Sue.

"Nah. If I know Katherine, she's got Harry shacked up somewhere for the weekend," commented Ann.

"Then why did they find Harry's kayak in the Atlantic and Kat's car at Stage Harbor?" asked Tina.

"I don't know. But you'll all be sorry you wasted the whole afternoon worrying when they're found," Ann said as she got up to leave.

"Someone will call you if anything happens," Dee said to Ann.

"You do that," was all Ann said as she left.

"She's a little pissy, wouldn't you say?" said Sue watching Ann walk out.

"Who knows," replied Tina. "Ann's got her own agenda."

"Yeah, and Paulie's on her agenda tonight," said Sue giggling.

"Get us all another round," Tina said to Dee.

It was clear that the ladies were all worried about the events of the day, all except Linda, and Ann.

Antonio arrived at the Coast Guard Station about twenty-five minutes after leaving Sundancers. He met Detective Simpson at the front door.

"Let's go around to the helipad. The chopper will be here in a few minutes," Simpson said to Antonio.

They went around to the side of the building to where there was a parking lot that didn't have any entrance or exit. It had a large white circle painted on it indicating the landing zone for the helicopter. The two looked south east as they heard the sound of the rotors grow louder.

"There it is," said Antonio pointing to the sky.

The chopper came in and hovered just above the landing zone, and then softly landed. The power was turned off on the helicopter and within a few minutes, all was quiet. The door to the chopper opened. Pilot Captain John Wagner got out. He walked over to Detective Simpson.

"We brought the kayak and life vest back," he said as he slid the door to the side of the chopper open. Seaman Martin began to slide the kayak out the door. Captain Wagner grabbed the end and assisted Martin in setting it on the tarmac.

"That's Katherine's," said Antonio as he walked over to where the kayak had been placed.

"You sure?" asked Detective Simpson.

"I'm sure. That thing has been outside my kitchen every day for weeks now. See her name written on it? Harry did that."

"This is her life vest also," said seaman Martin, handing the life vest out of the chopper to Captain Wagner.

"Yep, that's hers," said Antonio. "That one and the other one you had me look at are the two Harry loaded onto his Jeep on Friday."

Detective Simpson turned to Antonio. "Thanks for coming down and positively identifying these things Antonio. It'll help move my investigation along."

"No problem," said Antonio. "Can I go now?"

"Sure. I'll call you if I need you again," said Detective Simpson.

"Do you have my cell number, Detective?" asked Antonio.

"No. Why don't you let me have it? That way, I can get in touch with you faster if you're not at work."

"Ok." Antonio gave him his cell number.

On his way back to Sundancers, Antonio called the bar. Dee answered.

"Dee, they found Katherine's kayak. That's why they wanted me to come down, to positively identify it."

"Anything else?" she asked, not sure she really wanted an answer.

"I'll tell you all about it when I get back. Detective Simpson said he'd call if they need me for any more identification help. I'm going to stop at home for a few minutes on my way back to pick up a clean shirt. Call me on my cell if I'm needed for anything or if the Detective calls."

"Ok Antonio. Thanks for calling."

When she hung up, everyone was looking at her. She took a minute to compose herself. She put her hand on her forehead as she spoke.

"They found Katherine's kayak. Antonio's on his way back here. He said he'd tell us what he knows when he gets here."

Chapter 38

Around the same time as when the helicopter resumed its search after dropping the pink kayak off, a commercial fishing boat, the King Fish, hooked into something in about a hundred feet of water about a mile from where Harry's kayak had been recovered. The captain of the King Fish, Walter Owens, had been jigging for cod in an area he thought contained a few old wrecked ships. At first, he thought he had hooked into a wreck. But as he applied pressure, whatever he had on the line started to come up. It didn't fight but did move.

He would reel down to the water and then pull up with all he could to gain some line back from whatever he had on the line way down deep. Then he repeated the same motions again and again until he could finally see something coming to the surface. At first, he thought he had hooked some junk but as the end of his line reached the surface he said, "Holy shit."

He looked into the water and could now see the figure of a body. As it broke the surface, he could see the legs, arms, hands and headless body. He stopped reeling and let the body remain at surface level. He used a long pole he had on board with a hooked end to turn the body around. As he did, he turned away. The head was missing. The neck was shredded where it should have been attached to the head. It looked like a shark had bitten the head off.

He ran to the console of his boat. He picked up the marine radio mike and set the channel to the Coast Guard Station.

"Coast Guard, this is Captain Walt Owens of the King Fish, come in."

"King Fish, this is Coast Guard, Chatham. What can we do for you?"

"I just hooked a body while cod fishing."

"Say again, you hooked a body?"

"Yes. I was fishing in about a hundred feet of water about two miles southeast of Monomoy when I hooked into a body on the bottom."

"Can you tell if it's a man or woman?"

"Hold on."

He went to the back and reached down to touch the body. He felt the chest. He could not feel any breasts nor bra. He went back to the cabin and picked up the mike.

"I think it's a man."

"Is there hair on the head and can you tell what color the hair is?"

"Hell no, the head's missing."

"Did you say the head's missing?"

"Yes."

"How about the sex. Can you look down there?"

"Wait a minute."

Owens went back to the body and pulled the pants down.

"It's definitely a man."

"Ok Captain. We have a helicopter in the area and I'm going to dispatch it to your location. Can you give me your coordinates?"

"Sure."

Captain Owens looked at his GPS. He gave his coordinates to the Coast Guard operator.

"Thanks Owens. You'll see our chopper soon. They'll pick up the corpse."

"Ok. Owens out."

Commander Collins was summoned to the operations room at the Coast Guard station. The operator told her about the King Fish snagging a body and of the current coordinates of the King Fish. Collins picked up the mike and set the channel to the chopper.

"Captain Wagner, this is Commander Collins."

"Go ahead Commander."

"Captain, we just had a call from a fishing boat, the King Fish. The captain on board said he just hooked a body while fishing. He's not far from Monomoy. Can you rendezvous with the King Fish and retrieve the body?"

"Sure Commander. We're about half way down Monomoy now about two miles out over the Atlantic. Give me the King Fish's coordinates and we'll set our course for there."

Commander Collins provided the coordinates.

"Hess, did you get those?" Wagner asked his co-pilot.

"Got it."

"We're on our way Commander. I'll call you when we are returning."

"Thanks Captain."

Co-pilot Hess put the coordinates into the GPS. They made a slight turn and were on an intercepting course with the King Fish.

A few minutes later, Captain Owens heard the chopper before he actually saw it. The chopper came in pretty low over the water. It hovered about fifty feet over the boat. Crewman Martin motioned to Captain Owens to use his marine radio. Captain Wagner called the boat.

"King Fish, we're here to pick up the corpse you found."

"It's still on the line in the water along side the back of my boat," said Owens.

"Can you bring it on board the boat?"

"I'd rather not. The thing has no head," Owens said in a high-pitched voice.

Captain Wagner spoke into his headset to seaman Martin. "Go down in the basket and retrieve the body Martin."

"Ok Captain."

Tim Martin extended the winch arm out of the copilot. He attached the basket to the end of the cable. Then motioned to co-pilot to lower him down. Hess lowered Martin to the water. Martin was about twenty feet behind the boat. He instructed captain Owens to put a rope around a leg or arm of the corpse and to throw him the line. He told Owens not to cut the fishing line until he had the rope. Owens did as told.

Ten minutes later, Martin had pulled the headless corpse into the basket and was on his way back up to the chopper. When he was back inside the chopper, Hess said, "Is it a mess?"

"Not at all. All the blood must have ran out and the ocean cleaned the body. Look. The body's as white as can be."

The corpse was devoid of any color but white.

Captain Wagner called Owens back and thanked him for his help. He told Owens they would take the body back to the Coast Guard Station. The chopper turned back to the northeast and flew away.

Owens stowed his gear and set his attention on returning to port. He had enough excitement for one day.

En-route back to the station, Captain Wagner called Commander Collins.

"Commander, we retrieved a body from the King Fish. It looks to be that of a male, middle aged. I'd guess six feet or so but it's hard to tell with the head missing."

"Does the corpse have any identification in his pants pockets?" asked Collins.

"Hold on, I'll have Martin check."

"No. Martin says it looks like he was wearing sweat pants or those things a bicyclist wears."

"Ok. Bring the body back. I'll contact the coroner."

Captain Wagner signed off continuing the trip back to the Coast Guard Station. Commander Collins called the coroner and Detective Simpson. The coroner said someone would be at the station within a half hour. Simpson hadn't even made it back to the police station yet so he turned around and headed back to Chatham. Simpson pulled over on the side of the road to call Antonio Davies. He entered Antonio's cell number. The call went to voice mail. Simpson pressed end and then called Sundancers.

Ron answered the phone.

"Sundancers."

"Is Antonio there, this is Detective Simpson."

"He hasn't returned from Chatham yet Detective. Do you want me to have him call you?"

"No, just ask him to come back to Chatham if you would."

"Ok Detective. I can do that."

When Ron hung up, Dee said, "Who was that?"

"It was Detective Simpson. He wants Antonio to come back to Chatham."

"Did he say why?"

"No."

"Antonio was going to stop by his house on his way back. I'll call him."

Dee picked up the phone and called Antonio. He answered on the first ring.

"Antonio, it's Dee. Detective Simpson just called again and he wants you to come back to Chatham right away."

"Did he say what for?"

"No. Just that he wants you to come back."

"Ok. I'm on my way."

Chapter 39

Antonio pulled into the Coast Guard Station in Chatham again. This time, he parked behind the coroners van. He walked up to the main door. Detective Simpson greeted him.

"Sorry to have to call you back so soon Antonio, but they've found a body."

"Is it a man or woman?" Antonio asked his voice shaking.

"The pilot thinks it's a man. We'll know for sure after the coroner checks the corpse out."

Simpson pointed to the sky as the chopper was approaching. The two of them walked over to the helipad.

A woman was waiting there with a gurney. On the back of her smock, it said Coroner.

The helicopter landed and the side door slid open. Seaman Martin jumped out. He helped the coroner move the gurney to the door and slid a body out onto it. Then he got back into the chopper and closed the door.

The chopper took off again headed southeast.

Antonio looked at Detective Simpson and said, "Where are they going now?"

"I don't know but I don't think the search is over yet."

"So they're still looking for another body?"

"That or a living person."

The coroner wheeled the gurney to a side door at the station. The doors swung open and she wheeled the gurney inside.

Detective Simpson said, "Come with me Antonio. I'll want you to identify the body if you can."

They walked through the same side door and into a well lit room. The coroner was taking a tarp off the body.

"June, this is Antonio Davies from Sundancers. He's here to ID the body," Detective Simpson said to June Nevins, the coroner. "We think this might be Mr. Harry Adams. He's the owner of Sundancers."

"Hello Mr. Davies. Nice to meet you, although it could have been under better circumstances."

Antonio shook her hand.

As she peeled back the tarp, Antonio gasped at the sight of a body with no head. He didn't recognize the body as Harry's because the body had no head.

June looked at Antonio and asked, "Have you ever seen these clothes before?"

"Not that I can recall, but who knows what Harry might have been wearing. He only took up kayaking this year."

"Does Mr. Adams have any distinguishing marks on his body that you're aware of?" June asked Antonio.

"Gee, other than a scar on his forehead, I don't know."

"Well, that's not going to help in this situation. Do you know if he had a regular doctor?"

"I'm sure he did. He got prescriptions for back pain not too long ago so he must have been seeing someone."

"Good. Antonio, if you can find out, let the Detective know and he'll contact his doctor. We can match the blood type and it's possible his doctor would know about any other body markings."

"What about his finger prints. Harry's are probably on file somewhere." asked Antonio.

"You're right Antonio," said Detective Simpson, "Since Harry owned the bar, his prints are probably on file. I'll have it checked out."

"I'll send you over a copy of the prints from this corpse when I'm done Detective. Then you can match them up with what you have on file."

"Thanks June. That should tell us if this is Mr. Harry Adams or not."

"Now you two can go. I need to finish my work."

Detective Simpson and Antonio walked to the door. They talked for a minute outside before getting into their respective vehicles.

"Detective, do you think its Harry?"

"I don't know Antonio. But the coroner will find out. When I get those prints, I'll have them scanned in our database. We should know from that."

"Can you call me and let me know if the prints are Harry's?"

"I'll call as soon as I hear from her. But if it's Mr. Adams, I'll have to contact the next of kin first."

"I understand. Thanks."

Antonio got into his car. He was sweating heavily. He wiped the sweat from his brow and took a deep breath. He said, "I need a drink."

He drove erratically on the way back. At one point, he found himself doing sixty miles per hour along Route 28, normally a road with a speed limit of 30 to 40 mph. A lot of things were going through his mind. He didn't know what he would say when he got back to Sundancers.

All the way back to Sundancers, all he could think about was the headless corpse. About the only thing the coroner could confirm was that the body was a male. She didn't know the age, height or anything else at this point. She could only tell that he was a male as a result of cutting the pants off the corpse.

.

Chapter 40

Dee thought about the events of the past two days as she stood in the back corner of the bar. She was in a daze. Ron called her twice but she didn't respond. Finally, he walked over to her. She had her head down staring at an empty glass. He shook her arm.

"Dee, you ok?"

"I don't know Ron. I was thinking about Harry and Katherine. If I hadn't told them about the seals and the cut from Stage Harbor to the outside of Monomoy, they might not have gone out there."

"You can't blame yourself, Dee. You only meant to give them information about the area. It was still their decision to go where they did."

"That's easy for you to say Ron. You didn't send them out there."

"Well, lets keep working. It'll take our mind off the situation. Antonio should be back soon. Maybe he'll have some information."

Dee went back to bartending. She took care of half of the bar and the high tables in the bar area, Ron took care of the other half and the waitress station.

The door to Sundancers opened and in walked Linda and Paul. Dee looked at them, "I thought you two just left?"

"We did. But Linda couldn't get past Harry and Katherine being missing. She wanted to be here."

"I told Paulie he could come home with me once all this is over," said Linda.

"Can I get you something?" asked Dee.

"Sure, I'll have a Bud and get Linda a martini."

Dee got them drinks. About fifteen minutes after they came back in, Ann showed up.

"Where you been Ann?" asked Paul.

"Waiting for you to show up," she said as she walked past him and Linda.

"Oh, I forgot," was all Paul said as he sipped his beer.

Linda leaned into him, "Paulie, did you have a date with Ann and forgot about it?"

"Guess I did."

"Oh, she'll not forget about that. I guess it's a good thing I'm here to take you under my wing."

"Guess so," was all he could say.

Ann kept walking past them taking up a seat next to Sue Kent.

Antonio pulled into the parking lot and parked right at the front door. He came in. Immediately, Dee knew something was wrong. Antonio was sweaty. His hair was a mess. His face was red. He didn't say a thing but went right around the corner and behind the bar. He poured himself a shot and a beer. He downed both. Then he repeated it again. As he poured the third shot, Dee said, "What happened?"

"When I went over there the second time, they had found Katherine's kayak and life vest, but no Katherine."

He downed the third shot and poured another.

He continued, "Then, I got the call to go back before I could return here. When I got back the third time, the coroners van was at the station. When the chopper landed, they took a body off of it."

"You're kidding?" Ron said in anticipation.

Antonio stopped with his head down. Then he looked up and around at everyone. Eventually, he mustered the courage to continue.

"The medical examiner took the body inside and they asked me to come in to identify it."

"Who was it Antonio?" Dee asked in a shaky voice.

"All I know is it was a male."

Dee started to cry. "Oh Harry."

"So they had found Harry floating in the ocean?" Ed asked.

"I don't know," said Antonio.

"Apparently, a fisherman hooked the body and brought it to the surface and then called the Coast Guard. The helicopter was still searching nearby so it was diverted to the fishing boat to pick up the body."

Kenny came over to Antonio and said, "I don't understand Antonio. If they found the body, how come you don't know if it was Harry or not? Didn't they ask you to identify him?"

"They did, but the body had no head."

Everyone in the place gasped. They hadn't been prepared for anything like that.

"Oh, my god," said Dee as she broke out in a full cry.

"Harry was decapitated?" Tina asked.

"The medical examiner said it looked like a shark had bitten his head off."

"What a horrible way to die," exclaimed Linda.

"The coroner said she wouldn't know the cause of death until an autopsy has been completed. Right now, they are still trying to positively identify the body."

Dee said, "What about the other markings on Harry's body. They could identify him from those."

"I didn't know of any other markings on his body, Dee. So Detective Simpson was going to have the finger prints of the corpse matched to the database at the station to see if the body belonged to Harry."

"Or someone else," Ron added.

Tina said, "Did they look down there? Harry has a unique mark on his private part."

"You're right," Dee added.

Antonio looked at both of them. His eyebrows went up.

"Care to tell me what this unique mark is?" he said looking at the two.

"Sure. He has a birth mark on the shaft," said Tina.

"Yeah, just past the tip. It's about the size of a dime," added Dee.

Antonio looked at the two in amazement. He wondered how both of them knew.

"I'll pass that information along to the Detective," said Antonio as he downed the forth shot. He went into the kitchen taking his cell phone out as he walked. When he got there, he called Simpson.

"Detective, a few of the women here at Sundancers tell me Harry has a birthmark on his private part. They said it's unique, round, and the size of a dime."

"I'll pass that along to the ME."

"Did you get the finger prints yet?"

"Yes. We're running a search now."

"Can you call me once you have an answer?"

"Like I told you before, Antonio, I'll have to notify next of kin first."

"Ok. But please call as soon as you can."

"I will."

Detective Simpson called the coroner.

"June, it's Detective Simpson. I have some information that might help us put a name to the corpse."

"What do you have Detective?"

"A few of the ladies at Sundancers told Antonio that Harry Adams has a birthmark on his penis. They said it is just past the tip, shaped like a dime. You might want to look and see if there's anything there like that."

"Hold on a minute, let me check."

She looked at the part in question from multiple directions. Then she came back on the phone.

"There's no birthmark on this one."

"You sure?"

"I'm sure. I've looked close up and it's clean."

"Ok."

Simpson hung up and walked back to the computer room. He asked the clerk, Rene, if the database search had found anything yet matching the prints the ME had sent over.

"Nothing yet Detective."
"Rene, call me if you get a hit."
"Will do."

Simpson started to walk down the hall when Rene called him back.
"Detective, we got a hit."
Simpson walked back into the room.
"What do we have?"

"The prints belong to a Charles Chamberlin. It looks like he was involved in some minor charge a few years ago.
"Are you sure?"
"Hey Detective, the computer is 99.9% accurate."
"Charles Chamberlin, huh."
"That's the name."

The phone rang at Sundancers. Dee answered it.
"Sundancers."
"Is Antonio there? It's Detective Simpson."
"Hold on."

Dee called Antonio out of the kitchen.
"It's Detective Simpson for you."
Antonio walked over and took the phone from Dee.
"Yes Detective. What have you found out?"

There was a silence in the bar. Antonio took a deep breath and said, "So you'll call me back right after you have notified the next of kin? Thank you Detective."
Antonio hung up the phone.

"What did he tell you," asked Kenny.

"He said they have identified the body. As soon as they notify the next of kin, he'll call me back."

"Was it Harry?" asked Dee.

"He didn't say Harry's name because he's required to notify the next of kin first. But it must be. Otherwise, why would he call me back?"

"Oh, no," Dee started to cry again.

So did Tina Fletcher and Ann Benard. Sue Kent put her head on her arms on the bar and sobbed.

"He said he'd call you back after he contacted someone in Harry's family?" asked Ron.

"That's what he said."

"So what do we do now?" Ron asked.

"I don't know. Let's just finish up the day and see what happens tomorrow."

Antonio turned and walked back into the kitchen with his head down. He had absolutely no expression on his face. It was clear he was stunned.

Chapter 41

Harry and his friends, Don Lombard and Pete Nickels, had met up in Boston. They spent Friday night at a few bars. On Saturday, they got up at noon and went to a local pub for lunch. By the time they had eaten, it was after three.

Harry said to Don, "Why don't we go back to your place and get some rest. If we keep up this pace, I won't be able to go kayaking tomorrow."

Pete said, "You're kidding Harry. You're going kayaking tomorrow? Since when did you become the outdoors type?"

"It's got to involve a woman," said Don laughing.

"He's right Harry. Whose the woman?"

"Ok. There's this woman who started working for me recently. She's a ten."

"Oh, now we get it Harry. So are you actually going kayaking or is it just an excuse to get her alone?"

"You guys only think of one thing."

Don said, "And exactly what are you thinking about Harry? Kayaking?"

"No, really. I'm supposed to go kayaking with her tomorrow."

"Sure," said Pete.

"Ok Harry. We can go rest a little before the game. But only for an hour or two.

Harry was glad the two agreed to take a break. They had been drinking since last night when he got there. He wasn't in the same form as he'd been when they were younger but his friends apparently were still in drinking shape. They went back to Don's and rested for two hours. Harry was asleep on the sofa when Pete shook his arm.

"Time to go Harry. Game starts in two hours."

"Ok."

Harry got up, went to the sink and put water on his hands. He threw the water into his face and rubbed it. As he looked into the mirror, he said to himself, "How will I ever survive this?"

Ten minutes later, they were on their way to Fenway.

They decided to go into Boston Beer Works for an hour or so prior to the game. The place was jammed. Harry wanted to get a table but Don and Pete just wanted to hang out by the bar watching the women. Harry saw a table open up and he took it. He motioned for Don and Pete to join him.

"I've got to get something to eat," said Harry looking a little under the weather.

"Me too," added Pete.

"I've got my dinner right here," said Don holding up his beer.

"How do you do it Don? We aren't as young as we used to be," Harry said.

"Harry, we're not that old. What have you been doing down there on Cape Cod?"

"Kayaking?" Pete asked.

"Must be the women," Don added.

"No. I don't drink as much as we used to. Even though I own a bar, I have to play it cool."

"Sure, we understand," said Don.

"Come down sometime and you'll see."

"Didn't we do that last year? You tried to set us up with those middle-aged women. Don got lucky but all I got was the cold shoulder," Pete complained.

"Hey Pete, no one told you to hit on that woman who was dating a cop."

"Harry introduced me to her."

Harry said, "She's the one who recently came to work for me."

"So what happened to the cop?" Pete asked.

"He died."

"Oh," Pete said.

"And now you're doing her?" Don asked.

"It's not like that guys. She's a nice person."

"That's what I thought when you introduced me to her last year. But she just blew me off."

"Pete, you had your pick of three women who would have happily taken care of you. But no, you had to go off on your own. I can't help it if you always make the wrong choice in women," Harry chided him.

"Well, I guess it's easier if you own the bar," Pete responded.

"It does have its benefits," said Harry.

Harry and Pete ordered burgers and fries. The three sat and drank a few beers. After eating, they decided to go into the game. The place was packed for a Saturday night game. It was a close game and the Red Sox won 6 - 5 in thirteen innings.

The guys didn't get back to Don's until 3 am. Harry had celebrated too much and knew there was no way he was going to make it back to Cape Cod to go kayaking for Sunday. He didn't want to call but knew Katherine would be waiting for him if he didn't so he placed a call to her cell phone. The phone went immediately to voice mail. Harry was glad it did.

"Katherine, it's Harry. I'm still in Boston. I just got in from the game and its after three a.m. I don't think I'm going to make it back to the Cape in time to go kayaking on Sunday. I'm really sorry to have to cancel, but I'll make it up to you. I'll call you when I get in."

He hung up knowing she would get the message in the morning. He'd have to make it up to her in some way during the week. He put his phone in his pocket. Then he went into the living room to talk with Don.

"I've got to get back to Cape Cod at a reasonable time tomorrow Don. Do you have an alarm clock?"
"Yeah. Its in my bedroom."
"Can I borrow it for the night?"
"I'll set it for you. What time do you want to get up?"
"Let's see. If I get up at ten, shower and hit the road, I could be back early afternoon."
"Ok. I'll set it for ten," Don said.
Pete had gotten up to go to the kitchen for a couple more beers. He came back in handing both Harry and Don another one.

"To a Red Sox victory," Pete declared.

The all touched glasses and drank.

Don put on some 60's music. The three sat there listening for the next few hours, reminiscing about their youth and drinking more beers.

At a little after five, Harry said, "I've got to get to sleep."

"Me too," said Pete.

"Ok, Harry, you get the sofa. Pete, you get the day bed in the other room."

Pete having slept on the uncomfortable day bed the previous night said, "Harry can have the day bed."

"Ok, Harry, you get the day bed. Pete the sofa."

Don got up heading for his bedroom. As he left the living room, Harry said, "Don't forget to set the clock for 10 am, Don."

"Got it," was all Don said.

Harry went into the room that had the day bed. It was actually in a screened porch. He found a blanket and throw pillow and made a make shift bed for himself. He lay down and closed his eyes.

When he woke, it was full daylight. He looked at his watch. It was two forty five. He jumped up and walked into the living room. Pete was just stirring.

"I can't believe its two forty five," said Harry in an exasperated voice.

"After two huh," was all Pete said.

"Yeah, Don was supposed to get me up at ten."

"Well, guess he didn't," Pete said.

Harry knocked on Don's bedroom door.

"Go away," could be heard from inside.

Harry opened the door.

"Don, you were supposed to wake me up by ten. Didn't you set the alarm?"

"I did set it. I called out to you when it went off. You mumbled something and went back to sleep. I figured you had changed your mind."

Harry closed the door. He walked back into the living room.

"Did he forget to set the alarm?" asked Pete.

"He said it went off and he called me but I didn't get up."

"I don't know. I didn't hear anything."

"I guess he could have. We drank so much yesterday, I was probably still in the bag when he called out to me this morning."

"Hey, it happens," Pete said.

Harry made coffee. He brought Pete a cup and one for himself. Harry sat in an oversized chair and Pete just picked his head up to take a sip. They talked about scheduling another outing. Finally, Harry stood up and stretched.

"Well, I've got to get going. Tell Don I'll call him."

"Ok Harry. We had a good time."

"Sure did. See you Pete."

"Yeah," Pete said putting his head back down on the couch and closing his eyes.

Harry closed the door behind him. He got into his car and drove off. It was going on five o'clock. Where had the day gone?

Chapter 42

The employees and patrons of Sundancers were waiting for Harry's next-of-kin to be notified of his death. The Detective would contact them next. The anticipation was making everyone anxious. When the phone rang again, Ron answered it.

"Sundancers."
"Who am I speaking with?" Detective Simpson asked.
"It's Ron Jessup."
"Is Antonio around?"
"Hold on."

"Antonio, it's for you."
Antonio came out of the kitchen again. He took the phone from Ron.
"This is Antonio. Oh, hi Detective."
He listened for a minute. Then he said, "No kidding."
His demeanor changed from sadness to a slight smile. He hung up the phone and turned to Dee.

"It wasn't Harry."

"What?" she said.

"Detective Simpson said the prints didn't match Harry's. Plus, the body didn't have the birthmark you and Tina said it should have had."

"Did he say who the prints matched?" asked Ron.

"Yes, Charles Chamberlin."

The women who had been there for a celebration were just hanging around to get some information about Katherine. When Antonio said Charles Chamberlin's name, they all looked at each other in astonishment.

Dee put her arms around Antonio. "Are they sure it wasn't Harry?"

"Well, Simpson said the prints weren't Harry's."

"So, the body you saw with no head doesn't belong to Harry?"

"That's right," said Antonio smiling.

"Hooray," Dee said with excitement.

"Don't celebrate too much Dee. Harry hasn't been found yet."

"But the body they found in the Ocean didn't belong to Harry," she insisted.

"Yes, that particular body wasn't Harry's," Antonio said.

"So Harry might still be out there?" was a comment from Ed from the other side of the bar.

"We need to think positive," Dee said in a critical way giving Ed a nasty look.

Antonio turned to Tina, "Didn't one of you go out with Charles Chamberlin?"

"Ann Benard did some weeks ago," said Tina as she turned and then yelled, "Ann, you better come hear this."

Ann Benard came over to where Tina and Antonio were standing. Antonio said to her, "Did you go out with Charles Chamberlin a few weeks ago?"

"Yes. I met him here at the bar one day. We went to the beach and then to my place."

"Well, Detective Simpson said the dead man's prints matched his."

"Holy shit," was all Ann could say.

She thought for a few minutes and then said, "Charles knows Katherine. Could he have been kayaking with her?"

The women seated at the high tables in the bar area were very loud and animated in their conversation. Up to this point in the day, they had been rather quiet but after Antonio's announcement regarding Charles Chamberlin, they were all being very vocal. Dee walked over to them to see if they wanted to order anything else.

"Can I get you ladies anything else?" Dee asked.

Sharon Kelly said, "I can't believe Charles is dead. They need to find Katherine."

"Hey, she did what she said she would do," said Theresa Lee.

"But did he have to die?" asked Carol Tindle.

"Katherine couldn't have had any role in his death, could she?" Sarah Jacobs asked.

Ann Pierce said, "Well, Katherine knew Charles. And she did get him to return our funds yesterday. Maybe they had something going?"

"Not Katherine," said Carol.

"So you women all knew Charles Chamberlin?" Dee asked them.

"Yes. Like we said earlier, that's why we're here today," said Ann Pierce.

"We were supposed to meet Katherine here to celebrate. She got him to return all our missing funds to us yesterday," said Theresa Lee.

"Maybe she didn't get him to do it. Maybe she did it," said Sharon Kelly.

"Does it really matter?" asked Sarah Jacobs.

"True. All we wanted was to get our money back," Ann Pierce added.

"Maybe Katherine wanted more," commented Theresa.

"Well, I liked Charles. He really helped me out," Ann Pierce said."

"He won't be helping you any more," said Sharon.

"But what about Katherine?" asked Carol.

Dee went back to the bar. She spoke to Ron.

"Something really strange is going on here Ron."

"Why do you say that?"

"The ladies over there all said Chamberlin had taken money from each of them. Don't you remember the case where a number of widows here on Cape Cod were missing significant sums of money after their husband's had died?"

"Yeah, I remember something about it."

"Well, that group seated over there said they were the victims."

"You're kidding?"

"No. And they said Katherine played a role in them getting their money back."

"Just how did they say Katherine did that?"

"Well, something about getting the funds from Chamberlin. They said they all got their missing funds plus a nice return sent to them yesterday morning. They also said they were notified by Katherine via e-mail of the funds transfer yesterday."

"Do you think that had anything to do with Chamberlin dying?"

"I don't know and now Katherine's missing."

"Wow. You think he found out?"

"Who knows but I think there's a lot more here than meets the eye."

"You could be right."

Chapter 43

The night had been a night of mood swings. The regulars were all happy that the identity of the corpse found at sea didn't belong to Harry. But Harry was still missing, as was Katherine. The sun had set and it became very dark. The sky had been filled in with clouds obscuring the heavens from view. Dee and Ron continued their duties bartending. Antonio went back to work in the kitchen.

About an hour after sunset, Antonio had been cooking in the kitchen when he looked out back and noticed the lights on in Harry's office. He went out into the bar to talk with Dee.

"Dee, did you leave the lights on in Harry's office?"
"No. I turned them off after I got the bank out of the safe."
"Well, they're on."
"Then someone's in there."
Dee walked over to the door and looked out towards Harry's office.

"That's Harry's brother's car," she said as she went back behind the bar.

"What's he doing here?" asked Antonio. He hesitated, as he was about to say something else. Dee noticed his hesitation and said, "What is it, Antonio?"

"Simpson told me he had to notify the next of kin. What if it was Harry?"

"Oh, no," yelled Dee. "It was Harry."

Just then, Harry walked out of the kitchen.

"It was Harry what?" he asked.

Everyone held their breath for a minute. They couldn't believe what they were seeing.

"What's this all about?" Harry asked as he walked behind the bar.

"Oh, Harry. You were dead," said Dee as she put her arms around him and hugged him.

Tina came over and gave him a big kiss and hug as well.

"What's going on here?" he asked.

"They found your kayak. Then they found a body. It's head was missing and we all assumed it was you," Ron said.

"What do you mean they found my kayak? It's over at Katherine's."

"No it isn't," said Antonio.

"I had to go to the Coast Guard Station in Chatham to identify it. Your kayak was found out in the Atlantic Ocean."

"What about Katherine?"

"She hasn't been found yet," said Antonio.

"Didn't you go kayaking with her this weekend, Harry?" Dee asked him.

"No. I did pick up the kayaks on Friday but then I went to Boston to meet up with some friends. We went to the Sox game on Saturday and partied too much Saturday night. I called Katherine and left her a message telling her I wasn't in any shape to go kayaking on Sunday. She must have gone with someone else."

"Oh, I think she went with someone else alright," added Antonio. "She must have gone kayaking with Chamberlin."

"Harry, Katherine called here Saturday night and said something about kayaking and being in trouble and being in a fog somewhere on the ocean. We just assumed you were with her."

"Well, I wasn't."

"So it must have been Charles," said Sharon Kelly as she walked up to the bar.

She put out her hand to Harry and introduced herself.

"Sharon Kelly. I knew Charles Chamberlin. My friends and I were here to celebrate with Katherine. We've been hanging around hoping she would show up."

"I can't help you Ms. Kelly. I just got back into town a few minutes ago. I haven't even gotten my phone messages yet. Maybe one of them is from Katherine."

"Well, let us know if you find out," Sharon said to Harry as she turned and walked back to the other ladies she had been seated with.

Everyone shook Harry's hand or hugged him. He was still a little hung over from his trip to Boston but he went along with the festive mood.

At one point, he said to Dee, "I'm going to my office for a few minutes. I want to see if I have any messages. I'll be right back."

Harry walked out and back to his office. He sat at his desk and picked up his cell phone. He called in for messages. There were two from Katherine. The first message was a picture of a seal on a beach. He saved the picture and then selected the next message. He looked at the time. It was from very early in the morning on Sunday. He wondered why he hadn't gotten the message earlier when he used his cell to leave Katherine a message. He dismissed any concern because it wasn't the first time his messages had been delayed. He pressed one to hear the message.

"Harry, it's Katherine. I went kayaking with Charles Chamberlin yesterday morning. We were having a good time. The weather was nice at first so we went through the place Dee had told us about and ended up on the Atlantic Ocean side of Monomoy. There were quite a few seals and we followed them in our kayaks. I took a picture of a seal when we stopped to rest on the beach and I sent it to your cell phone. When we tried to turn around to return, we found ourselves getting overtaken with a fog. Somehow, we got turned around and lost. Charles ended up falling in the water after being capsized by a wave. I lost track of him in the fog. Then I spent the night on the ocean. The sun's just starting to come up and the fog has lifted. I think I can see land and I'm trying to paddle there now. The water conditions have become very rough. I almost tipped over a number of times. I should have waited for you. I hope to see you later today. If I'm not back by the time you get this message, then."

The call ended there. He didn't know if something had happened to her, the phone or if the message storage had run out. He felt incomplete at not hearing the rest of her message. Harry hung up the phone and went back into the bar. When he got there, he recalled the message Katherine had left him. When he was done, Dee said, "That's all?"

"That's it. The call ended. I don't know why, but it did," was all Harry could say.

Ron stepped up and said, "Everyone, drinks are on me."

He and Dee made everyone their favorite drink. As they all took hold of their drinks, Ron made a toast.

"To Harry. We're glad you're all right."

They all held up their glasses and drank. Harry felt good although he wasn't sure how he felt about Katherine.

After participating in the celebration, Antonio went back into the kitchen. He called Detective Simpson.

"Detective Simpson."
"Detective, it's Antonio from Sundancers."
"What can I do for you Antonio?"
"I thought you should know, my boss Harry Adams just showed up."
"What do you mean showed up?"
"Apparently, he had gone to Boston for the weekend and he just got back. When he did, he checked his voice mail and had a message from Katherine. You'll want to talk with Harry about it."
"Is he there now?"
"Yes."
"If you would, please tell him I'm on my way over and I would like to talk to him."
"Will do."

Antonio went back into the bar. He told Harry of his call to Detective Simpson. Harry said he would be in his office if the Detective came in.

It was less than thirty minutes later when Detective Simpson came in. He asked for Harry. Dee buzzed Harry's office and Harry asked her to send the Detective to the office. She pointed the office out.

Simpson introduced himself to Harry and sat down. For the next half hour, they talked and discussed the situation. Harry called his home phone at one point allowing Detective Simpson to listen to the message from Katherine. After the call, Simpson said, "I guess they ran into bad weather kayaking. We'll never know what actually happened."

"What about Katherine?"

"We'll keep looking."

Detective Simpson thanked Harry for his time and left. Harry went back into the bar to rejoin the celebration even though he wasn't really in a partying mood.

Chapter 44

Katherine's body had not been found. The search continued for another few days but was eventually called off. The kayaks were returned to Harry and he gave them to Clint for use in his kayaking business.

The women who had thought they were victims of Charles Chamberlin were all made whole thanks to the actions Katherine had taken before she went kayaking. Katherine didn't have any relatives anyone knew of so no one was contacted. A notice was placed in the Cape Cod Times regarding disposition of her estate. Andrew Dunn was the only person to respond. At the hearing held to dissolve her estate, it was disclosed that she had a Will, and left everything to Andrew.

The body of Charles Chamberlin sat in the coroners vault for a month. Detective Simpson could not find a next of kin for Chamberlin. One day, the funeral director from Doane, Beal and Ames contacted the Coroners Office. June Nevins took the call.

"Ms. Nevins, this is Robert Henderson. I'm the funeral director at Doane, Beal and Ames in Harwich."

"Yes, Mr. Henderson, what can I do for you?"
"Do you have a body of a Charles Chamberlin in your freezer?"
"Yes. No one has come forward to claim the body."

"Well, an anonymous person has come forward and made a donation to my funeral home hoping to provide Mr. Chamberlin with a proper burial."
"Well, you'll have to get a release from Detective Simpson at the Dennis Police Department before I can release the body to you."
"Ok. I'll call him."

Mr. Henderson called Dennis PD.
"My name is Robert Henderson. I'd like to speak with Detective Simpson."
"One minute."

There was a pause while he was put on hold.
"This is Detective Simpson, how can I help you Mr. Henderson?"
"Ms. Nevins from the Coroners Office said I needed to get your permission in order to give Mr. Charles Chamberlin a proper burial."
"Why would you want to do that?" Simpson asked him.
"I received a donation from an anonymous donor sufficient to provide Mr. Chamberlin with a burial."
"And do you know who this anonymous donor was?"
"No. I found a note and fifteen thousand dollars cash in my business mailbox asking that the funds be used to

provide Mr. Charles Chamberlin with a burial. The note told me where to go to find Mr. Chamberlin's body."

"Do you have the note and the money?" Simpson asked.

"I do. The note's typed and looks like it came off a computer printer. It's not signed. The fifteen thousand is in a bank envelope so I think it was all drawn out of an account and put in a teller's envelope. But the envelope didn't have anything written on it that would identify a bank."

"So you're telling me you don't think there's any prints on the money or way to trace the letter. Is that so?"

"That's what it looks like to me."

Simpson decided to go with what he had and to get the body release forms.

"Leave the note with me. I'll have it checked out."

Simpson typed a few things into his computer. Then a document printed. He signed it and handed it to Mr. Henderson.

"This should do it."

"Thank you Detective. Now I can get on with a proper burial for Mr. Chamberlin."

"I'll send a fax over to the ME and instruct her to release the body to you."

"Thank you Detective."

"Your Welcome."

Simpson thought about it for a minute. Should he try to find out if someone had withdrawn fifteen thousand from one of the local banks recently? Then he decided it probably wouldn't get him anywhere. So he let it go.

At the end of the week, a service was held at Doane, Beal and Ames for Charles Chamberlin. Detective Simpson was there to see who showed up. Mr. Henderson had arranged for a minister from a local church to say a few words before taking the simple casket to the cemetery.

A few minutes before the short service was to begin, the door to the funeral home opened. In walked Sharon Kelly, Carol Tindle, Theresa Lee, Ann Pierce and Sarah Jacobs.

The casket was closed. The five sat next to each other a few rows in front of Detective Simpson. Only Carol Tindle expressed any sympathy for Chamberlin. The other women all sat there showing no emotion at all.

When the short service was done, Mr. Henderson asked if anyone was going to the cemetery. No one answered. The women all got up and walked out together. Detective Simpson followed them. Outside, he caught up with the women.

"Ladies, why are you all here?" he asked them.

"While we didn't like what he did to us, the result in the long run turned out to our benefit," said Theresa Lee.

"What do you mean?" asked Simpson.

"We all got our missing funds back from Mr. Chamberlin," said Sharon Kelly.

"Plus a nice return," added Sarah Jacobs.

"Then it was true that Mr. Chamberlin acted in good faith when he took or should I say, invested your money."

"He could have handled it better, but yes, we got our money plus a nice return back," said Theresa Lee.

"You ladies should consider yourselves fortunate," Simpson said.

"Oh, we do," replied Ann Pierce.

"We're just sorry Katherine couldn't be here with us," said Carol Tindle.

"Yes, isn't it a shame she didn't make it," Simpson said as he turned to walk away.

"Wait a minute Detective. Did you find her body?" asked Theresa.

"Not yet."

"But you're still looking, right?" asked Carol.

"Not actively. The case is cold, and has moved from rescue to recovery. But the file will remain open. Have a good day ladies."

Simpson turned and walked to his car. As he walked he wondered what really happened to Katherine Sterns. Maybe it was Katherine who paid for Chamberlin's burial, or maybe one of the other women.

About a week later, a biologist team from the National Seashore was evaluating a rook of seals on the south tip of Monomoy Island. The team had traveled along the west side of the island hoping to make land near the tip of the island in order to get close to the seals without disturbing them. After landing on the west side of the island tip, the two biologists walked along the dunes keeping out of sight of the seals. As they rounded the tip, they could see over a thousand seals lying on the beach. Biologist Mark Trump spoke in a whisper to his partner, Biologist Nancy Glenn, "Nancy, let's try to get right up to the seals through those dunes." He pointed to a path between the dunes leading down to the beach.

"Keep low Mark. They haven't seen us yet."

"What's up with all those seagulls landing in the middle of the seals?" Asked Nancy.

"They look like they are feeding on something."

"Maybe a dead seal."

"Maybe."

The two carefully approached the seals. They got to within a hundred feet when the seals started to act up. Their arrival had been detected. The seals started to stir with some going into the water.

"Well, there's no sense trying to hide anymore, they know we're here," said Mark as he stood up taking pictures.

Nancy made a few notes in her book trying to estimate the size of the rook.

"Looks like a thousand, maybe more," she said.

"Yeah, I agree."

They walked forward towards the area where the seagulls were still working. Nancy was the first to spot it.

"Look, those seagulls are working on what looks like a body."

Mark walked closer.

"You're right. It's definitely a body."

Nancy walked to within a few feet, "It's the body of a woman. Look there, her bra is still on."

The seagulls had made a mess of the body. It had been picked over quite a bit. The body still had pants on. Mark walked up to it and bent over.

"There's something in the pocket."

"Can you get it out?"

"Maybe."

Mark reached into the pocket and pulled out a zip-lock bag. Inside, there was a cell phone.

"Any identification?" asked Nancy.

"Just this cell phone."

"The authorities should be able to tell who it is by looking up the number if the phone still works."

Mark turned the phone on. It came to life. As it did, he pressed a few keys and was able to see the phone number. He read it to Nancy.

"Nancy, call the Coast Guard and let them know we found a body. Give them the phone number and let them see if they can figure out who this is."

"Will do."

Nancy called the Coast Guard station. She gave them the information and was told someone from the Coast Guard would be at their location within the hour. They were asked to remain with the body until it could be picked up.

"The Coast Guard will come pick up the body. They said they would be here within the hour and asked that we stay until they can pick it up."

"Ok. Let's finish up our research. They should be here by then."

The biologists finished up their research over the next half hour. They were sitting near the corpse when they heard the sound of a helicopter approaching.

"That should be the Coast Guard," said Mark looking to the north.

"I can see its insignia," said Nancy. "It's them."

The chopper landed about fifty feet away from the two biologists. The body was put in a body bag and removed from the beach. The crewmen from the Coast Guard thanked the Biologists and the chopper took off headed back to the station.

Detective Simpson got a call from Commander Collins of the Coast Guard.

"Detective, this is Commander Collins from Chatham Coast Guard Station."

"Hello, Commander. What can I do for you?"

"We retrieved a body from Monomoy today. We think it's the missing kayaker you'd been looking for."

"Did the body have any identification?"

"Only a cell phone. The biologists who found the body were able to turn the phone on and get the cell phone number."

Commander Collins read the number to Simpson.

"Thanks Commander. I'll check the number out and get back to you."

When Simpson hung up the phone, he went to operations and had the cell number checked. It belonged to Katherine Sterns. He already knew she had no immediate family to contact, so he decided to let her friends know about the discovery.

Detective Simpson made a call to Sundancers.

"Is Harry Adams available?"

"Hold on."

"This is Harry, how can I help you?"

"Harry, it's Detective Simpson."

"Hi Detective, what can I do for you?"

"Nothing really. I just wanted you to know we found a body washed up on Monomoy today. Looks to be the Sterns woman."

"Really?"

"Yes. The body was in pretty bad shape. A team of biologists doing research on the Monomoy seals came across it earlier today."

"How did they identify her?"

"They found a cell phone in her pocket. When I checked on the number, it was definitely her phone."

"Do you have the number, Detective?"

"Yes."

Simpson read the number to Harry.

"That's her cell number," was all Harry could say.

"We're going to have the medical examiner look at the body and get a positive ID from dental records, but I'm pretty sure it's the Sterns woman."

"Do you want me to identify the body?"

"The body is in pretty bad shape. It must have been on the beach for a few days mixed in with the seals. I don't think a visual identification is possible."

"Thanks for calling Detective. Can you let me know once a positive ID has been made?"

"Sure. I'll call you when I know something."

Harry hung up the phone stunned. He walked into the bar and got a shot and a beer.

"What's wrong Harry?" Dee asked.

"I just talked to Detective Simpson. They found Katherine's body today on Monomoy."

Dee couldn't talk. She came around from behind the bar crying and hugged Harry.

Antonio came out of the kitchen after hearing the commotion.

"What's up?" he said as he stood behind Harry.

"They found Katherine's body," said Harry as he downed the shot and beer.

8950574R0

Made in the USA
Charleston, SC
28 July 2011